Constance Santego

Wisdom of a Soul

Dr. Constance Santego has been practicing and teaching *The Nine Spiritual Gifts, Granted From Spirit,* for over twenty-five years. She lives in British Columbia, Canada, with her husband.

www.constancesantego.ca

Published by
Editor & Interior Layout: Dr. Constance Santego
Book Layout: ©2017 BookDesignTemplates.com
Cover Design: Jennifer Louie
Soft Cover ISBN: 978-1-990062-47-6
eBook ISBN: 978-1-990062-48-3

Created and published in Canada. Printed and bound in the United States of America
Ordering Information: csantego@gmail.com

ALSO BY DR. CONSTANCE SANTEGO

FICTION
The Nine Spiritual Gifts Series:
Journey of a Soul – (Vol 1 Michael)
Language of a Soul – (Vol 2 Gabriel)
Prophecy of a Soul – (Vol 3 Bath Kol)
Healing of a Soul – (Vol 4 Raphael)
Miracles of a Soul – (Vol 5 Hamied)
Knowledge of a Soul – (Vol 6 Raziel)

NONFICTION
The Intuitive Life, The Gift of Prophecy, Third Edition
Fairy Tales, Dreams and Reality… Where Are You On
Your Path? Second Edition
Your Persona… The Mask You Wear
Angelic Lifestyle, A Vibrant Lifestyle
Angelic Lifestyle 42-Day Energy Cleanse
Archangel Michael's Soul Retrieval Guide
Tesla and the Future of Energy Medicine
Beyond Tesla: *Advancing the Science of Energy Healing*
Tesla's Code: *Mastering Energy, Frequency, and
Creative Power*
Scaling Beyond 6 Figures: *Strategies for Health &
Wellness Professionals*
Beyond the Mind: *Harnessing the Power of Astral
Projection for Creative Awakening*
Bend, Don't Break: *Finding Your Way Back to
Abundance*
Ring Therapy: *A Guide to Healing and Balance*
Ring Therapy Pocket Guide
Floraopathy™: *The Art and Science of Vibrational
Healing with Essential Oils*

SECRETS OF A HEALER, SERIES:
Magic Of Aromatherapy (Vol I)
Magic Of Reflexology (Vol II)
Magic Of The Gifts (Vol III)
Magic Of Muscle Testing (Vol IV)
Magic Of Iridology (Vol V)
Magic Of Massage (Vol VI)
Magic Of Hypnotherapy (Vol VII)
Magic Of Reiki (Vol VIII)
Magic Of Advanced Aromatherapy (Vol IX)
Magic Of Esthetics (Vol X)
The Reiki Master's Manual (Vol XI)

ADULT COLORING JOURNALS
SERIES - ZEN COLORING:
Quantum Energy and Mindful Living Journal (Vol 1)
Reiki Energy Journal (Vol 2)
Nine Spiritual Gifts Journal (Vol 3)
I Forgive Journal (Vol 4)

SERIES – COLORING PROSPERITY:
Genie-Inspired Mandalas and Wealth Journal (Vol 1)
Entrepreneurial Mindset Reboot (Vol 2)

SERIES – HARMONIC MIND CODE:
Harmonic Mind Code Coloring Journal (Vol 1)

FOR CHILDREN
I am Big Tonight. I Don't Need the Light!

Cast of Characters

Some of the Residents of New York City, USA, and other places.

Alexandra (Lexi) Elizabeth Constantine:
Fashion designer in Upper East Side Manhattan.
Daughter of beloved parents—Olivia and
Marcus Constantine (Italian). Was a Fiancée to
Reverend Edward Julien Hawthorne. Her boss
was Sebastian. Friends with co-worker Southern
belle, Sherie. Was going to be engaged to Neo,
but is in love with Redington.

Susannah Grace Constantine:
Lexi's belated sister and now guardian angel.
Lived in Dumbo (Down Under the Manhattan
Bridge Overpass). She was an antique collector
for Aryeh Jacob Kofman and dated Billy
Randazzo.

**Olivia Sarah Constantine (Maiden name,
Austin)**: Mother to Lexi and Susannah.
Widowed housewife. Parents were from
England. She lives in Dyker Heights, Brooklyn,
NY. Deceased.

x   Dr. Constance Santego

Reverend Edward Julien Hawthorne: Was a mortician and minister of his family's funeral home in Brooklyn. Was a Fiancé to Alexandra (Lexi). Casandra was his secretary. He had an accident and forgot everything. Another soul took over his body at the time of his death and lived as a walk-in.

Sophea (Tamara Reeve): Past Psychic medium and teacher of many of the Spiritual Gifts. Was a Fiancée to Greg Masones. Still owns her grandmother's brownstone in Brooklyn Heights. Now lives in Katmandu, Naples—in a monastery and is a monk.

Detective Ferguson "Red" Redington: Was 1st-grade homicide investigator, Manhattan Bureau – Midtown South Precinct, Shield number 1323, NYPD. Lives in Far Rockaway Beach, Queens, on Long Island, NY. His family comes from England. Now is a FBI agent.

Greg Masones (AKA Julian D'Angelo): At large. Accountant for the Genovese crime family. Italian immigrant. Son of Serena D'Angelo. Was Tamara's fiancé.

Sebastian: Lexi's boss at the fashion house.
Sherie: Lexi's co-worker at the fashion house.
Isabella Jackson: Famous actress. She moved around to wherever her next movie was being filmed. Friends with Lexi, Edward, and

Main Angel of each Novel

Book 1 – Archangel Michael
"Warrior"
Companion Book – Archangel Michael's Soul Retrieval Guide.
Book 2 – Archangel Gabriel
"Messenger"
Companion Book – Your Persona... The Mask You Wear.
Book 3 – Bath Kol
"Daughter of the Voice," the Holy Ghost, and Gabriel
Companion Book – The Gift of Prophecy.
Book 4 – Archangel Raphael
"God Has Healed"
Companion Books – Secrets of a Healer Series.
Book 5 – Archangel Hamied
"Miracles"
Companion Book – Secrets of a Healer, Reiki,
Book 6 – Archangel Raziel
"The Keeper of Secrets and The Angel of Mysteries."
Book 7 – Archangel Uriel
"Light of God"

Wisdom of a Soul
The Gift of Wisdom

A Novel
7th in the series, The Nine Spiritual Gifts
'The Gift of Wisdom'
Dr. Constance Santego

Vol 7

Dedicated

to all souls that possess

the gift of Wisdom!

Wisdom of a Soul

The Nine Spiritual Gifts

In the New Testament my favourite story is "The Gifts."
Corinthians 1, Chapter 12, Verse 4-11
(Maybe a little differently worded
depending on which Bible you have).

The variety and the unity of gifts
There are many different gifts, but it is always the same Spirit; there are many different ways of serving, but it is always the same Lord. There are many different forms of activity, but in everybody it is the same God who is at work in them all. The particular manifestation of the Spirit granted to each one is to be used for the general good.
To one is given from the Spirit the gift of utterance expressing **wisdom**; to another the gift of utterance expressing **knowledge**; in accordance with the same spirit to another, **faith**, from the same Spirit; and to another, the gifts of **healing**, through the same Spirit; to another, the working of **miracles**; to another **prophecy**; to another, the power of **distinguishing spirits**; to one, the gift of **different tongues** and to another, the **interpretation of tongues**. But at work in all these is one and the same Spirit, distributing them at will to each individual.
The New Jerusalem Bible

Awaken to the spirit world, for there lie your gifts granted by Spirit.

Dr. Constance Santego

Fact:

All biblical references, science, legends, and myths are real *(slightly changed to fit the character.* This novel was written as a story inspired by Spirit, to give you, the reader a new perspective, a new way to learn, and a new opportunity to empower your life.

Many locations and all characters are fictional.

Prologue

In the quietude of the ancient monastery, where the stones themselves whispered secrets of ages past, there existed a library. This was no ordinary repository of books, but a sacred chamber where the scrolls of wisdom were preserved under the watchful eyes of time-honored guardians. Within these walls, the air was thick with the scent of old parchment and myrrh, an ambiance that seemed to transcend the mundane world.

Here, the Wisdom of the Soul was not merely a concept, but a living, breathing presence. It was said that the scrolls contained the distilled essence of countless enlightened beings who had walked the earth, their insights captured in the intricate script that danced across the fragile pages. These were the teachings of Tobias, a sage whose understanding of the soul's journey had illuminated paths for those who sought truth beyond the material veil.

The monastery stood secluded in a forgotten valley, surrounded by mountains that touched the heavens. It was a place of refuge for those wearied by the world's cacophony, a sanctuary where the soul could speak and be heard. Here, seekers of wisdom came to study the ancient texts, hoping to glean understanding that would guide them through life's labyrinth.

Among these seekers was Lexi, a young acolyte whose spirit burned with a desire for knowledge. Her journey was not just of the mind, but of the heart, driven by a quest to understand the deeper currents that guide one's destiny. Accompanied by the enigmatic Redington, a man of the world with secrets of his own, Lexi delved into the teachings of Tobias, each scroll unraveling mysteries that were both profoundly personal and universally resonant.

But the wisdom of the soul was not without its perils. For within the depths of enlightenment lay shadows, aspects of the self that must be confronted and understood before true wisdom could be embraced. As Lexi and Redington navigated the challenges laid forth by Tobias' teachings, they found themselves not only learners of the sacred texts but also players in a cosmic drama that had been unfolding since the dawn of time.

This is their story, a tale woven from the threads of ancient wisdom, human frailty, and the enduring quest for understanding. It is a narrative that invites the reader to explore the vast landscapes of the soul, to discover the luminous truths hidden within the shadows of their own hearts.

Thus begins "Wisdom of the Soul," a journey into the depths of being, where every heartache and triumph, every loss and discovery, contributes to the unfolding of the greatest mystery of all—the mystery of oneself.

4 Dr. Constance Santego

Chapter 1

The tranquility of the Nepalese monastery, usually undisturbed except by the routine chants and the soft flutter of prayer flags, was subtly disrupted this crisp morning. As Lexi and her friends engaged in a meditative session in the monastery's lush gardens, a slight commotion at the entrance caught their attention.

Kesia, who was seated closest to the path leading to the monastery gates, was the first to notice the figure striding toward them. Tall and imposing, the man's familiar gait brought a mixture of surprise and relief to her face. "Redington!" she exclaimed, disrupting the meditative silence.

Lexi turned sharply, her eyes widening as she recognized the figure approaching them. "Redington? What are you doing here?" Her voice was a mix of happiness and bewilderment.

Redington, wearing a light smirk that didn't quite reach his eyes, stopped in front of them, his chest heaving slightly as if he had been walking briskly. "I could ask you the same, Lexi. You vanish off to Nepal, and the next thing I hear, you're laid up with a fever that's giving you visions. Thought I'd better come and see things for myself."

As the initial surprise settled, Isabella brought over an extra cushion for Redington, and they all sat in a loose circle under the shade of a sprawling Bodhi tree. Redington looked around, taking in the serene surroundings before his gaze settled back on Lexi. "I've been tracking movements back in New York. Things are... unsettled. Your name came up more than once in connection with some artifacts that have gone missing," Redington explained, his tone serious. "When I couldn't reach you, I decided it was time to check in personally."

Lexi listened intently as Redington detailed the disturbances back in New York, her mind racing with the implications. The artifacts, the battles—she had believed them all to be the fevered illusions of a mind gripped by illness. His words, however, painted a far different reality.

"Artifacts? Missing? But…I thought it was all a dream..." Lexi murmured, her confusion palpable. She glanced at Isabella, Kesia, and Sophea, seeking confirmation or perhaps denial.

Before anyone could respond, a wave of dizziness washed over Lexi. Her vision blurred, the colors and sounds of the monastery garden melting into a whirl of indistinct shapes and distant echoes. "I... I don't feel—" Lexi managed to whisper before collapsing, unconscious, her friends rushing to catch her.

As darkness enveloped her consciousness, Lexi found herself in another place, another time. The harshness of the monastery's simple aesthetics gave way to the opulent splendor of ancient Greece, the air filled with the scent of olive trees and the distant roar of the Aegean Sea.

Lexi stood atop a high cliff overlooking a bustling city below. She was dressed in flowing robes, a crown of laurel leaves adorning her head, and the people in the streets below bowed in reverence as they looked up at her.

In this past life, Lexi was venerated as Thea Lexiana, a deity embodying wisdom and equilibrium. She resided over a vibrant city nestled between rolling hills and the azure embrace of the Aegean Sea. The architecture was a testament to human ingenuity inspired by divine influence, with temples and palaces that gleamed white under the sun.

Thea Lexiana's presence among her people was a daily affirmation of her guardianship. Her ethereal form glided through the city's stone-paved streets, her robes barely touching the ground, her movements accompanied by a gentle luminescence that seemed to harmonize the very air around her. When she moved, a trail of soft, golden particles lingered in the air, and when she gestured, subtle currents whispered promises of harvests and harmony.

As a goddess, Thea Lexiana's duties were manifold. She was the custodian of the celestial balance between the mundane and the divine. Her powers included bestowing knowledge to philosophers, granting foresight to seers, and infusing rulers with the wisdom to govern justly. Her temple, a magnificent edifice atop the city's highest hill, was a focal point of spiritual energy, where she mediated conflicts and dispelled any growing darkness with her light.

She was revered not just for her power but for her wisdom. Her council—comprised of demigods, spirits of ancient heroes, and incarnations of natural forces—met under the dome of her temple. They debated courses of action, interpreted omens, and strategized on maintaining the delicate equilibrium of the cosmic scales…

Chapter 2

In the ethereal space between consciousness and the dream world, Lexi found herself enveloped in a tranquil expanse of azure skies and endless horizons. The air around her shimmered with a gentle, golden light, calming her senses. She recognized this as a realm of higher guidance, a place beyond the ordinary, where the archangels often met with those seeking wisdom.

As she oriented herself, a figure appeared in the distance, approaching her across the vast, cloud-like ground. The figure's presence was commanding yet benevolent, surrounded by a soft radiance that intensified as he drew nearer. It was Uriel, the Archangel of Light and Wisdom, his features both stern and kind, his eyes reflecting the depths of knowledge he guarded.

"Lexi," Uriel's voice resonated in the serene expanse, echoing like a gentle wind. "You have been brought here at a pivotal moment, both in your journey and the broader tapestry of the celestial balance."

Lexi, feeling the gravity of his words, replied with a mix of reverence and urgency. "Uriel, I've had visions that confuse yet enlighten me. They speak of past lives and the ongoing battles between light and shadow. How do these visions connect with my path?"

Uriel gestured to the space around them, where faint images began to coalesce into scenes of Lexi's previous incarnations—lives filled with trials, wisdom, and the pursuit of balance. "Each life you've lived, each role you've embodied, has been a step on the stairway of your soul's evolution. You are being prepared, Lexi, for a role that transcends your earthly experiences."

The scenes shifted, showing Lexi in various eras, each time playing a crucial role in maintaining harmony. Uriel continued, "Your visions are not mere echoes of the past; they are lessons imbued with the knowledge necessary for your upcoming challenges."

Lexi absorbed the scenes, each memory a piece of a larger puzzle. "And the artifacts? The battles? How do they fit into this?"

"They are metaphors, my dear. The artifacts represent tools of enlightenment, while the battles symbolize the conflicts within every soul between the higher self and the lower instincts. Your role, as ever, is to mediate, to bring light to darkness, understanding to ignorance."

Uriel's form began to glow brighter, his next words carrying a weight that Lexi felt in the core of her being. "There is an upcoming convergence, a critical point where the earthly and the divine will align more closely than usual. Your experiences, your wisdom, are crucial in guiding this alignment toward harmony."

Lexi, empowered yet humbled by Uriel's affirmation, nodded. "What must I do, Uriel? How do I prepare?"

"Continue to seek knowledge, to embrace the wisdom offered by your experiences. Stay true to your path of balance and be ready to act as a guardian when the time comes. Remember, the light you carry within can illuminate not only your path but also the paths of others."

As the vision began to fade, Uriel's voice echoed one last time, "Balance is not achieved through force, Lexi, but through understanding, through the gentle guiding of energies to create harmony. You are not alone in this journey. We are here, always, guiding, supporting, watching."

Lexi awoke from the vision with a start, the morning sun casting gentle rays through the window of her room in the monastery. The vividness of the encounter with Uriel lingered in her mind, each word a beacon in the fog of her uncertainty.

She rose, her spirit invigorated despite her physical weariness, and walked into the tranquil gardens of the monastery to meet her friends. As they gathered, Lexi shared her visionary encounter with Archangel Uriel, each detail unfolding like a sacred script.

Together, they discussed the implications of her visions and Uriel's counsel. As the day progressed, the monastery's peaceful environment provided the perfect backdrop for contemplation and preparation for the challenges that lay ahead.

With each conversation, each moment of silence, Lexi and her friends grew more aligned with their spiritual paths, ready to face the convergence Archangel Uriel had foretold, their hearts and minds fortified by the wisdom of the archangels.

Chapter 3

The monastery's tranquil mornings were typically filled with the soft sounds of meditative chants and the flutter of prayer flags in the gentle breeze. However, for Redington, this serenity only deepened his sense of alienation. Standing apart from the group, he watched as Lexi and her friends immersed themselves in their spiritual discussions, their faces alight with passion and belief.

Redington's gaze lingered on Lexi, his heart conflicted. The stark contrast between his world of facts and evidence and the mystical realities Lexi embraced was never more pronounced than here, in this remote sanctuary of spiritual seekers. His feelings for her, complex and unresolved, added another layer to his inner turmoil.

He turned away, his thoughts wandering back to his days as a detective in New York City. There, the world made sense, defined by clear lines and tangible evidence. His transition to the FBI had only reinforced his reliance on concrete data and rational explanations. Yet, here he was, surrounded by ancient walls echoing with prayers and prophecies that defied logical understanding.

Redington decided to take a walk around the monastery grounds, hoping the physical activity would clear his mind. As he wandered through the gardens, the vibrant colors of the flowers and the serene landscapes seemed to mock his discomfort.

"Why am I even here?" he muttered to himself, frustration simmering beneath his calm exterior. "I should be back in New York, working on cases, not chasing visions and mystical artifacts."

Despite his skepticism, Redington couldn't deny the evidence he had seen with his own eyes—the inexplicable phenomena surrounding the artifacts, the undeniable power they wielded, and Lexi's profound transformations. These experiences challenged every fiber of his pragmatic soul.

As he walked, he stumbled upon a secluded part of the garden, where an old monk was tending to the plants. The monk looked up at Redington, his eyes reflecting a deep, unspoken understanding. "Troubled are the steps that walk the path of confusion," the monk said in a gentle, measured tone.

Redington stopped, taken aback by the monk's insight. "I'm not one for riddles," he replied curtly, his defenses up.

"The truth is not a riddle, young man," the monk continued, returning to his gardening. "But often, it is hidden beneath layers of doubt and denial. Sometimes, what we fight against the most is what we need to embrace to move forward."

These words struck a chord in Redington. He considered his constant struggle to dismiss the spiritual aspects of their quest as mere distractions. "And if I find this truth you speak of and it goes against everything I believe?" he questioned, not expecting any answer that would ease his skepticism.

"Then you will have found a greater truth, and your belief will have led you there," the monk replied without looking up.

Redington left the monk to his gardening and continued his walk, the monk's words echoing in his mind. As he pondered, he realized that his journey here might be more about understanding his own barriers and biases than about debunking the beliefs of Lexi and her friends.

Later that evening, as they all gathered for dinner, Redington watched Lexi laughing and sharing with her friends. He felt an unfamiliar pull to join in, to share not just in their meals but in their discussions. Maybe, he thought, it was time to explore this path, not as a skeptic but as a seeker. Perhaps, in understanding their beliefs, he could reconcile his feelings for Lexi and find his place in this strange, new world.

That night, as Redington lay in his simple room at the monastery, he resolved to take a more active role in their spiritual discussions and explorations. It was a decision born not out of sudden belief but out of a desire to understand, to bridge the gap between his world and theirs.

Chapter 4

Sophea began the day's gathering at the monastery with an engaging narrative, drawing her audience into a vivid depiction of a past era. "Once upon a time, in a village cradled by lush hills and serene streams, there lived a sage named Eliam. Renowned across the lands for his deep understanding and wise counsel, people from far and wide sought his guidance for their most complex dilemmas," she narrated, her voice filling the great hall where Lexi, Isabella, Kesia, and the other monks were seated, absorbed in her storytelling.

"One bright morning, a spirited young boy named Tobias approached Eliam with a burning question," Sophea continued. "He asked, 'Elder Eliam, everyone speaks of wisdom as if it were a treasure more precious than gold. But what, truly, is wisdom? And how might one find it?'"

Eliam, with a warm twinkle in his eyes, invited, "Come, walk with me." As they wandered through the verdant meadows, he shared his insights. "In the sacred texts of our ancestors, wisdom is described as a guiding light in darkness, the very first gift of creation, woven into the fabric of the earth at the dawn of time. According to the Proverbs of Solomon, wisdom calls out to those who listen, offering life and favor from the Creator."

As they reached a fork in the road, Eliam paused and gestured toward the paths. "Wisdom, Tobias, is knowing which path to choose, aware that each step impacts not only oneself but others around us. It teaches us to live in harmony with the earth and with each other."

Kesia, intrigued, leaned forward and asked, "Sophea, how does one practice this wisdom daily?"

Sophea replied, "Just as they continued their walk, they came upon a farmer whose cart was stuck in the mud. Without hesitation, Eliam and Tobias helped free the cart. Eliam explained to Tobias that wisdom also involves knowing when to lend a hand, to act with kindness and consideration without waiting to be asked."

"The writings of James tell us that if anyone lacks wisdom, they should ask the Creator, who gives generously to all without finding fault. True wisdom comes from above and is pure, peace-loving, considerate, and sincere," Sophea quoted as Eliam would have.

Back at the village's edge, they stopped by a well, where Eliam drew water for them to drink. He imparted, "Remember, my boy, wisdom is not merely about knowing or speaking, but in living righteously. It's the practical application of knowledge, the quiet humility that comes from understanding the Creator's will."

Tobias, his mind teeming with thoughts and questions, eagerly asked, "How can I begin to gain wisdom?"

Eliam advised, "Begin by fearing the Lord, for that is the foundation of all wisdom. Cherish His teachings, walk in His ways, observe, listen, and reflect on everything around you, and always be ready to learn."

Lexi, reflecting on the narrative, posed a question, "How did Tobias use this wisdom as he grew older?"

Sophea smiled, pleased with the question. "As Tobias matured, his daily life was filled with Eliam's teachings. He sought wisdom in every aspect of life, observing the natural world and deeply engaging with elders and scholars. One autumn day, while at the market, he resolved a dispute between two merchants by reminding them of the community's need for harmony, displaying his acquired wisdom."

"Years later, as Eliam's time drew near, he asked Tobias to continue guiding the villagers. Tobias embraced this role, teaching others about the virtues of wisdom, using nature and the

Creator's laws as his guidebooks. He shared stories of King Solomon, whose request for wisdom above all else granted him not only wisdom but wealth and long life because his priorities were aligned rightly."

Sophea concluded, "Tobias' wisdom became a beacon, guiding many. He wrote down his life's lessons, creating a book that continues to light the way for those seeking to live wisely. And just as Tobias sat beneath the old oak, teaching new generations, so does the spirit of wisdom continue, as long as there are those who seek it with sincere hearts."

The monks, inspired by the story, reflected on their own paths to wisdom, contemplating how they, too, could embody these teachings in their daily lives, guided by the examples of Tobias and Eliam.

Chapter 5

In the monastery's great hall, the air hummed with the quiet murmur of eager anticipation as Sophea prepared to continue her tale of Tobias. The monks, Lexi, Isabella, Kesia, and others, gathered closer, their eyes reflecting the glow of the oil lamps.

"As Tobias began to pen his reflections beneath that ancient oak," Sophea began, her voice weaving through the silence, "He thought of how wisdom, much like the mighty tree under which he sat, requires a firm foundation."

Isabella, always curious about the depths of spiritual truths, raised her hand gently. "How did Tobias view the challenges he faced? Did he see them as obstacles or opportunities?"

Sophea nodded appreciatively at the question. "Ah, Isabella, Tobias saw each challenge as a seed from which wisdom could grow. He believed that overcoming obstacles was a way to deepen one's roots in wisdom. Every hardship was an opportunity to practice the virtues he learned from Eliam and the scriptures."

She continued, "As Tobias wrote, he recalled a particular day, one that marked a turning point in his understanding of wisdom's virtues. It was during a harsh winter when the village faced a great famine. Tobias, then a young man, saw his fellow villagers despairing. He remembered Solomon's wise administration during Israel's plentiful times and his efforts to prepare for years of want."

Kesia, whose interest often lay in the practical applications of faith, leaned forward. "But how did Tobias apply these lessons? How did he help his village?"

"Tobias organized the villagers to share their remaining stores of food," Sophea explained. "He taught them to create reserves during the times of harvest, guided by Solomon's example. This not only sustained them through the winter but also strengthened their community bonds. Tobias showed them that wisdom must lead to action, that it should uplift not only oneself but also those around us."

Lexi, thoughtful and introspective, spoke up. "Did Tobias ever doubt his path? The weight of such leadership must have been heavy."

Sophea smiled gently at Lexi's insight. "Indeed, Lexi, Tobias did feel the weight. Yet, he found strength in prayer and meditation. He believed that each step guided by wisdom was a step toward greater harmony with the Creator's will."

Sophea paused, allowing the monks to absorb the narrative. "Under that old oak tree, as he wrote, Tobias reflected on the branches of wisdom—how they spread wide and offered shade and shelter to all who sought refuge. He wrote about the virtues of wisdom—patience, humility, generosity, and courage. Each virtue was like a branch, essential for the fullness of the tree's canopy."

As the night deepened, Sophea turned the pages of her own book, a copy of Tobias' writings. "Here, listen to Tobias' words," she said, reading aloud. "'Just as the oak stands firm through storms and winds, so must we stand firm in our virtues. Let patience be your root, humility your trunk, generosity your branches, and courage your leaves.'"

The story carried on, filling the hall with echoes of ancient wisdom and the rustle of turning pages. As Sophea spoke, the monks envisioned Tobias, the sage under his oak, writing his legacy into the dusk of his days.

"And so," Sophea concluded as the first light of dawn crept through the windows, "Tobias' legacy teaches us that wisdom is not just a gift to be received but a lifelong journey of nurturing and growing the virtues within us, spreading its shade far beyond our own reach."

The monks sat in reflective silence, each contemplating the depth of Tobias' life and teachings, inspired to carry the torch of wisdom in their own journeys.

Chapter 6

As the evening prayers concluded and the sun dipped below the horizon, casting a serene glow over the monastery grounds, Lexi and her friends gathered in the small, cozy lounge used by the guests for quiet reflection and casual conversations. With its soft cushions and warm tapestries, the room felt inviting, a stark contrast to the austere meditation halls.

Redington, who had spent the day away from Sophea's storytelling session, walked in just as the group settled in. His presence, always slightly aloof yet intriguing, brought a subtle shift in the atmosphere. The girls, still immersed in the day's teachings about wisdom and spiritual growth, were eager to share their insights and curious about Redington's day.

"Good evening," Redington greeted them, his voice carrying a hint of curiosity mixed with his usual reserve. He took a seat somewhat apart from the group, his posture relaxed yet guarded.

"Evening, Redington," Lexi responded, her voice warm and welcoming. "We missed you at Sophea's session today. It was enlightening."

Isabella, always keen to bridge gaps, chimed in, "Yes, it was about the virtues of wisdom and the stories of a sage who lived by them. It made us think about our own paths."

Kesia, her eyes bright with the fervor of the day's learnings, leaned forward slightly. "Sophea shared how wisdom isn't just about knowledge but about applying it to make meaningful changes. It's about the impact we have on others and the world."

Redington nodded, his expression thoughtful. "Sounds interesting," he admitted, though his tone suggested he was still grappling with the practical implications of such philosophical discussions.

Sophea, joining the group a bit later, noticed Redington's slightly detached demeanor and decided to engage him directly. "Redington, I sometimes wonder how you reconcile the concrete realities of your work with the spiritual nuances we delve into here."

Redington sighed, a rare moment of openness crossing his features. "Honestly, it's not easy. I deal with facts, evidence, and things I can see and prove. All this," he gestured loosely around the room, "It's harder to grasp. But..." he paused, looking around at the earnest faces, "I'm trying to understand. Not just for my sake, but perhaps because it matters to you all."

Lexi smiled gently at this, appreciating his effort. "That means a lot, Redington. Maybe think of it this way—wisdom, like what we discussed today, isn't just metaphysical. It's also about understanding deeper truths about human nature, what drives us, and how we can better navigate our lives."

Redington considered this, his gaze settling on Lexi. "I suppose there's a kind of wisdom in recognizing that there are different kinds of truths, including those that aren't so easily quantified."

Isabella, ever the peacemaker, added, "And maybe it's about finding a balance between those truths, integrating them in ways that make sense to us, individually and together."

As the conversation flowed, Redington found himself more engaged, asking questions and sharing a few challenges from his experiences as an FBI agent. The evening slowly turned into a deep exchange of ideas, blending practical experiences with philosophical insights.

Before they knew it, the monastery's clock chimed late into the evening, signaling that it was time to retire. As they stood to leave, Lexi turned to Redington, her expression sincere. "Thank you for joining us tonight, Redington. It's good to have you be part of these conversations."

Redington nodded, a subtle shift in his demeanor suggesting that he too valued the connection. "Thank you for having me," he replied, a slight smile touching his lips as he headed to his quarters.

As the group dispersed, there was a mutual feeling of contentment and camaraderie. They had shared a part of themselves, blending their diverse perspectives into a richer tapestry of understanding. For Redington, the evening had opened a small window into a world he had kept at bay, hinting at the possibility that perhaps, these spiritual pursuits had a place even in the structured confines of his own beliefs.

Chapter 7

As the morning light filtered through the stained-glass windows of the monastery, casting colorful patterns on the stone floor, Sophea opened the next chapter of Tobias' teachings. The monks, now familiar with the rhythm of these gatherings, settled into a reflective silence, eager to absorb the wisdom passed down through the ages.

"Today, we explore the Streams of Thought," Sophea began, her voice calm and clear. "Tobias likened wisdom to the rivers that meander through our village. These streams, always in motion, are pure and vital, cleansing and nurturing all they encounter on their journey to the sea."

Isabella, her curiosity piqued by the analogy, raised a hand. "Sophea, how does this comparison help us understand the nature of wisdom?"

Sophea nodded appreciatively at the question. "Just as a river continuously flows and renews itself, so does wisdom remain ever pure, untainted by falsehood. It brings life and clarity wherever it goes, purifying our thoughts and actions." She paused, ensuring the analogy settled within each listener. "Tobias believed that purity in wisdom was crucial, for it is from purity that peace and gentleness flow."

She continued, drawing from the ancient texts, "In the writings of James, we are reminded that the wisdom from above is first pure, then peaceable, gentle, and willing to yield. Tobias reflected on these qualities, emphasizing how true wisdom does not force its way but flows naturally, guiding us gently and yielding when necessary to avoid harm."

Kesia, reflecting on the practical applications of these teachings, asked, "How can we cultivate this type of wisdom in our daily lives?"

"By nurturing our inner life like a gardener tends to a riverbank," Sophea responded. "We must remove the debris of selfish desires and the silt of arrogance that can cloud our judgment. By doing so, we allow the pure waters of wisdom to flow freely, guiding our actions with peace and gentleness."

Lexi, always keen on understanding deeper spiritual truths, inquired, "But, what does it mean to be 'willing to yield'? How does this attribute connect with wisdom?"

Sophea smiled warmly at Lexi's thoughtful question. "To be willing to yield is to recognize that our personal understanding may be limited. It means being open to the perspectives and needs of others, much like a river that bends and shifts its course around obstacles. This flexibility prevents conflicts and promotes harmony within our community."

She then guided the monks in a contemplative exercise. "Let us envision our thoughts as streams of water. Where do they rush too hastily? Where might they need purification? Contemplate how you can allow the waters of wisdom to cleanse and renew your mind, making it a source of life and peace for others."

As the monks meditated on these questions, the room filled with a profound silence, each person internally exploring the pathways of their own thoughts.

Sophea concluded the session with a final reflection. "Remember, the streams of wisdom are always moving, always pure. They cleanse and give life, flowing through us and extending beyond us. As Tobias taught, let us strive to keep the waters of our wisdom pure and peaceable, for this is how we will nourish and enrich the lives of all we touch."

With that, the chapter closed, leaving the monks with much to ponder about the purity of their own wisdom and the impact of their thoughts and actions on the world around them. The teachings of Tobias, like the rivers he so cherished, continued to flow through the hearts and minds of those who sought to live wisely.

Chapter 8

As the next gathering in the monastery's great hall began, Sophea opened her ancient, leatherbound copy of Tobias' writings. The monks, now deeply engaged in the unfolding narrative, listened intently as she introduced the new chapter, titled "The Winds of Wisdom."

"Tobias often wrote about the nature of wisdom, comparing it to the gentle winds that sweep across our lands," Sophea began, her voice resonating softly throughout the hall. "He believed that just as the wind has the power to refresh and renew, so does wisdom have the ability to bring peace and nurture growth among us."

Isabella, reflecting on her own experiences, asked, "Sophea, could you share how Tobias applied this gentle wisdom to resolve conflicts?"

Sophea nodded and turned the pages to a well-worn section. "There are many stories, but one in particular stands out. Once, during a severe drought, tensions rose in the village over the remaining water sources. Disputes threatened to divide the community. Tobias, recalling the peace-loving nature of divine wisdom, stepped forward not with force, but with a calm presence and soothing words."

She continued, "Much like a cooling breeze on a stifling day, Tobias' approach alleviated the heat of anger among the villagers. He facilitated discussions that led to the creation of a fair water-sharing agreement. His interventions were gentle yet effective, mirroring the way wind spreads seeds to fertile ground, allowing new life to grow where it is most needed."

Kesia, always keen to understand the practical implications, queried, "How can we embody this kind of wisdom in our own interactions, especially in moments of tension and disagreement?"

"Kesia, we must strive to be like the wind," Sophea answered thoughtfully. "This means approaching conflicts with a soft demeanor and a willingness to listen. It requires us to understand the underlying issues at heart and to speak words that soothe rather than provoke. By embodying this gentle force, we can help guide those in conflict toward resolution and understanding."

Lexi, interested in deepening her spiritual practice, sought clarification. "Sophea, is there a specific mindset or practice that can help us cultivate this gentle wisdom?"

"Indeed, Lexi," Sophea responded. "Mindfulness is key. Being fully present in the moment allows us to sense the emotional climate of a situation and respond with the appropriate gentleness. Regular meditation on the teachings of our faith can also attune us to the subtleties of human interaction, just as one becomes sensitive to the changes in wind direction."

As Sophea concluded her lesson, she invited the monks to close their eyes for a guided reflection. "Imagine yourselves as the wind," she instructed softly. "Feel the power you have to cool anger, to spread seeds of peace, and to refresh the weary. Contemplate how, in your daily interactions, you might use this power to foster harmony and understanding."

The room filled with a serene silence as each monk internalized the metaphor, considering how they might live out the wisdom of the wind in their own lives.

Sophea finished the session with a gentle reminder, "Let us carry this wisdom forward like a soft breeze, using our presence to bring peace wherever we go, just as Tobias did. Remember, the true strength of wisdom lies not in its force, but in its nurturing touch and ability to guide change subtly and gently."

With that, the monks rose from their seats, feeling renewed and inspired, ready to practice the gentle winds of wisdom in their own lives, embodying the teachings of Tobias to cultivate peace and understanding in a world that often felt as harsh as a midsummer's day.

Chapter 9

The monastery's great hall, filled with the quiet rustle of robes and the soft light of morning, provided a serene backdrop as Sophea prepared to share the next chapter of Tobias' legacy. The monks, each now familiar with the depth and breadth of Tobias' wisdom, gathered with a sense of reverence and eager anticipation.

"Today, we turn to a chapter in which Tobias likened wisdom to the canopy of a grand oak tree," Sophea announced, her voice echoing softly in the high-ceilinged hall. "He saw wisdom not merely as a personal virtue but as a shelter that extends its branches to protect and consider all who seek refuge beneath it."

Isabella, always moved by the symbology of nature in spiritual teachings, asked, "Sophea, how did Tobias use this idea of the 'canopy of consideration' in his travels and teachings?"

Sophea nodded, pleased with the question, and began, "Tobias often traveled to distant towns, where disputes and misunderstandings between people were common. In one town, a long-standing feud between two families threatened to erupt into violence. Tobias arrived, not as a judge imposing decisions, but as a mediator, offering the shade of understanding and compassion."

She continued, detailing Tobias' approach: "Much like the oak's branches provide shelter from the harsh sun, Tobias provided a space for each side to express their grievances safely. He listened intently, ensuring that his advice considered the well-being of both families, not favoring one over the other. His wisdom helped them see their shared interests and the potential for peace, guiding them toward reconciliation."

Kesia, who had a keen interest in the practical applications of these teachings, reflected aloud, "It seems that wisdom, like the oak's canopy, is both protective and nurturing. How can we cultivate such wisdom that considers and shelters all?"

"Indeed, Kesia," Sophea responded, "To cultivate such wisdom, we must develop deep empathy and the ability to listen truly. It begins with stepping out of our own perspectives and entering the shade of others' experiences. This shift allows us to understand their pains and hopes, much like the oak tree feels the wind and bears the weight of the snow."

Lexi, intrigued by the transformational aspect of this wisdom, asked, "How did Tobias ensure that his own considerations didn't cloud his judgment?"

"A vital question, Lexi," Sophea affirmed. "Tobias practiced what we call 'self-emptying'—setting aside his own biases and desires to fully receive the stories and needs of others. This practice allowed him to act as a true conduit of wisdom, channeling solutions that were fair and nurturing for all involved."

As the discussion drew to a close, Sophea invited the monks to a moment of reflection. "Let us each consider how we might extend our own canopy of consideration. Think of ways you can provide shelter and empathy in your interactions, whether in resolving small disputes or in offering comfort to those in distress."

The monks sat quietly, pondering the vastness of wisdom's canopy and their role beneath its shelter. They visualized themselves as oaks, roots deep in spiritual understanding, branches wide in compassion, leaves whispering peace.

Sophea concluded, "As we move through our day, let us walk gently, mindful of the shelter we carry within us, ready to extend the cool shade of consideration to all who cross our paths, just as Tobias did under the vast canopy of his wisdom."

With that, the monks rose, inspired to carry forth the lessons of the oak tree's canopy into their daily lives, each step guided by the profound sheltering wisdom of Tobias.

Chapter 10

The cool evening air brushed against the stone walls of the monastery as Lexi found herself walking toward the small garden that overlooked the valley. The stars began to pierce the twilight, casting a serene glow on the paths lined with prayer flags. She was deep in thought, reflecting on the day's lessons, when she noticed a familiar figure leaning against the garden's low wall.

Redington stood gazing out over the landscape, his posture relaxed but with an air of contemplation. As Lexi approached, he turned, offering her a small, introspective smile. "Evening, Lexi," he greeted, his voice carrying a hint of something pending on his mind.

"Evening, Redington," Lexi replied, joining him at the wall. "You've been quite the elusive figure these past few days. Sophea's sessions have been insightful. We missed having you there."

Redington chuckled softly, "I bet they were. But no, I've been walking, thinking... exploring the streets of Nepal. It's a fascinating place, full of life and so different from what I'm used to."

Lexi nodded, understanding his need for space and clarity, especially given his skepticism about the spiritual discussions that filled their days at the monastery. "It sounds like a journey in itself. What did you discover out there?"

"More than I expected," Redington admitted. "But, Lexi, that's not the only reason I wanted to talk to you tonight." He paused, searching for the right words. "I've been thinking about our time here, what we've experienced together and separately. And, well, I've come to realize that maybe it's time for me to head back to New York. And I was hoping you might consider coming with me."

Lexi felt a surge of mixed emotions. The request was unexpected, yet it resonated with a part of her that longed for the familiar streets of New York City. "Back to New York? What's waiting for us there, Redington?"

"There are cases, responsibilities I left behind," Redington explained. "And I think there's more for us to explore, not just about the artifacts or our mission, but about ourselves. New York could give us that chance. Plus, I need your help with a few things that are tied to what we've learned here."

Lexi considered his words, the weight of the decision pressing on her. She thought about the lessons of wisdom and the spiritual journey she had embarked on in Nepal. "And what have you been up to these last few days, apart from walking and thinking?"

"Just that, really," Redington said, looking out over the valley again. "Walking the streets, watching the people, trying to understand this part of the world, and figuring out where I stand in all of this. It's given me a lot of clarity, and I think New York might do the same for you."

Lexi felt the sincerity in his voice and recognized the growth in his perspective. "I'll think about it, Redington. There's a lot here for me, too. These teachings... they're changing me. But I won't deny that New York is calling me in a way it hasn't before."

Redington nodded, appreciating her openness. "Take your time, Lexi. I'm not rushing this. Just think about what could be next for us, for our mission, and maybe for whatever else is between us."

They stood together in silence, the night deepening around them, each lost in their thoughts but comforted by the other's presence. Finally, Lexi smiled softly, breaking the quiet. "Let's see what the next few days bring, Redington. And thank you, for thinking of me for this next part of your journey."

As they parted ways for the night, the possibility of returning to New York with Redington lingered in Lexi's mind, a new chapter waiting to be written against the backdrop of the bustling city. Yet, the spiritual teachings of the monastery still echoed in her heart, a reminder of the balance she sought to achieve in her life.

Chapter 11

As the monastery settled into the quiet of the night, Lexi found herself restless, the conversation with Redington echoing in her mind. She had always felt pulled in multiple directions—her past in New York, her present in Nepal, and the uncertain paths of her future. She finally drifted into a fitful sleep, her thoughts swirling with the possibilities Redington had laid before her.

In her dream, she found herself standing in a vast, open field, under a sky painted with stars. The air around her vibrated with a gentle, luminous energy, and in the distance, a figure approached. It was Archangel Uriel, bathed in a soft, golden light, his presence both comforting and awe-inspiring.

"Lexi," Uriel's voice resonated, clear and calm, "you stand at a crossroads, each path laden with its own lessons and trials."

Lexi looked around, noticing multiple paths radiating out from where she stood. "Uriel, I am torn. New York calls to me, offering a chance to return to my roots, but something here in Nepal holds me back."

Uriel nodded, his eyes reflecting a deep understanding. "The pull you feel toward New York is not just about returning to what you know. It's about applying what you've learned, about testing your growth. However, your journey here is not yet complete. There are lessons still waiting for you in these mountains, teachings that are essential for your spiritual evolution."

Lexi listened, her heart torn between the comfort of familiarity and the growth promised by her current path. "How do I choose? How do I know which path is mine to walk?"

Uriel gestured to the sky above, where the stars seemed to brighten. "Look to the stars, Lexi. Just as they guide travelers in the night, let your inner light guide you. You already know which path to follow. Trust in that knowledge."

He continued, "Your stay in Nepal is not about putting aside the future but about enriching it. Every moment here weaves itself into the tapestry of your life, strengthening you, preparing you for what lies ahead."

Lexi felt a sense of peace wash over her as she absorbed Uriel's words. "And what of the challenges in New York? Should I just leave them unanswered?"

"Challenges will always await you, Lexi. But you will return to them stronger, wiser, if you allow yourself the time to learn what can only be taught here. This is a time for deepening, for grounding yourself in the spiritual truths that will be your anchor no matter where you are."

As the dream began to fade, Uriel's final words lingered in the air, "Stay the course here, Lexi. Let your heart be your compass. It will not lead you astray."

Lexi awoke early the next morning, the first rays of sunlight streaming through her window. The vividness of the dream with Uriel left her feeling invigorated, with a newfound clarity. As she rose from her bed, her decision was firm in her mind. She would stay in Nepal for now, embracing the lessons and spiritual growth it offered.

Chapter 12

As the early morning sun cast a gentle glow through the monastery's stained glass, Sophea opened the worn pages of Tobias' writings to the next chapter. The monks gathered in the great hall, their presence a testament to their commitment to understanding the deeper virtues of wisdom.

"Today, we delve into the essence of sincerity, a virtue that Tobias held in high regard," Sophea began, her voice resonant and clear. "He often compared wisdom to a fruitful tree, underlining that just as a tree must bear fruit, so too must wisdom manifest in sincere actions that nourish and sustain relationships."

Isabella, drawn to the metaphorical richness of the discussion, asked, "Sophea, could you share how Tobias demonstrated this sincerity in his dealings?"

Sophea smiled, acknowledging the depth of the question. "Certainly, Isabella. There are many stories, but one stands out. On his journeys, Tobias once encountered a merchant who was accused of dishonesty. Instead of dismissing the merchant based on rumors, Tobias met with him to understand his side of the story. By approaching the situation with an open mind and a sincere heart, Tobias was able to uncover the truth: the merchant had been falsely accused."

She continued, "This act of sincere engagement not only cleared the merchant's name but also restored his dignity and respect within the community. Tobias taught us through his actions that sincerity builds bridges of trust and respect between individuals."

Kesia, always eager to apply these teachings practically, queried, "How can we cultivate such sincerity in ourselves, Sister?"

"To cultivate sincerity, we must first cultivate self-awareness and integrity," Sophea explained. "We must align our inner values with our outward actions, ensuring that we do not wear masks or harbor hidden motives. Tobias often meditated on his intentions before acting, a practice that helped him maintain his sincerity."

Lexi, reflecting on the challenges of maintaining sincerity, added, "But Sister, in our daily lives, we often face situations where being sincere can lead to conflict or discomfort. How did Tobias handle such challenges?"

"That is a profound observation, Lexi," Sophea replied. "Tobias faced similar dilemmas. However, he believed that the discomfort brought on by sincerity was a small price to pay for maintaining one's integrity and the trust of others. He often said that true wisdom is devoid of deceit and that sometimes, the hardest truths, delivered sincerely, are the most crucial for growth and understanding."

Encouraged by the monks' thoughtful engagement, Sophea invited them to a moment of reflection. "Let us each think about an instance where we might have compromised our sincerity. Contemplate how you could have handled it differently, keeping Tobias' example in mind. Consider how you can apply sincerity in your interactions today, ensuring your actions bear the fruit of trust and respect."

The monks closed their eyes, each internally examining the moments where sincerity could have altered the course of their actions for the better.

Sophea concluded the session with a final thought. "Remember, the fruits of wisdom—like those of a tree—are not hidden but are visible to all. Let us strive to ensure that our fruits, borne of sincerity, are wholesome and nurturing, enhancing the lives of those we touch."

With that, the monks dispersed, each carrying with them the resolve to live more sincerely, inspired by the teachings of Tobias and guided by the wisdom of their beloved Sophea.

Chapter 13

The monastery's garden was bathed in the warm, golden light of the late afternoon sun as Lexi made her way to the spot where she and Redington had shared a profound conversation the night before. She found him there, gazing contemplatively at the horizon where the sun was beginning to set, casting long shadows across the vibrant blooms and verdant foliage.

Redington turned at the sound of her approaching footsteps, his expression a mixture of hope and resignation. He had sensed the internal struggle Lexi was undergoing, a battle between her deep-seated ties to New York and the spiritual calling that held her in Nepal.

"Redington," Lexi began, her voice reflecting a newfound clarity and determination. She paused, taking a moment to gather her thoughts, ensuring her words carried the weight of her decision. "I've given it a lot of thought. My path is here, for now. There are things I need to learn, growth I need to undergo before I can return to New York."

She watched him closely, gauging his reaction. Redington's features softened, his initial disappointment giving way to understanding. He had always admired Lexi's commitment to her growth and her courage to follow her heart, even when it led her away from him.

"I had a feeling you might say that," Redington replied, his voice low but supportive. He stepped closer, bridging the gap between them, his eyes locked on hers. "And I respect your decision, Lexi. Just know that whenever you're ready, New York will be there. And so will I."

His words, sincere and unwavering, touched Lexi deeply. She felt the bond between them strengthen, a silent acknowledgment of the respect and care that underpinned their relationship. Lexi reached out, her hand lightly touching his arm in a gesture of gratitude and connection.

"Thank you, Redington," she said, her smile soft but sad, acknowledging the complexity of their situation. "Your understanding means more to me than you know. And knowing that I have your support makes this decision a little easier."

They stood together in silence for a few moments, each lost in their thoughts, sharing the serene beauty of the setting sun. The garden around them seemed to hold its breath, a witness to the pivotal moment in their lives.

Finally, Redington spoke, breaking the reflective quiet. "I'll miss having you around, Lexi. But I guess this is part of your journey, and I want what's best for you. I'll be back in New York, sorting out the chaos, waiting for the day you decide to return."

Lexi nodded, her heart heavy yet hopeful. "And I'll be here, learning and growing. We'll both be on our paths, but I believe they'll cross again. Until then, let's keep pushing forward, wherever we are."

As the sun dipped below the horizon, casting a final glow that seemed to set the sky aflame, Redington and Lexi parted ways, each stepping back into their separate lives yet carrying a piece of this shared moment with them. They knew that whatever the future held, the connection they had fostered here, amidst the ancient wisdom of the monastery and the quiet whispers of the Nepalese hills, would endure.

Redington walked away first, his figure slowly blending into the twilight shadows, leaving Lexi to watch the last light of the day vanish, her spirit buoyed by the belief that she was exactly where she needed to be.

Chapter 14

In the quietude of the monastery's morning, Sophea prepared to unfold another chapter from Tobias' profound teachings. The monks, now deeply invested in the narratives and lessons shared, assembled with an air of anticipation, ready to explore further the virtues of wisdom through biblical history.

"Today, we journey back to the stories of King Solomon, a figure whom Tobias often referred to as the epitome of biblical wisdom," Sophea announced, her voice imbued with reverence for the ancient tales. "Tobias used Solomon's life to illustrate the heights of wisdom and the perils of straying from its path."

Lexi, a bit distracted from last evenings farewell to Redington, but intrigued by the historical aspect, asked, "Sophea, could you tell us how Tobias interpreted Solomon's humble request for wisdom?"

Sophea nodded, turning the pages to the relevant passages. "When young Solomon ascended to the throne, he made a humble request to God, asking not for long life, riches, or the defeat of his enemies, but for an understanding mind to govern his people wisely. God, pleased with this request, granted Solomon not only great wisdom but also riches and honor beyond any king before or after him," she recounted, echoing the scriptural story (1 Kings 3:5-12).

"This story," Sophea continued, "served as a pivotal lesson in Tobias' teachings—highlighting that true wisdom begins with humility and the desire to serve others well, rather than seeking personal gain."

Isabella, reflecting on the implications, queried, "How did Tobias use Solomon's wisdom in his own life and teachings?"

"Tobias often recounted Solomon's wise judgment in the case of the two mothers claiming the same baby," Sophea replied. "Solomon's proposal to divide the living child revealed the true mother's love, as she chose to give up her claim to save her child's life. This story was used by Tobias to emphasize the depth and practicality of wisdom in resolving conflicts by uncovering the truth hidden in human hearts" (1 Kings 3:16-28).

Kesia, always keen to understand the moral of the story, asked, "What caution did Tobias offer from Solomon's life?"

Sophea sighed softly, recognizing the gravity of the tale. "Despite his wisdom, Solomon eventually strayed from the path. His wealth and many alliances led him to idolatry, compromising his commitment to God, which ultimately led to his kingdom's division. Tobias used this part of Solomon's story as a cautionary tale, warning that no amount of wisdom can safeguard us if we lose sight of our foundational values and succumb to complacency or pride" (1 Kings 11).

She encouraged the monks to reflect, "Let these stories remind us that wisdom must be continuously nurtured and aligned with ethical and spiritual integrity. Like Solomon, we may start well, but we must remain vigilant not to stray from the path of wisdom."

As the lesson concluded, Sophea invited the monks to a quiet meditation. "Consider your own requests to God and reflect on how you can emulate Solomon's initial desire for wisdom in your daily responsibilities. Ponder too on how you might avoid the pitfalls that even the wisest can fall into."

The monks bowed their heads, each silently contemplating the dual lessons of Solomon's rise and fall, inspired to cultivate a humble and steadfast heart in their pursuit of wisdom.

Sophea closed the book gently, knowing that the stories they had explored would resonate deeply, guiding the monks as they navigated the complexities of life with wisdom as their beacon.

Chapter 15

The night wrapped the monastery in a blanket of stillness, only the faint sound of rustling leaves and distant animal calls filling the air. Lexi, her mind still resonant with the day's lessons about Solomon, drifted into sleep with thoughts of wisdom and its profound implications swirling in her dreams.

In her dream, she found herself standing in a vast library, its shelves towering with ancient texts and scrolls. The air was thick with the scent of aged parchment and cedar. As she walked down the aisles, she came upon a table where a single book lay open, illuminated by a shaft of light that seemed to emanate from the book itself. She knew instinctively that this was no ordinary place—it was a dreamscape formed by her subconscious, mingled with the celestial influence of her guardian, Archangel Uriel.

As she approached the table, Uriel appeared beside her, his presence commanding yet comforting. The room seemed to brighten at his arrival, the shadows dancing away from the light that surrounded him.

"Uriel," Lexi greeted, her voice echoing slightly in the vast hall of knowledge.

"Lexi," Uriel responded, his tone warm and encouraging. "You seek understanding of the lessons taught today—the wisdom of Solomon and the teachings of Tobias. What troubles your heart?"

Lexi gestured to the open book, its pages filled with the stories of Solomon. "Today's lessons... they spoke of wisdom's heights and its perils. Solomon asked for wisdom to serve his people, yet he fell into pride and lost his way. How can I, or any of us, hope to hold onto wisdom without falling into the same traps?"

Uriel nodded, understanding her concern. "Solomon's story is a reminder that wisdom is not just about the accumulation of knowledge or even the ability to apply it judiciously. It is also about maintaining humility and spiritual integrity. His early request was pure, but as he grew in power, he forgot that wisdom should serve to connect us more deeply with divine truths, not just earthly governance."

Uriel moved closer, placing his hand on the book. The pages turned as if caught by a gentle breeze, stopping on the passage of Solomon's humble prayer for wisdom. "True wisdom,"

Uriel continued, "Is a constant journey, not a destination. It requires a continual recommitment to the virtues that originally defined it— humility, service, and devotion."

Lexi absorbed his words, the significance of the dream growing clearer. "So, wisdom is more about the journey than merely the outcomes or achievements it brings?"

"Exactly," Uriel affirmed. "And it is in the journey that you must find balance, constantly realigning yourself with the divine source of all wisdom. Solomon lost his balance, swayed by wealth and earthly power. Your challenge is to learn from his rise and his fall— to embrace wisdom as a way of being, integrated fully into every aspect of your life."

The archangel's words resonated deeply with Lexi, each syllable echoing around the dream library. "Reflect on this, Lexi. Reflect on your own requests for guidance. Consider how you can embody the humility and devotion that Solomon initially showed, and be mindful of the pitfalls of complacency and pride."

As the dream began to fade, Uriel's voice lingered, a soft but clear bell in the quiet of the subconscious: "Carry this understanding back into your waking life. Let it guide you in your quest for wisdom, grounding you as you continue your spiritual journey."

Lexi awoke just as the first light of dawn crept through her window. She lay in bed for a few moments, pondering the dream. Uriel's visit had given her much to consider—about wisdom, its maintenance, and its integration into her life. She felt a renewed sense of purpose, ready to meet the day with the lessons of the dream fresh in her mind, guiding her steps like the ancient wisdom of Solomon guided by divine light.

Chapter 16

The vibrant cacophony of New York City was a stark contrast to the tranquil solemnity of the Nepalese monastery. As Redington stepped out of the JFK airport, the familiar rush of the city greeted him like an old friend. The honking taxis, the bustling crowds, and the towering skyscrapers were all part of the intricate tapestry that was his home.

Driving through the busy streets toward the FBI field office, Redington's mind was a mix of focused determination and lingering thoughts of Nepal. Images of Lexi and the serene gardens of the monastery floated through his mind, juxtaposed against the gritty reality of his New York life.

Settling into his office, Redington was immediately briefed on a new case—a series of art thefts that seemed to have implications far beyond simple burglary. The stolen pieces were ancient artifacts, each with significant cultural and historical value. The pattern suggested that the thief was not just a common criminal but someone who understood the deeper significance of these items.

As Redington dove into the case files, his recent experiences in Nepal subtly influenced his perspective. He couldn't help but recall the discussions about wisdom and integrity, and how they intersected with the responsibilities of power and knowledge. Each stolen artifact was a piece of history, a fragment of collective wisdom passed down through ages, now ripped from its context for personal gain.

The case led him to a suspect, a renowned but reclusive art collector known for his obsession with ancient civilizations. Surveillance footage from the last theft showed a figure that matched the collector's description. Redington decided to confront him directly, hoping to appeal to his better nature rather than just his fear of prosecution.

Meeting the collector in his sprawling uptown mansion, and after being searched by the security men guarding the mansion, Redington was struck by the opulence that surrounded him. Every room was filled with priceless artifacts, each displayed with a curator's care yet lacking the soulful reverence they deserved.

"Mr. Hartley," Redington began, choosing his words carefully, his thoughts still influenced by his recent philosophical learnings, "These pieces you've taken, they're not just valuable in terms of money. They carry the wisdom and stories of the cultures they come from. They're meant to be shared, not hidden away for personal enjoyment."

Hartley scoffed, his demeanor haughty. "Agent Redington, you speak of wisdom and sharing as if they are more important than possessing the greatest collections. What does it matter where they are kept?"

Redington looked around, his gaze settling on a stolen 12th-century scroll depicting the journey of a great Asian philosopher. "Wisdom, Mr. Hartley, like the stories on this scroll, is meant to enlighten, to reach people, to teach us about where we come from and possibly where we're going. When you hoard these pieces, you're not just stealing objects; you're stealing opportunities for understanding and growth."

The conversation seemed to unsettle Hartley, his expression faltering slightly. Redington pressed on, "Imagine using your resources not to hide these treasures, but to support museums and educational institutions. Share your passion in a way that benefits others, not just your ego."

As Redington spoke, he realized he was not just making a case for the return of the artifacts but was also negotiating for a larger moral victory. This wasn't just about solving a case; it was about restoring balance, about ensuring that the wisdom encapsulated in these artifacts continued to serve humanity as intended.

As Redington stepped out into the bustling night, the city lights danced around him, casting a shimmer across the streets wet with a recent rain. Although he hadn't secured enough evidence to arrest Hartley for the theft of the artifacts, he left the collector in a contemplative silence, pondering the weight of his words. Walking away, Redington sensed a profound shift within himself—a deeper recognition of his role, extending beyond mere law enforcement to that of a guardian of wisdom. His experiences in Nepal had sparked a transformation, subtly reshaping his approach to his duties. This change was now manifesting in his work, influencing him in ways he had not foreseen, as he navigated the complexities of his profession with a newfound perspective on justice and morality.

Back at his condo, overlooking the shoreline, Redington reflected on his day. The case was still open, but he felt a sense of accomplishment that went beyond his usual satisfaction of solving crimes. He was beginning to understand that every choice he made, every case he solved, could contribute to a larger good, a greater balance. It was a lesson in wisdom, slowly permeating his thoughts and actions, guiding him not just as an agent but as a person seeking to do right in a complex world.

Shaking his head, *Great I am losing my mind and starting to think like the girls.*

With that thought he went and poured himself a double.

Chapter 17

As the soft light of dawn spread across the monastery's walls, the monks gathered for another session with Sophea. The air was filled with a thoughtful silence as they prepared to dive deeper into the teachings of Tobias and the wisdom of the scriptures. Kesia, who had been pondering the interconnections between diverse spiritual paths, raised a question that reflected her curiosity.

"Sophea," Kesia began, her voice reflecting genuine intrigue, "as a Buddhist monk in Nepal, how have you come to know so much about these biblical stories, and how do you see them connecting with Buddhist teachings?"

Sophea smiled warmly, appreciating the thoughtful nature of the question. "Kesia, that is a wonderful inquiry," she replied. "My journey into the biblical scriptures began many years ago when I sought to understand the universal truths that thread through all great religions. In studying the Bible, I found profound teachings on wisdom, compassion, and integrity, which resonate deeply with Buddhist principles."

She continued, "Both Buddhism and Christianity teach us about the importance of compassion, selflessness, and the pursuit of spiritual wisdom. While the stories and contexts differ, the core messages of love, understanding, and ethical living are remarkably similar. For instance, just as Solomon asked for wisdom to better serve his people, the Buddha taught that wisdom is essential for enlightenment and for alleviating suffering in the world."

Isabella, intrigued by this synthesis of ideas, asked, "How do you integrate these teachings in your daily practices, Sister?"

Sophea nodded thoughtfully. "In my daily practice, I strive to embody the virtues that both religions uphold. Meditation and prayer guide me toward inner peace and wisdom, much like how Solomon sought knowledge to govern wisely. The Buddhist practice of mindfulness helps me remain aware and sincere in my actions, echoing the biblical teachings on sincerity and truth."

Lexi, always seeking practical applications, wondered aloud, "Could you give us an example of how these integrated teachings might help us resolve conflicts or deal with challenges?"

"Certainly, Lexi," Sophea responded. "Consider the biblical story of Solomon's judgment and the Buddhist teachings on understanding and compassion. When faced with a conflict, I try to see the deeper truths in each side, much like Solomon did. At the same time, I practice compassion to understand the suffering of each person involved, which is a fundamental aspect of Buddhism. This dual approach helps in finding solutions that are wise and compassionate, benefiting all parties."

Encouraged by Sophea's explanations, Kesia mused, "So, in a way, the wisdom from these teachings helps build bridges between different beliefs and cultures, fostering greater understanding and peace."

"Exactly, Kesia," Sophea concluded, her eyes alight with the joy of shared understanding. "By exploring and respecting the wisdom in different traditions, we can find common ground and enrich our own spiritual journeys. This interconnectedness not only deepens our own faith but also helps us to see the world as a more interconnected and harmonious place."

As the session drew to a close, the monks reflected on the universal themes of wisdom and compassion, inspired to carry these teachings into their interactions and to view the diverse spiritual paths of the world as varied expressions of the same underlying truths.

Chapter 18

The following morning, as the monks assembled once more in the peaceful ambiance of the monastery's great hall, Kesia's thoughts lingered on the broader aspects of spiritual teachings, particularly those touching on the nature of reality and existence. Inspired by the previous discussions, she posed another thoughtful question to Sophea.

"Sophea," Kesia began, her voice tinged with curiosity, "we've discussed practical wisdom and ethical living from both Buddhist and biblical perspectives. But what about metaphysics? How do the metaphysical aspects of Christianity and Buddhism compare or contribute to our understanding of these teachings?"

Sophea regarded Kesia with an approving nod, recognizing the depth of her inquiry. "That's an excellent question, Kesia," she replied. "Metaphysics, which explores the fundamental nature of reality, existence, and the universe, plays a significant role in both Buddhism and Christianity, though in quite different ways."

Sophea paused to gather her thoughts before continuing. "In Christianity, metaphysics often deals with understanding the nature of God, the creation of the universe, and the relationship between the material and spiritual worlds. Concepts such as the Trinity, the incarnation of Christ, and the resurrection are central, offering insights into the nature of divine existence and its interaction with the human world."

She shifted slightly, signaling a transition in her explanation. "Buddhism, on the other hand, typically focuses on the nature of the self and the illusion of permanence. It teaches about Anatta, or 'non-self,' and Anicca, 'impermanence.' These concepts challenge our conventional understanding of self and reality, pushing practitioners toward a realization of Emptiness, which is devoid of inherent existence but interconnected with all things."

Kesia listened intently, absorbing the nuances of the comparison. "So, how do these ideas influence our spiritual practices or our daily lives?" she asked, eager to connect these metaphysical concepts with practical applications.

Sophea smiled, pleased with Kesia's eagerness to apply these teachings. "In practical terms, understanding these metaphysical concepts can deeply influence how we live our lives. For Christians, the belief in a benevolent creator and an eternal life affects choices and ethical behavior, encouraging a life aligned with divine will and the hope of salvation. This fosters a sense of purpose and moral responsibility."

"In Buddhism," Sophea continued, "the realization of non-self and impermanence can lead to a reduction in selfishness and clinging, promoting a life of detachment, compassion, and mindfulness. This helps practitioners live more harmoniously with the transient nature of life, reducing suffering caused by attachment and aversion."

Lexi, reflecting on the discussion, added, "It sounds like both approaches, although different in their metaphysical foundations, ultimately guide us toward greater wisdom and compassion."

"Exactly, Lexi," Sophea affirmed. "While the metaphysical views might differ, the end goal of both paths is to lead us to a deeper understanding of ourselves and our place in the cosmos, fostering a life of virtue and spiritual depth. By studying these principles, we learn not only about the seen but also about the unseen, encouraging us to live more thoughtfully and conscientiously."

As the monks nodded in agreement, the session concluded with a shared sense of enrichment and a renewed commitment to explore further the metaphysical teachings of their respective faiths, each striving to bridge the gap between philosophical understanding and everyday living.

Chapter 19

The monastery's great hall was filled with a contemplative quiet as the monks settled in for another session with Sophea. Each was eager to continue their exploration of Tobias' teachings, which resonated deeply with their own spiritual quests. Today's discussion promised to delve into the interconnectedness of life and the wisdom inherent in nature.

"Tobias often spoke of the profound lessons that nature itself teaches us about the Creator's laws and the harmony we must strive to maintain with the world around us," Sophea began, her voice echoing softly in the serene space. "He described the seasons, each with its own role and beauty, the flora and fauna that adapt to the rhythms of life, and the overarching cycle that connects them."

Isabella, always intrigued by the practical implications of spiritual teachings, asked, "Sophea, could you elaborate on how Tobias used these natural cycles to illustrate the principles of wisdom?"

"Certainly, Isabella," Sophea replied. "Tobias observed how each season serves a specific purpose in the natural world. Spring brings renewal, summer nurtures growth, autumn heralds harvest, and winter allows rest. He saw these cycles as metaphors for the stages of our own lives and believed that by understanding and respecting these natural processes, we learn to live in synchrony with the Creator's design."

She continued, "For instance, Tobias taught that just as plants do not resist the changing seasons but rather adapt to them, we too should embrace the changes in our lives, recognizing them as opportunities for growth and learning."

Kesia, reflecting on the dynamics of personal growth, inquired, "How did Tobias suggest we apply these lessons of adaptation and growth to our spiritual practices?"

"Tobias advocated for a life that mimics the resilience and adaptability of nature," Sophea explained. "He encouraged mindfulness of our environment and responsiveness to life's changes as they come. For example, he admired how trees bend in the wind and how animals prepare for the changing seasons, seeing these as lessons in humility and preparation."

Lexi, always keen to deepen her spiritual understanding, wondered, "What specific actions did Tobias recommend to help us live more harmoniously with nature and by extension, with each other?"

"Tobias emphasized the importance of living sustainably and respectfully within our environments," Sophea responded. "He urged his followers to observe the natural world not as a resource to be exploited, but as a sacred space to be cherished and preserved. This meant practicing moderation, caring for the earth, and ensuring that our actions contributed positively to the world around us."

Sophea then guided the monks in a meditation. "Let us each reflect on the natural world around us. Think about the trees, the rivers, the animals, and the air. Contemplate how we are all part of this beautiful, intricate system of life. Consider how we might live in a way that honors and preserves this harmony."

The monks closed their eyes, each contemplating the interconnectedness of life and their role within it. They visualized themselves as part of the natural cycle, contributing to the balance and beauty of the environment.

As the session ended, Sophea concluded, "Let us carry forward the wisdom Tobias shared, respecting the natural rhythms and laws of creation. Just as the world nurtures us, so must we nurture it, living each day with intention and gratitude for the bounties it offers."

With these thoughts, the monks were inspired to approach their day with a renewed sense of responsibility and connection to the world around them, embodying the lessons of wisdom that Tobias so eloquently taught.

Chapter 20

As the evening shadows lengthened across the monastery grounds, Lexi found her mind deeply engaged with the day's lessons and discussions. The intricate tapestry of metaphysical concepts and practical wisdom woven by Sophea had left her both inspired and introspective. Seeking clarity and perhaps a deeper understanding, Lexi retired early, her heart open to the celestial guidance that often visited her in dreams.

As she drifted into sleep, her consciousness seemed to expand beyond the confines of the monastery walls, reaching into a realm where time and space blurred into irrelevance. There, in the serene vastness of her dreamworld, Lexi once again encountered Archangel Uriel, his presence as comforting and majestic as ever.

They stood together in a luminous space, an ethereal library where scrolls and books floated freely, each glowing with a soft, internal light. Uriel gestured toward a scroll that hovered before them, its pages filled with ancient symbols and writings.

"Uriel," Lexi began, her voice echoing slightly in the celestial quietude, "today's teachings stirred many questions within me about the nature of reality and our place within it. How do these spiritual lessons connect with the challenges we face in our daily lives?"

Uriel's gaze was kind and understanding. "Lexi, the teachings you absorb, the stories of Solomon and the wisdom of Tobias, are more than mere narratives. They are mirrors reflecting the fundamental truths of existence—about the interplay between the transient and the eternal, the self and the universe."

He reached out, touching the scroll, which then shimmered more brightly. "Consider Solomon's wisdom and his eventual downfall. It is a potent reminder of the delicate balance needed between worldly knowledge and spiritual integrity. It shows us that true wisdom is not just about understanding the laws of the world but aligning them with the laws of the spirit."

Lexi listened intently, absorbing Uriel's words as the scroll before them displayed scenes from Solomon's life, highlighting his achievements and his failures.

"Solomon's journey teaches us about the responsibilities that come with knowledge and power," Uriel continued. "Each decision you make, each action you take in your own life, should be weighed with a similar awareness. Wisdom, true wisdom, involves seeing beyond the immediate, beyond the surface of things, and understanding the deeper implications of your actions."

The images on the scroll shifted, showing Lexi moments from her own life, her decisions, and their impacts on others. "Your journey, much like Solomon's, is about navigating these complexities, making choices that align with both your earthly roles and your spiritual path."

Lexi felt a surge of understanding, a connection between the archaic stories and her personal experiences. "How can I ensure that my choices reflect this balance, Uriel? How can I guard against the pride and complacency that ensnared Solomon?"

Archangel Uriel smiled, his eyes alight with a profound depth. "Always strive to cultivate humility, Lexi. Seek counsel, as you do, from those who walk different paths but share the same destination. Let their wisdom and your experiences guide you. And above all, remain connected to the divine source from which all true wisdom flows. Pray, meditate, and reflect, allowing these practices to anchor and guide your spirit."

As the dream began to fade, Uriel's voice followed Lexi back toward waking consciousness. "Remember, Lexi, wisdom is not just about the knowledge you acquire but about how you apply it to serve the greater good, to harmonize the spiritual and the material in your life."

Lexi awoke just as the first light of dawn crept through her window, her heart filled with peace and a renewed sense of purpose. Uriel's visitation had provided not just answers but a clearer path forward, intertwining the ancient wisdom with her modern challenges, guiding her to live a life of thoughtful balance.

Chapter 21

The relentless rhythm of New York City seemed to carry a more ominous undertone as Redington pored over the case files spread out in front of him. The latest investigation was drawing him into uncharted territory—a disturbing series of crimes linked by dark undercurrents far surpassing the usual motivations of greed or revenge.

The case was composed of seemingly disconnected incidents: a mysterious arson at a historical church that had long been a pillar of the community, the theft of ancient occult texts from a collector's private library, and a sequence of violent assaults, each marked by an unsettling precision. Each crime scene bore cryptic symbols that hinted at a nefarious purpose, suggesting those involved were not merely fringe criminals but part of a group dabbling in dangerously arcane rituals.

Redington's analytical mind wrestled with the eerie implications as the investigation deepened. He learned from experts in religious symbolism and occult practices that the symbols were linked to ancient summoning rituals thought to bridge our world with demonic realms. The thought sent a shiver down his spine as he sat in his dimly lit office late one evening, the city's sounds a ghostly echo to the sinister puzzle unfolding before him. His mind occasionally drifted back to the tranquility of the monastery in Nepal, its serene teachings clashing with the dark reality he faced.

Determined to find the missing link in the chain of bizarre events, Redington arranged a meeting with Professor Elena Mirov, an anthropologist renowned for her expertise in religious cults and esoteric traditions. They met in a secluded café, far from the relentless pulse of the city. Over coffee, she shared her insights, tracing her finger over the images of the symbols that Redington had captured on his camera.

"These are not merely random occult markings," Professor Mirov explained, her voice low and urgent. "They belong to a very specific ritualistic practice believed to bridge our world with darker realms. The individuals behind this don't just believe in these myths—they're actively trying to enact them."

Redington felt the weight of her words. "What's their endgame?" he asked, tension threading his voice.

Professor Mirov leaned in, her expression grave. "The texts and contexts suggest a quest for power—dark, ancient powers they believe can be summoned to serve their will. They think controlling these entities will grant them influence over natural and metaphysical forces. However, history is littered with accounts of such practices ending in disaster—both for the practitioners and the innocent."

Armed with this chilling knowledge, Redington recognized the urgency of the situation. These perpetrators were not merely a threat to public safety; they posed a danger on a potentially existential level. He swiftly organized a specialized task force, directing them with a newfound urgency, understanding that conventional methods would barely scratch the surface of this deep-rooted evil.

As the investigation progressed, every new clue seemed to pull him deeper into a shadowy world, challenging his foundational beliefs and reliance on tangible evidence. Yet, Redington found himself drawing on both the detective skills honed on New York's gritty streets and the spiritual wisdom absorbed in Nepal's serene landscapes. This unique blend of factual investigation and intuitive understanding was becoming his guide through the labyrinth of the occult and the arcane.

Navigating this complex case, Redington started to see patterns and connections that others might dismiss. His approach, balancing the seen with the unseen, the known with the mysterious, was beginning to reshape not just his methods, but also his worldview. The darkness he was uncovering was vast and deep, but he was determined not to let it consume him or the city he swore to protect. As he left his office late into the night, the chilling realization of what he was up against was clearer than ever. Yet, so was his resolve to stop it, armed with every tool at his disposal—from his badge to the esoteric wisdom that now coursed quietly through his veins.

Chapter 22

As the soft light of early morning filtered through the monastery windows, casting a serene glow over the gathered assembly, Sophea prepared to share another chapter from Tobias' cherished writings. The monks, their minds, and hearts open, readied themselves for the profound insights that the day's teachings promised.

"Today, we explore one of the more introspective chapters Tobias wrote," Sophea began, her voice gentle yet filled with a deep reverence for the subject matter. "He likened wisdom to a divine whisper—subtle, not often loud or overt, but deeply impactful and ever-present."

Isabella, intrigued by the metaphor, asked, "Sophea, how did Tobias describe finding and recognizing this whisper of wisdom in our daily lives?"

Sophea nodded appreciatively at the question. "Tobias urged his readers to cherish the quiet moments that life offers—moments of solitude, early morning hours, or peaceful evenings. He believed that it is in these still times that one can best hear the soft whisper of wisdom. He encouraged an attitude of deep listening, a kind of spiritual receptivity where one is open to the guidance of the Creator, attuning oneself to the subtle intuitions that guide our decisions."

She paused to let the words sink in, then continued, "Tobias wrote about the importance of being present in each moment, mindful of the thoughts and decisions that shape our actions. He saw wisdom as an ever-present guide, akin to the gentle touch of a breeze that one can only feel when still."

Kesia, always eager to apply these teachings, reflected, "How can we cultivate such an environment or state of mind that enhances our ability to listen to this whisper?"

"To cultivate such a state," Sophea responded, "Tobias recommended regular practices of meditation and prayer. These are not just acts of faith but also disciplines of the mind, training us to quieten the noise of everyday life and focus on the deeper truths. He also suggested spending time in nature, as the natural world itself teaches us about the rhythms and cycles that encourage reflective thought."

Lexi, considering the practical aspects of these teachings, asked, "What are the signs that we are truly hearing and following this divine whisper of wisdom?"

"That's a thoughtful question, Lexi," Sophea replied. "Tobias believed that when we are aligned with this divine whisper, our actions manifest peace, compassion, and integrity. Conflicts diminish, and relationships strengthen. There is a sense of harmony between our inner intentions and our outward behaviors, and our choices consistently reflect our deepest values."

Sophea then invited the monks to a silent meditation. "Let us sit in silence for a few moments," she instructed. "Focus on your breath, and allow your mind to settle. Invite the whisper of wisdom into your consciousness. Listen for what it might be guiding you to understand or to do."

The room filled with a profound silence, each monk internally seeking that subtle yet powerful divine whisper. After some time, Sophea gently brought the session to a close.

"As we continue our day," she concluded, "Keep your hearts and minds open to the whisper of wisdom that surrounds us. Remember Tobias' advice: wisdom is like a divine whisper, always present, guiding us gently yet profoundly. Let it guide your steps and breathe life into your actions."

With that, the monks slowly rose, each carrying with them a renewed intention to seek out and heed the whispers of wisdom in their everyday lives, inspired by the teachings of Tobias and guided by the compassionate hand of Sophea.

Chapter 23

As night enveloped the monastery, Lexi retired to her small, austere room, her mind still echoing with the day's teachings on the subtle whispers of wisdom. The concept of divine guidance being a gentle, almost imperceptible nudge rather than a clamorous declaration had struck a deep chord within her. As she drifted off to sleep, her thoughts were a meditative reflection on the day's lessons, inviting the possibility of a divine whisper even in her dreams.

In the quiet sanctuary of her dream, Lexi found herself walking through a dense, misty forest. The air was cool, and the path underfoot was soft, covered with a blanket of fallen leaves. The gentle rustling of the trees and the distant call of a nightingale created a symphony of natural sounds. It was here, in this serene dreamscape, that Archangel Uriel appeared beside her, his presence as calming and majestic as ever.

"Uriel," Lexi greeted him, her voice a mere whisper blending with the forest sounds.

"Lexi," Uriel responded, his tone conveying warmth and wisdom. "You seek understanding of the divine whispers, the subtle guidance that shapes your path."

Lexi nodded, looking around at the tranquil forest that seemed to breathe with life. "Yes, I want to understand how to listen, how to truly hear what these whispers are guiding me to do."

Uriel smiled gently, motioning for her to sit on a nearby fallen log. As they sat, the environment seemed to quieten even more, the mist softly enveloping them in a cocoon of privacy and peace.

"Wisdom's whispers," Uriel began, "Are not always through words. They are often felt, experienced as moments of clarity, peace, or intuition. They guide you subtly, influencing your choices with a gentle yet profound presence."

He paused, allowing Lexi to absorb his words. "In your daily life, these whispers can be drowned out by noise, haste, and distraction. Here, in your dream and in places like the monastery, you find the silence necessary to hear them more clearly."

"How can I make space for this silence in my everyday life?" Lexi asked, genuinely curious.

"Create moments of stillness," Uriel advised. "Regularly engage in practices that quiet the mind—meditation, prayer, walks in nature. These are not merely activities but openings, spaces you create to welcome the whisper of wisdom."

Uriel stood, offering Lexi a hand to rise as well. They began to walk slowly along the path, the mist starting to lift, revealing the lush greenery of the forest in greater detail.

"Remember," Uriel continued, "The signs that you are in tune with this wisdom are evident when your actions bring peace to your heart, when they align with your deepest values, and when they foster harmony in your interactions with others."

Lexi felt a profound sense of understanding settling in her heart. The dream, though a construct of her subconscious, carried the weight and warmth of truth.

As the dream began to fade, Uriel's voice echoed softly, "Let the divine whisper guide you, Lexi. Trust in its presence, and let it inform your steps with grace and wisdom."

Lexi awoke just as the first light of dawn was filtering through her window. She lay in silence for a few moments, savoring the peace and clarity the dream had brought. The day awaited with its usual demands, but she felt renewed, equipped with a deeper understanding of how to integrate the divine whispers of wisdom into the fabric of her daily life.

Chapter 24

As the morning light illuminated the pages of Tobias' writings, Sophea prepared to share a blend of history and virtue, merging the legacy of Tobias' influential book with his teachings on the virtue of temperance. The monks, already deeply engrossed in the wisdom of the past chapters, readied themselves for yet another enriching session.

"Tobias' insights on temperance were profound," Sophea began, her voice resonating with admiration for the ancient sage. "He likened temperance to a well-tended orchard, where each tree, carefully cultivated, yields the finest fruit. He drew parallels with how King Solomon organized his kingdom, dividing it into districts, appointing leaders according to their strengths and capabilities to ensure the kingdom's prosperity and balance" (1 Kings 4:7-19).

"As Tobias' book was meticulously copied by scribes and spread across distant lands, it became more than just a manuscript; it became a beacon of wisdom, guiding countless seekers on how to lead a balanced and moderated life. Just as the orchard needs the gardener's hand to maintain harmony and productivity, our lives, too, require the temperance to manage our resources and passions wisely," she explained.

Isabella, intrigued by the historical spread of the book, asked, "Sophea, how did Tobias' teachings on temperance influence the communities that adopted his book?"

Sophea smiled, pleased with the question. "The communities that embraced Tobias' teachings found great value in the principles of temperance. Leaders learned to govern with restraint and foresight, much like Solomon. They understood that unchecked desires could lead to discord and imbalance, just as an untended orchard eventually falls into disarray."

She continued, "Generations passed, and with each, Tobias' teachings deepened in the hearts of those who followed his path. The oak tree under which he once sat and taught grew ever more majestic, symbolizing the enduring and growing influence of his wisdom."

Kesia, always looking for practical applications, inquired, "How can we, in our modern lives, apply Tobias' teachings on temperance to achieve a more balanced life?"

"To embody temperance today," Sophea responded, "we must be mindful of how we allocate our time, energy, and resources. It means practicing self-control, setting boundaries, and prioritizing long-term wellbeing over immediate gratification. This might look like choosing to spend time in meditation or community service rather than in pursuits of fleeting pleasures."

Lexi, reflecting on the depth of the teachings, noted, "It seems that temperance, much like the oak tree, requires time and patience to truly embed itself in our lives."

"Exactly, Lexi," Sophea affirmed. "Temperance is not cultivated overnight but through consistent practice and reflection. It is about making thoughtful choices repeatedly, which eventually shape the course of our lives, much like the daily care that shapes the orchard."

As the session drew to a close, Sophea encouraged the monks to spend the day in contemplation of their own lives. "Consider the areas where temperance could bring more harmony and balance. Reflect on how you might cultivate your personal orchard of virtues."

The monks dispersed, inspired by the legacy of Tobias and the metaphor of the orchard, each pondering how to integrate the virtue of temperance into their lives to bear the best fruits of their own endeavors. Tobias' teachings, preserved in his book and echoed beneath the ancient oak tree, continued to inspire and guide all who sought its wisdom, promising a legacy that would flourish for generations to come.

Chapter 25

After the morning session with Sophea, the air around the monastery seemed to hum with the echoes of ancient wisdom, resonating deeply with the monks who were gathered there. Lexi, inspired and thoughtful from the teachings on temperance, sought a quieter corner to reflect more personally on what had been shared. She found Kesia and Isabella sitting under the sprawling branches of an old tree in the monastery's serene garden—a spot that seemed to beckon for deeper conversations.

Joining her friends, Lexi shared her desire to delve further into the day's lessons. "Sophea's interpretation of Tobias' writings really struck a chord with me," she began, her voice soft but filled with intrigue. "The idea of temperance as a well-tended orchard—it's such a vivid image. It makes me think about what I'm cultivating in my own life."

Isabella nodded, her eyes reflecting the dappled sunlight filtering through the leaves. "It's a beautiful metaphor, isn't it? It shows that temperance isn't just about restraint but about nurturing the right things in the right way. Like carefully choosing which tree to plant in the orchard and where to plant it."

Kesia, always practical, added her perspective. "I've been thinking about how to apply this to our daily routines. It's about balance, right? Not letting one aspect of life overwhelm the others, but giving each the attention it deserves."

Lexi considered this, turning over a fallen leaf in her hand. "It's about intentionality," she mused. "Choosing to spend our energy in ways that bring about the best outcomes, not just for ourselves but for everyone around us."

The conversation drifted toward personal experiences, with each sharing moments where they felt they had either succeeded or struggled with maintaining balance. Isabella spoke of her efforts to balance her spiritual practices with her responsibilities at the monastery, while Kesia discussed her challenges in managing time between community service and personal growth.

Lexi listened intently, then shared her own reflections. "Being here, away from the chaos of my previous life, has taught me a lot about what

I truly value. The teachings on temperance are timely. They remind me that every choice has an impact, like each tree affects the health of the orchard."

Isabella smiled, looking up at the old tree above them. "This tree is probably centuries old. Think about how many seasons it's seen, how many storms it's weathered. It's a testament to the strength that comes from growing slowly, steadily."

Kesia nodded in agreement. "And just like this tree, the teachings of Tobias aren't meant just for the short term. They are principles to live by, principles that grow deeper and stronger with time."

As the afternoon shadows began to lengthen, the three friends agreed to spend a part of each day discussing their progress and challenges in applying the teachings. They saw this as a way to keep each other accountable and to deepen their understanding of temperance.

The session under the oak concluded with a shared commitment to mindful growth. Lexi felt a renewed sense of purpose, bolstered by the support of her friends and the timeless wisdom of Tobias. The teachings, much like the shade of the oak, provided a protective canopy under which they could each grow, fostering virtues that would extend far beyond the walls of the monastery.

Chapter 26

In the serene ambiance of the monastery's great hall, as a gentle morning light streamed through the stained glass, Sophea prepared to guide the monks through yet another chapter of Tobias' profound wisdom. Today's lesson centered on the virtue of fortitude, a quality that Tobias illustrated with the metaphor of a steadfast mountain.

"Tobias wrote about the mountain as a symbol of strength and resilience," Sophea began, her voice imbued with the gravity of the subject. "He admired how mountains endure the elements, standing firm against the winds and storms. Similarly, he explored the fortitude shown by King Solomon in undertaking the monumental task of building the Temple—a venture that required immense physical, emotional, and spiritual strength" (1 Kings 5-6).

Isabella, always thoughtful, asked, "Sophea, how did Tobias draw lessons from Solomon's experience for personal growth?"

Sophea nodded, pleased with Isabella's insightful question. "Tobias saw Solomon's resolve as a direct parallel to the challenges we face in our own spiritual journeys. Just as Solomon remained committed to the construction of the Temple despite its daunting challenges, Tobias encouraged his readers to remain resolute in their convictions and steadfast in their pursuit of wisdom. He believed that personal adversities, much like the harsh weather faced by a mountain, are opportunities to demonstrate our spiritual strength and commitment."

Kesia, reflecting on her own challenges, inquired, "How can we develop such fortitude in our daily lives, especially when faced with personal trials?"

"To cultivate fortitude," Sophea replied, "Tobias suggested that we must anchor ourselves in our faith and the teachings of wisdom, much like a mountain roots itself in the earth. He recommended regular spiritual practices such as meditation, prayer, and studying sacred texts to build inner strength. Additionally, he emphasized the importance of community support, reminding us that just as mountains are part of a range, we are not alone in our struggles."

Lexi, intrigued by the metaphor, wondered, "What specific actions did Tobias recommend to handle moments when our resolve might weaken?"

"Tobias advised that in moments of doubt or weakness, we should remind ourselves of our greater purpose and the rewards of perseverance," Sophea explained. "He often reflected on how Solomon celebrated the completion of the Temple, a moment of great fulfillment and joy that followed years of steadfast effort. Tobias encouraged his followers to visualize the 'temple' they are building in their lives, be it personal growth, service to others, or spiritual enlightenment."

Encouraged by the depth of the discussion, Sophea guided the monks into a brief meditative exercise. "Let's close our eyes and imagine ourselves as mountains," she instructed. "Feel the strength within you, the solidity of your convictions, and the height of your aspirations. Consider the 'temple' you are building with your life. Draw upon the mountain's strength to help you progress toward completing your task, no matter the adversities."

As the meditation ended, the monks felt renewed, each carrying with them the image of the mountain—a symbol of their own fortitude and a reminder of the endurance required to overcome personal challenges and achieve their spiritual goals.

Sophea concluded, "Remember, the path of wisdom is not always easy, but like the mountain, we must strive to rise steadfast and strong, anchored in our faith and purpose. Let Tobias' teachings guide us to be resolute and courageous, as we continue to build the temples of our lives."

With these words, the monks left the session inspired to embody the virtue of fortitude in all aspects of their lives, strengthened by the wisdom of Tobias and the steadfastness of the mountain metaphor.

Chapter 27

As the investigation deepened, Redington's days became a blur of shadowy leads and clandestine meetings. The city that never sleeps seemed even more restless under the cloud of the sinister case that was unfolding. Redington, driven by a relentless commitment to unearth the truth, felt the weight of urgency with each passing night.

The task force had pinpointed a network of suspects linked to the occult practices, each member more elusive than the last. Surveillance operations and data analysis had revealed a potential hub of activity—an abandoned warehouse on the outskirts of the city that seemed to pulse with secretive energy after dusk.

Redington decided on a direct approach, leading a late-night raid on the warehouse. As his team prepared, the air was tense with the anticipation of what they might find. They breached the warehouse under the cover of darkness, tactical lights piercing through the inky blackness inside.

The interior was a labyrinth of ancient symbols and eerie artifacts, more akin to a dark temple than a storage facility. As they moved deeper, they stumbled upon a chilling scene: an elaborate altar setup, complete with ancient relics and disturbing iconography, all arranged for what appeared to be a summoning ritual.

In the shadows of the warehouse, they caught several cult members, cloaked and chanting, seemingly in the midst of their dark rite. The arrests were swift, but the real victory was the discovery of extensive evidence linking the group to the recent crimes. The confiscated items included stolen artifacts, ancient manuscripts, and an array of occult paraphernalia, each item sending chills down the spines of the officers present.

In the aftermath of the raid, as dawn began to break, Redington stood outside the warehouse, watching his team secure the area. The pre-dawn silence was a stark contrast to the adrenaline-fueled chaos of just hours before. He felt a mix of relief and foreboding; while they had disrupted a potentially catastrophic ritual, the full scope of the cult's intentions remained a haunting mystery.

Returning to his office, Redington poured over the items recovered. Among them was a journal belonging to the cult's leader, filled with ramblings about harnessing demonic powers to instigate a new world order—one ruled by shadows and chaos. The writings were erratic but revealed a chilling level of conviction and detailed knowledge of ancient dark rituals.

It was then that Redington realized the battle was far from over. The arrests had cut off one head of the hydra, but the ideology and the threat it posed were far-reaching. He pondered the next steps, knowing that the cult's beliefs could inspire others to continue their sinister work.

Driven by a newfound resolve, Redington reached out to Professor Mirov again, seeking deeper insights into the cult's beliefs and how they might prevent further escalation of their activities. Together, they delved into historical accounts of similar cults, searching for strategies that had effectively dismantled such groups without driving them further underground.

As Redington immersed himself in the study, the line between his professional duties and personal crusade began to blur. He was no longer just solving a case; he was warding off an encroaching darkness that threatened to seep into the very fabric of the city.

Each piece of evidence, each expert consultation, fortified his resolve but also deepened his understanding of the complex interplay between belief and power. Redington found himself drawing not just on his law enforcement training but also on the spiritual resilience he had honed in Nepal. The wisdom of balance, the understanding of light and shadow, played through his mind as he strategized his next moves.

As Redington prepared for the challenges ahead, he knew he was not just protecting the city from crime, but also from a darkness that sought to undermine the very essence of order and light. The fight was personal, each step forward a testament to his evolution not just as a detective, but as a guardian of the city's soul.

Chapter 28

The morning light shone brightly into the monastery's great hall as the monks gathered around Sophea, ready for the next lesson drawn from Tobias' life and writings. Today's discussion promised to explore the profound relationship between justice and wisdom, a theme that resonated deeply within the spiritual community.

"Tobias was greatly inspired by the wisdom of Solomon, particularly by his famous judgment in the case of the two mothers claiming the same baby," Sophea began, her voice steady and imbued with the gravity of the subject. "This story, found in the scriptures, highlights Solomon's acute sense of justice and his ability to discern the truth in a seemingly impossible situation" (1 Kings 3:16-28).

Sophea paused for a moment before continuing, "From this, Tobias developed the metaphor of justice as a field that requires careful cultivation and nurturing. Just as a farmer tends to his fields to yield a fair harvest, so must a society or community foster conditions where fairness and justice can flourish."

Isabella, always keen to connect these teachings with real-world applications, asked, "Sophea, how did Tobias suggest we cultivate such a field of justice in our own communities?"

"Tobias believed that the cultivation of justice begins with individual actions," Sophea explained. "He urged his readers to practice fairness in their daily interactions and to make decisions that consider the well-being of all parties involved. This includes being mindful of our biases and striving to understand multiple perspectives before rendering judgments."

Kesia, looking for deeper understanding, inquired, "What role did Tobias assign to wisdom in achieving justice?"

"Tobias emphasized that true wisdom is indispensable in the pursuit of justice," Sophea responded. "He argued that wisdom allows us to see beyond surface appearances and to discern the deeper truths of any situation. Just like Solomon, who used his wisdom to uncover the true mother of the child, we too must use our wisdom to navigate complex social and ethical challenges, ensuring that our decisions contribute to a balanced and fair society."

Lexi, thoughtful and introspective, questioned further, "Can you share how Tobias addressed the mistakes or injustices that inevitably occur despite our best efforts?"

"That's a significant aspect of Tobias' teachings," Sophea acknowledged. "He recognized that humans are fallible and that injustices do occur. Tobias encouraged a system of accountability where errors can be openly acknowledged and corrected. He advocated for compassion and forgiveness as essential components of justice, enabling communities to heal and move forward from conflicts."

Encouraged by the monks' engagement, Sophea led them in a reflective exercise. "Let us each think about a recent decision we made. Reflect on whether it was fair, how you arrived at it, and how it might have been perceived by others involved. Consider what adjustments, if any, could be made to enhance fairness and justice."

The monks closed their eyes, each contemplating their own experiences and decisions in light of Tobias' teachings on justice.

As the reflection ended, Sophea concluded, "Remember, the field of justice we cultivate in our community will determine the health and harmony of our collective lives. Let us strive to embody the wisdom of Solomon and the teachings of Tobias in every decision, fostering a just and equitable environment for all."

With these words, the monks were inspired to continue their day with a renewed commitment to fairness, justice, and the wise cultivation of their communal field, guided by the profound lessons from Tobias' life and teachings.

Chapter 29

As the morning sunlight streamed into the monastery's hall through the ornate windows, creating patterns of light and shadow on the stone floor, the monks gathered around Sophea for another enriching lesson from Tobias' teachings. Today's session focused on the virtue of patience, a quality that Tobias likened to the careful cultivation of a vineyard.

"Tobias often reflected on the nature of patience through the metaphor of a vineyard," began Sophea, her voice imbued with a serene calm. "He saw the growth of vines and the eventual harvest as a perfect analogy for understanding the importance of timing and the rewards of patience in our lives."

She continued, drawing parallels from biblical history, "Tobias particularly admired how Solomon demonstrated patience in his negotiations with King Hiram of Tyre. These negotiations were crucial for acquiring the cedar wood and skilled craftsmen needed for constructing the Temple" (1 Kings 5:1-12). "Solomon's ability to negotiate effectively over time ensured that he secured the best resources, showing that patience can lead to achieving great ends."

Isabella, intrigued by the practical applications of this virtue, asked, "Sophea, how did Tobias suggest we cultivate such patience in our own lives?"

Sophea nodded thoughtfully before responding. "Tobias believed that patience could be cultivated through daily practice and mindfulness. He advised his followers to observe moments in their lives where impatience surfaced and to consciously choose a more measured response. He emphasized the idea of waiting as an active state—mindfully preparing, rather than passively enduring."

Kesia, reflecting on her own experiences, inquired, "What are the signs that we are growing in patience, according to Tobias?"

"Tobias wrote that growing in patience is often signified by a decrease in stress and an increase in peace, even in situations that previously would have caused us frustration or anger," explained Sophea. "He likened this to a vineyard that grows stronger and more fruitful over the years. As we practice patience, our actions and reactions become more thoughtful and less impulsive, contributing to a more harmonious life."

Lexi, always keen to deepen her understanding, wondered aloud, "How did Tobias reconcile the need for patience with the necessity of timely action?"

"That's an excellent question, Lexi," Sophea replied. "Tobias recognized that wisdom lies in knowing when to act and when to wait. He advised that we should be like the wise vintner who knows the exact right moment to harvest the grapes—neither too early nor too late. This balance ensures the quality of the wine, just as our decisions, made at the right time, ensure the quality of our outcomes."

Encouraged by the depth of the discussion, Sophea led the monks in a brief reflective exercise. "Let us close our eyes and think of a situation that requires our patience. Envision yourself handling it as a skilled vintner tends to his vineyard. Contemplate the steps you can take to nurture this situation with care and attention, waiting for the right moment to act."

As the monks meditated on these thoughts, a sense of calm filled the hall. They each considered how cultivating patience might transform their interactions and decisions, enhancing their spiritual growth and personal peace.

Sophea concluded the session with a gentle reminder, "Let us move forward with the patience of a vintner and the wisdom of Solomon, trusting that our careful attention and timing will bring forth the best fruits in our lives, just as they do in the vineyard."

With these words, the monks dispersed, each carrying with them a renewed commitment to cultivating patience in their lives, inspired by the teachings of Tobias and the age-old wisdom of tending to a vineyard.

Chapter 30

As dawn broke, casting a soft golden hue through the monastery's tall windows, the monks gathered once more around Sophea in the great hall, ready for another insightful lesson from Tobias' teachings. Today's discussion centered on the virtue of humility, a trait Tobias profoundly admired and often exemplified through natural metaphors.

"Tobias likened humility to rivers that gracefully lower themselves to nourish the land and all living things they encounter," Sophea began, her voice resonating with the depth of the lesson. "He saw humility as essential for true wisdom, as it involves recognizing our limitations and the vastness of divine wisdom."

She continued, referencing the biblical King Solomon, "Despite his immense wealth and wisdom, Solomon showed his humility when he acknowledged his limitations before God, admitting his youth and inexperience when he became king and asking for divine wisdom to govern his people effectively" (1 Kings 3:7). "Tobias used this moment to highlight how even the wisest among us must remain humble, recognizing our need for guidance beyond ourselves."

Isabella, deeply moved by the analogy, asked, "Sophea, how did Tobias suggest we practice humility in our own lives?"

"Tobias advised his readers to practice humility by serving others and valuing their contributions as much as their own," Sophea replied. "He encouraged embracing moments of failure as opportunities for growth and learning, rather than as defeats. By doing so, we acknowledge our human limitations and open ourselves up to the wisdom that can only come from experiencing and overcoming challenges."

Kesia, seeking practical applications, inquired, "What are the signs that we are growing in humility, according to Tobias?"

"Tobias wrote that a growing sense of peace and a decreasing need to assert one's importance are clear signs of developing humility," explained Sophea. "He noted that as we learn to listen more and speak less, we begin to appreciate the value of all voices, not just our own. This shift is a strong indication that humility is taking root in our hearts."

Lexi, curious about the spiritual depth of humility, asked, "How does humility affect our spiritual growth, Sister?"

"Humility deepens our spiritual growth by allowing us to be more receptive to the truths we might otherwise miss if we were too focused on our own perceptions and beliefs," Sophea answered. "It opens us to a broader understanding of the divine and our place within it. Just as rivers gather strength and depth as they flow and descend, our spiritual lives gain depth and vitality as we lower ourselves in humility."

Encouraged by the monks' thoughtful engagement, Sophea guided them in a short meditative exercise. "Let us close our eyes and envision ourselves as a river, flowing gently across the landscape. Think about how the river enriches the land, supporting life along its banks. Reflect on how you can bring life and nourishment to others through your humility."

The monks sat in quiet reflection, each considering how they might incorporate the virtue of humility more fully into their lives, inspired by Solomon's example and Tobias' teachings.

As the meditation concluded, Sophea offered a closing thought: "Let us strive to embody the rivers of humility in all that we do, recognizing our limits but also the boundless possibilities that come from a humble heart. In this way, we allow the streams of divine wisdom to flow freely through us, enriching not only our lives but also those of everyone we touch."

With renewed inspiration, the monks dispersed, each carrying with them the serene and nourishing image of humility as a life-giving river, ready to apply the lessons of Tobias in their daily practices and interactions.

Chapter 31

The quiet murmur of anticipation filled the monastery's great hall as the monks settled into their seats for another lesson from Tobias' revered teachings. Today, Sophea prepared to delve into the virtue of good counsel, a theme Tobias richly illustrated with the metaphor of a forest.

"Tobias envisioned good counsel as a vast forest," Sophea began, her voice echoing softly through the hall. "In this forest, each tree represents a different advisor, and together, these trees contribute to the health and vitality of the woodland. Just as a forest thrives with a diversity of trees, so too does human understanding flourish with a variety of perspectives."

She continued, drawing from the biblical narrative, "Tobias often reflected on King Solomon's early reign, noting how Solomon's wisdom was partly due to his willingness to listen to his counselors. However, as recorded in the scriptures, Solomon's later decisions, particularly his rejection of wise counsel in favor of harsher measures suggested by younger advisors, led to great troubles, including the eventual division of his kingdom" (1 Kings 12:6-8).

Isabella, intrigued by the analogy, asked, "Sophea, how did Tobias suggest we apply the lesson of seeking diverse perspectives in our own decision-making processes?"

Sophea nodded, acknowledging the importance of the question. "Tobias advised that just as a wise king surrounds himself with various counselors, we too should seek the insights and advice of others in our own lives. He stressed the importance of listening not only to those who share our views but also to those who may offer contrasting perspectives. This, he believed, helps us avoid the pitfalls of narrow-mindedness and make more balanced, informed decisions."

Kesia, always looking for deeper insights, wondered, "What did Tobias say about the dangers of ignoring wise counsel?"

"Tobias warned that ignoring wise counsel can lead to decisions that are not only flawed but also potentially destructive," Sophea replied. "He used the example of Solomon's decision to increase labor and taxes, which ultimately led to rebellion and division. Tobias saw this as a clear lesson in the risks of dismissing experienced and balanced advice in favor of more appealing but shortsighted suggestions."

Lexi, reflecting on practical application, inquired, "How can we ensure that we are truly open to good counsel and not just hearing what we want to hear?"

"To truly benefit from good counsel, Tobias recommended cultivating humility and openness," Sophea explained. "He suggested that we should actively seek feedback and be ready to question our own assumptions. Moreover, he believed in the practice of regular reflection on the advice received, weighing it carefully against our values and long-term goals."

Encouraged by the thoughtful discussion, Sophea guided the monks in a brief reflective exercise. "Let us each consider a recent decision we faced. Think about the counsel you sought or might have overlooked. Reflect on how different perspectives could have influenced your decision and how you might integrate this lesson into future decisions."

The monks closed their eyes, each pondering the complex interplay of advice, perspective, and decision-making in their own lives.

As they concluded the reflection, Sophea offered a parting thought: "Let us strive to be like a forest rich in diversity, welcoming the wisdom of many counselors. In doing so, we build not only our individual wisdom but also the collective wisdom of our community."

With these words, the monks were inspired to seek and value diverse perspectives, carrying with them the image of a forest where every tree plays a vital role in the health of the whole. This lesson from Tobias would surely guide them in cultivating a community rich in wisdom and insight.

Chapter 32

With the adrenaline of the warehouse raid still coursing through his veins, Redington turned his full attention to the intricate network that underpinned the cult's sprawling operations. The raid had unearthed more than just illicit artifacts and eerie ceremonial altars; it had exposed the tip of a sinister iceberg, hinting at the depth and reach of the cult's influence across the city.

As he sifted through the evidence collected—each item meticulously tagged and recorded—Redington discovered an array of communications devices. These weren't just simple phones or tablets; they were encrypted with sophisticated software, clearly designed to shield the cult's activities from prying eyes. The initial forensic analysis cracked open a trove of data that mapped a vast web of contacts stretching across various sectors of the city. This network infiltrated unexpected places, from the upper echelons of financial institutions to the murky depths of the underground crime world, and even into political circles that were disturbingly high up.

The revelation of such a structured and influential network was deeply unsettling. It was clear that this was no ragtag group of occult enthusiasts; this was a well-organized syndicate with its tendrils coiled deep within the city's societal foundations. The cult had its fingers in numerous pies, manipulating events and people with a precision that spoke of long-term planning and deep-rooted infiltration.

Recognizing the gravity of the threat, Redington convened a series of strategic meetings with key figures in intelligence, cybersecurity, and law enforcement. In a secure room lined with monitors and buzzing softly with the hum of computers, they laid out the cult's network on digital maps, tracing the connections like a sprawling, sinister spiderweb.

The strategy to dismantle this network had to be multifaceted. Redington proposed a coordinated approach that included rigorous digital forensics to track financial transactions and communications, undercover operations to infiltrate the lower ranks of the cult, and continuous surveillance to monitor suspected members. Every agency brought its expertise to the table, forming a task force that was formidable in its scope and determination.

The ensuing weeks saw a hive of activity as the task force executed the strategy. Digital forensics experts worked round the clock, piecing together shredded data and tracing the digital footprints left behind by the cult's activities. Undercover agents, carefully selected for their skills and nerve, disappeared into their roles, gathering intelligence from the inside.

Simultaneously, surveillance teams kept a vigilant watch over suspected cult members, tracking their movements and intercepting communications where possible. Every piece of information was analyzed, every lead followed up with precision. The city became a chessboard, with Redington and his task force maneuvering strategically to corner their insidious adversary.

As the network began to unravel, arrests were made, assets seized, and several key figures were brought to light, their roles in the cult's activities laid bare. Each arrest, each piece of evidence gathered added to the picture of a cult that was as dangerous as it was ambitious, seeking power through dark and ancient forces that they believed they could control.

Throughout this intense period, Redington felt the weight of his responsibility acutely. The battle was not just against a criminal network; it was a fight to protect the city from a darkness that sought to engulf it from within. The challenge was immense, but Redington was not deterred. He knew that the road ahead was long and fraught with danger, but he was committed to following it to the end, driven by a resolve to keep the city safe from the shadows that threatened to consume it.

Chapter 33

In the stillness of the night, as the monastery settled under a blanket of serene darkness, Lexi found herself transported from her modest chamber to the luminescent realm of her recurring dreams. Here, amidst a celestial landscape, the presence of Archangel Uriel awaited her, more vivid than ever. His form shimmered with a gentle, golden light, casting a soft glow that seemed to warm the very air around him.

Lexi approached Archangel Uriel through a meadow bathed in moonlight, the grass beneath her feet glistening with dew. The air was fragrant with the scent of jasmine and lilac, enhancing the surreal beauty of the dream. Uriel, with his wings unfurled in majestic splendor, turned to greet her with a benevolent smile.

"Welcome, Lexi," Uriel's voice resonated with a calm authority, echoing slightly as if carried by the wind. "You have been pondering deeply about the nature of wisdom and counsel."

Lexi nodded, feeling an unspoken understanding flow between them. "Yes, I've been reflecting on the lessons of Tobias and the importance of diverse perspectives. It seems there is so much to consider, so much I am still learning."

Uriel stepped closer, the light surrounding him pulsing softly. "True wisdom, Lexi, is like the vast universe—ever expanding and infinitely complex. It requires not only the seeking of various voices but also the courage to act upon the truths you discover."

He gestured to the sky above, where stars began to align, forming intricate patterns. "Consider these stars," he continued. "Each one represents a piece of knowledge, a perspective, a life. Alone, they are points of light, but together, they form constellations, stories written in the heavens. You, too, must learn to connect these points in your life, to form your own stories of wisdom."

Lexi looked up, awe-struck by the celestial spectacle. "How can I ensure I am truly open to these perspectives and not just seeking confirmation for my own beliefs?"

Uriel's gaze was compassionate yet piercing. "You must cultivate a heart of humility and a spirit of inquiry. Ask questions, listen earnestly, and be willing to be transformed by what you learn. Wisdom is not just acquiring knowledge; it's a transformative process that reshapes your being."

He reached out, placing a hand on her shoulder. At his touch, a warmth spread through her, comforting yet invigorating. "In your journey, be like the river that shapes the landscape through which it flows—persistent, adaptive, and nourishing to all it touches."

The dream began to fade, the edges of the meadow blurring into the growing light of dawn. Lexi felt a gentle pull back to the waking world but held onto Uriel's final words.

"Remember, every person you meet, every story you hear, adds to the forest of your understanding. Let it grow wild and wide."

As Lexi awoke, the first light of morning filtered through her window, casting patterns on the stone floor. She sat up, filled with a renewed sense of purpose and a deep yearning to seek out the wisdom Uriel spoke of. With a quiet resolve, she prepared for the day, the image of the starlit sky etched in her mind, guiding her forward.

Chapter 34

As the early morning sun bathed the
monastery's great hall in a warm, golden light,
the monks gathered once more around Sophea
for their daily discourse. Today, they were to
explore the virtue of charity, beautifully depicted
by Tobias in his writings as a lush, thriving
garden.

"Tobias envisioned charity as a garden where
each act of giving is like sowing seeds that
bloom into beauty and joy across the
community," Sophea began, her voice imbued
with the gentle enthusiasm that this metaphor
inspired. "He drew upon the example of King
Solomon, noted for his unparalleled generosity
toward his workers and allies, which is well
documented in the scriptures" (1 Kings 10:23-
25).

"Solomon's kingdom was famed not only for its wealth but also for its spirit of abundance and giving. Tobias used these historical accounts to illustrate how a generous spirit can significantly enrich a community, making it robust and vibrant like a well-tended garden."

Isabella, always thoughtful and eager to connect these teachings to personal growth, asked, "Sophea, how did Tobias suggest we cultivate such a garden of charity in our own lives?"

"Tobias believed that charity begins in the heart and extends through our actions," Sophea replied. "He encouraged his readers to practice charity not only in giving materially but also in offering time, attention, and compassion to others. He taught that these acts of kindness purify our own hearts and spread joy much like water nourishes a garden, helping it to flourish."

Kesia, considering the practical implications, inquired, "What are some specific ways we can practice this kind of charity every day?"

"To practice daily charity, Tobias recommended simple acts like sharing food with those in need, providing a listening ear to someone going through a tough time, or volunteering in community projects," Sophea explained. "Each act, no matter how small, contributes to the growth of the communal garden of charity."

Lexi, reflecting on the deeper spiritual aspects of charity, asked, "How does practicing charity impact our own spiritual journey?"

Sophea nodded, appreciating the depth of Lexi's question. "Tobias taught that charity is transformative. It opens our hearts to the realities of others, diminishing our egocentric tendencies and fostering a spirit of unity. This transformation is akin to the way a garden transforms the landscape—it beautifies not only the external environment but also enriches the soil, making it fertile for new life."

Inspired by the discussion, Sophea guided the monks in a short meditation. "Let us close our eyes and envision ourselves walking through a garden of our own making, filled with the flowers of our charitable acts. Think about the colors, the fragrances, and the life that your garden brings to those who wander its paths."

As the monks visualized their gardens, a sense of peace and purpose filled the room. They contemplated the many ways they could contribute to their community's well-being through acts of charity, inspired by Tobias' teachings.

As they opened their eyes, Sophea concluded, "Let this image of a flourishing garden inspire us to cultivate charity in our lives. Remember, each act of giving, no matter how small, adds beauty and strength to the tapestry of our community."

Energized by these thoughts, the monks prepared to carry the spirit of charity into their day, each committed to nurturing their garden of generosity, guided by the wise teachings of Tobias.

Chapter 35

As the tranquil morning gave way to a serene afternoon, the monks assembled in the monastery's great hall, where the atmosphere was imbued with a sense of culmination and deep reflection. Sophea, with a subtle smile of profound satisfaction, prepared to share the final teachings from Tobias' revered writings. This session was to focus on the ultimate integration of all virtues into a harmonious whole, as Tobias had envisioned.

"Tobias, in his concluding reflections, described wisdom as a celestial harmony, a divine symphony that aligns the heavens with the earth," Sophea began, her voice echoing softly through the hall. "He saw this harmony as the perfect integration of all virtues, a reflection of the divine order that encompasses every aspect of our lives."

She continued, "Tobias brought together the virtues we have discussed—temperance, justice, fortitude, charity, and others—illustrating how each contributes to a broader, harmonious whole. He likened this to a symphony where every instrument, while distinct, is essential to the fullness of the music."

Isabella, moved by the metaphor, asked, "Sophea, how did Tobias suggest we apply this concept of celestial harmony in our daily lives?"

Sophea responded, "Tobias urged his readers to pursue wisdom relentlessly and to live by the virtues that reflect this harmony. He encouraged us to see our actions and decisions as notes in a larger divine melody. Just as a symphonist would, we must carefully consider how our individual actions contribute to the overall harmony of our community and the world."

Kesia, always keen to explore practical applications, inquired, "What specific practices did Tobias recommend to help us align more closely with this celestial harmony?"

"To align ourselves with this celestial harmony, Tobias recommended regular reflection on our actions and their impacts," Sophea explained. "He advocated for meditation, prayer, and the study of sacred texts to continually recalibrate our understanding and alignment with divine wisdom. He also suggested engaging in community service and dialogue, which allow us to test and refine our virtues in real-world settings."

Lexi, contemplating the spiritual depth of Tobias' teachings, questioned, "How can we inspire others to walk in these paths of harmony and wisdom?"

"Tobias believed that the best way to inspire others was by example," Sophea replied. "By embodying the virtues of divine harmony in our own lives, we naturally become beacons of wisdom for others. Tobias emphasized the importance of sharing our journey and struggles openly, which not only humanizes us but also encourages others to seek wisdom and join in the symphony."

Inspired by the discussion, Sophea guided the monks in a closing reflection. "Let us each consider how we might contribute to the divine symphony today. Think about your interactions, your decisions, and how you might align them more closely with the virtues we've explored. Imagine the impact of our collective harmony on the world."

As the monks meditated on these ideas, a deep sense of purpose filled the room. They visualized their lives as part of a grand orchestral piece, each action a note that contributed to the divine melody.

Sophea concluded the session with a call to action: "Let us go forth and live in harmony, not just within ourselves but with each other and the world. Let the symphony of celestial harmony guide every step we take and every decision we make."

With that, the monks rose, feeling empowered and aligned, ready to embody the celestial harmony that Tobias envisioned, each committed to making their part of the world a more harmonious and enlightened place.

Chapter 36

The monks gathered once again in the tranquil atmosphere of the monastery's great hall, where the filtered light cast peaceful shadows around them. Sophea, ready to share yet another profound lesson from Tobias' teachings, opened the ancient texts to a chapter that explored the gentle virtue of meekness.

"Tobias likened meekness to a meadow—soft, inviting, and resilient," Sophea began, her voice carrying the serene quality of the subject matter. "He used this beautiful natural imagery to express how meekness, far from being a weakness, is a strength that fosters growth and peace."

She continued, "In his reflections, Tobias often referred to Solomon's prayer for wisdom. Instead of asking for wealth, long life, or the defeat of his enemies, Solomon chose to ask for an understanding heart to govern his people effectively" (1 Kings 3:9). "Tobias saw this request as a perfect example of meekness, showing how it allows one to truly 'inherit the earth,' to appreciate and cultivate the beauty and bounty it offers."

Isabella, drawn to the practical aspects of these teachings, asked, "Sophea, how did Tobias suggest we cultivate such meekness in our own lives?"

"To cultivate meekness," Sophea replied, "Tobias recommended daily practices of reflection and meditation, focusing on the virtues of humility and gentleness. He believed that by understanding our own limitations and embracing gentleness in our interactions, we could develop a meadow-like resilience—soft yet strong."

Kesia, considering the implications of this virtue, inquired, "What benefits did Tobias see in meekness for leaders and citizens alike?"

"Tobias believed that meekness was crucial for effective leadership and harmonious living within communities," Sophea explained. "For leaders, it meant governing with compassion and empathy, ensuring decisions were made for the good of all rather than personal gain. For citizens, meekness facilitated peaceful coexistence, promoting understanding and cooperation over conflict."

Lexi, always eager to understand the deeper spiritual implications, questioned, "How does meekness impact our spiritual growth, Sister?"

"Meekness deepens our spiritual connections by fostering an openness to divine guidance," answered Sophea. "Tobias taught that a meek heart is like fertile soil, ready to receive the seeds of wisdom that the Creator sows. This condition of openness and receptivity enhances our spiritual insights and aligns us more closely with divine will."

Inspired by the depth of the discussion, Sophea led the monks in a brief meditative practice. "Let us close our eyes and imagine ourselves in a lush meadow, surrounded by the beauty of nature. Feel the softness of the earth underfoot, the gentleness of the breeze. Reflect on how you can bring this meekness into every aspect of your life, nurturing the growth of yourself and those around you."

As the monks meditated, they visualized themselves embodying the soft strength of a meadow, each committing to bring this sense of peace and resilience into their interactions and decisions.

Concluding the session, Sophea encouraged, "Let us strive to walk with the meekness of a meadow, gentle yet resilient, allowing us to truly inherit the beauty and bounty of the earth. May this virtue guide us in our leadership, our communities, and our spiritual journeys."

With a renewed sense of purpose, the monks rose, ready to practice the meekness Tobias extolled, each feeling more connected to the natural harmony and spiritual depth of their tranquil monastic environment.

Chapter 37

The monastery's great hall was filled with a contemplative quiet as the morning light gently illuminated the faces of the gathered monks. Sophea prepared to share insights from another chapter of Tobias' teachings, this time focusing on the vital virtue of hope, portrayed as a safe haven for the soul.

"Tobias envisioned hope as a sanctuary, a safe haven that offers refuge during storms of despair and a guiding light through the fog of uncertainty," Sophea began, her voice embodying the comfort and assurance that hope itself provides. "He drew upon the example of Solomon, who hoped for a peaceful and prosperous reign over his kingdom—a hope that was largely fulfilled during his rule" (1 Kings 4:20-25).

She continued, "Solomon's era of peace and prosperity exemplified how hope, when anchored in wise leadership and righteous living, can lead to real and tangible outcomes. Tobias used this historical reflection to illustrate hope's power not only as a spiritual aspiration but also as a practical force that shapes reality."

Isabella, always eager to connect these teachings with personal growth, asked, "Sophea, how did Tobias suggest we nurture hope in our own lives?"

"Tobias recommended engaging with practices that reinforce hope on a daily basis," Sophea replied. "This includes meditating on the scriptures, observing the cycles of nature, and participating in community acts that reaffirm the goodness and potential of humanity. He particularly admired how nature itself, through processes like the regeneration of forests after wildfires, shows us the resilience and renewal that hope can bring."

Kesia, reflecting on the challenges of maintaining hope in difficult times, inquired, "What guidance did Tobias offer for those times when hope seems hard to hold onto?"

"Tobias acknowledged that maintaining hope can be challenging, especially in times of personal or communal crisis," Sophea answered. "He encouraged his readers to remember past victories and lessons learned from difficult times, using them as fuel to sustain hope. He also stressed the importance of community support, reminding us that hope can be reignited and shared through encouragement and empathy from others."

Lexi, interested in the deeper implications, asked, "How does hope influence our actions and decisions, according to Tobias?"

"Tobias believed that hope acts as a compass, guiding our decisions toward future possibilities rather than current limitations," explained Sophea. "He taught that with hope, we are more likely to take positive actions and make decisions that contribute to healing and growth, both personally and within our communities."

Inspired by the depth of the discussion, Sophea led the monks in a brief reflective exercise. "Let us close our eyes and imagine ourselves in a haven of hope. Picture a place where you feel safe, peaceful, and hopeful. Reflect on how this place of hope influences your feelings, thoughts, and decisions."

As the monks meditated, a serene sense of possibility filled the hall, each monk visualizing their personal haven of hope and drawing strength from it.

Sophea concluded the session with encouraging words, "Let us carry this haven of hope within us, using it to navigate the uncertainties of life. Remember, hope is not just a feeling but a choice and a guide that leads us toward peace and prosperity, just as it did for Solomon."

With a renewed sense of purpose, the monks rose, ready to foster hope in their lives and their communities, inspired by Tobias' teachings and the enduring wisdom of Solomon's peaceful reign.

Chapter 38

As the moon cast its silvery light over the monastery, Lexi settled into her modest bed, her mind filled with the day's teachings and discussions. The virtue of hope, so eloquently discussed by Sophea, lingered in her thoughts, weaving into the fabric of her consciousness as she drifted into sleep. That night, Lexi found herself once again in the ethereal presence of Archangel Uriel, in a dream that felt as real and vivid as the waking world.

The setting of her dream was a vast, open plain under a starlit sky, where the grass whispered secrets with the wind, and the stars above seemed to sing in a silent symphony of light. Uriel appeared before her, his countenance serene and his wings reflecting the celestial glow of the cosmos.

"Lexi," Uriel's voice enveloped her, resonant and filled with warmth, "you have been reflecting deeply on hope and its power to guide and sustain."

"Yes, Uriel," Lexi replied, her voice steady yet full of wonder. "I've learned that hope is not merely a feeling, but a force—a guide through darkness and uncertainty."

Uriel nodded, a gentle smile gracing his features. "Indeed, Lexi. Hope is the beacon that lights the path when all else seems obscured. But it is also more; it is the very fabric that binds the tapestry of the universe. It connects every act of kindness, every gesture of love, every moment of courage."

He extended his hand, and as Lexi took it, they began to ascend, rising above the plain toward the stars. Below them, the world seemed to unfold as a map, rivers of light flowing across the landscape, weaving through the darkness.

"Look closely, Lexi," Uriel guided her gaze. "Each light represents a soul ignited by hope. See how they connect, how they spread, growing brighter against the night."

Lexi watched, mesmerized, as the lights expanded, linking together in a dazzling display of interconnectedness. "It's beautiful," she breathed, "but how can I carry this vision into my waking life? How can I hold onto hope when the darkness feels overwhelming?"

Uriel's grip tightened reassuringly. "Remember this vision, Lexi. Carry it in your heart as a reminder that no light is too small, no act of hope too insignificant. Each moment you choose hope, you contribute to this celestial tapestry."

He paused, allowing the scene to sink into Lexi's soul. "And when you feel the weight of despair, recall this unity, this connection. You are never alone in your journey; the hope you foster affects more than you can see or know."

As the dream began to fade, Uriel's final words echoed around her, "Let hope be your constant companion, your unwavering guide. Let it illuminate your path and inspire others to follow."

Lexi awoke just as dawn was breaking, the first gentle rays of sunlight spilling into her room. She lay there for a moment, the memory of the dream vivid and inspiring. Rising from her bed, she felt a renewed sense of purpose and clarity. Today, she would carry the light of hope, not just for herself, but as a beacon for all those around her. With Uriel's words etched in her heart, she was ready to face the day's challenges, guided by the celestial harmony of hope and interconnectedness.

Chapter 39

In the hushed ambiance of the monastery's great hall, where the early light filtered through the stained glass to lay patterns across the stone floors, the monks settled in for another session with Sophea. Today, she would discuss the virtue of courage, portrayed by Tobias as a steadfast citadel, a stronghold of strength and protection.

"Tobias drew upon the symbol of a citadel to represent courage — not just any courage, but the courage rooted in wisdom and faith," Sophea began, her voice echoing the resolve and fortitude of her subject. "He reflected on Solomon's bold decision to build the Temple in Jerusalem, a monumental undertaking that presented significant logistical and spiritual challenges" (1 Kings 5-6).

She continued, "Solomon's initiative required not only physical resources and manpower but also a deep conviction in his divine mission. Tobias admired how Solomon's courage was intertwined with his faith, driving him to undertake tasks that were daunting yet critical for his people's spiritual and cultural identity."

Isabella, drawn to the historical aspect, asked, "Sophea, how did Tobias interpret Solomon's actions as lessons for us in practicing courage today?"

"Tobias believed that true courage involves making decisions that uphold integrity and faith, even when faced with great risks," Sophea replied. "He taught that like a citadel, our courage should serve as a defense for our values and principles, protecting not only ourselves but also those who depend on us."

Kesia, reflecting on her own experiences, inquired, "What advice did Tobias give for cultivating such courage in our everyday lives?"

"To cultivate this kind of courage, Tobias recommended regular reflection on our deepest convictions and the purposes that drive our actions," Sophea explained. "He encouraged engaging in prayer or meditation to strengthen our spiritual foundation, which in turn fortifies our courage. He also suggested that we seek counsel from those we trust and admire, much like Solomon consulted Nathan the prophet."

Lexi, always seeking to understand the broader implications, asked, "How does courage, in this sense, impact our communities and societies?"

"Tobias wrote that when individuals exhibit true courage — the courage to make difficult decisions that honor their faith and integrity — it inspires and uplifts entire communities," Sophea elaborated. "Courageous actions set a precedent, showing others that despite challenges, it is possible to act in ways that are both brave and wise. This can transform a society, much like a citadel becomes a symbol of strength and resilience for a city."

Inspired by the profound nature of the discussion, Sophea guided the monks in a visualization exercise. "Imagine yourself as a citadel, strong and imposing. Inside your walls are your beliefs, your integrity, and your faith. Reflect on how you protect these treasures and how your courage allows you to act boldly in their defense."

As the monks closed their eyes and meditated on this imagery, a sense of quiet determination filled the room. Each monk visualized their personal citadel of courage, considering how they might fortify it further and the actions they could take to embody this virtue.

Concluding the session, Sophea encouraged them, "Let us go forth with the courage of a citadel, making decisions that reflect our highest values and defending the principles we hold dear. May our courage inspire and protect those around us, just as Solomon's boldness left a lasting legacy for his people."

With these motivating words, the monks dispersed, each carrying with them the image of a citadel of courage, ready to face the challenges of their paths with renewed strength and conviction.

Chapter 40

As the monks assembled in the tranquil environment of the monastery's great hall, light streamed through the clerestory windows, casting an ethereal glow that seemed to heighten the anticipation for Sophea's discourse. Today, she would introduce them to the concept of insight, which Tobias likened to an observatory—a place enabling a broad and far-reaching view.

"Tobias used the metaphor of an observatory to describe insight, suggesting it as a space from which one can see beyond the immediate, across vast distances, to grasp deeper truths and broader perspectives," Sophea began, capturing the monks' full attention with her vivid depiction.

She continued, "Tobias admired Solomon's request for an understanding mind, as it demonstrated the king's desire for profound insight to govern his people wisely" (1 Kings

3:11-12). "Solomon did not ask for wealth or power but for the wisdom to discern between good and evil, which shows his priority was to see and understand deeply, not just to rule."

Isabella, always keen to connect these teachings to practical applications, asked, "Sophea, how did Tobias suggest we cultivate such insight in our own lives?"

"Tobias believed that developing insight requires us to elevate our perspective, to rise above the mundane concerns and see the larger picture," Sophea replied. "He encouraged practices like deep meditation, thoughtful reflection, and the study of sacred texts, which help sharpen our understanding and expand our view."

Kesia, interested in the transformational aspect of insight, inquired, "What benefits does such insight bring to our personal growth and interactions with others?"

"Insight, according to Tobias, transforms the way we interact with the world," Sophea explained. "It allows us to anticipate consequences, understand others' motives and feelings, and respond with empathy and wisdom. In essence, it helps us navigate life's complexities with greater ease and effectiveness."

Lexi, contemplating the broader implications, asked, "How does this perspective of insight help us contribute to society?"

"Tobias taught that when we view life from an 'observatory' of insight, we can contribute to society by making decisions that are not only beneficial for the short term but also sustainable and fruitful for the long term," Sophea elaborated. "Just as Solomon's wisdom led to a prosperous and peaceful reign, our insightful contributions can foster harmony and progress within our communities."

Inspired by the discussion, Sophea guided the monks in a visualization exercise. "Imagine yourself in an observatory, high above the landscape, viewing the world around you. From this vantage point, consider the challenges you face. Think about how looking deeper and seeing wider can change your understanding of these challenges and your approach to solving them."

As the monks engaged in this reflective practice, they visualized their personal observatories of insight, considering how this elevated perspective could transform their understanding and actions.

Concluding the session, Sophea encouraged them, "Let us strive to maintain our position in the observatory of insight, using our enhanced perspective to guide our decisions and actions. May our insight illuminate paths not only for ourselves but also for those we lead and serve."

With renewed motivation, the monks left the hall, each committed to nurturing their capacity for insight, ready to apply their expanded perspectives to all aspects of their lives.

Chapter 41

In his relentless pursuit to unravel the complexities surrounding the resurgence of occult activities in New York, Redington embarked on a meticulous investigation into the city's historical undercurrents. Recognizing that the key to understanding the present lies in the echoes of the past, he ventured into the heart of the city's archives, a repository of forgotten truths and concealed wisdom.

As he stepped into the dimly lit rooms filled with towering shelves of aging documents, Redington felt a palpable sense of history enveloping him. The archives, with their musty scent of old paper and leather, seemed to whisper secrets of times long past. He spent days immersed in this sanctum, poring over yellowed newspapers, police records stained with the passage of time, and rare manuscripts that chronicled the city's occult history.

These documents painted a vivid picture of New York's early days, when the city was a burgeoning metropolis on the cusp of modernity yet deeply rooted in esoteric traditions. Redington discovered that many of New York's founding families were not merely influential pioneers but also custodians of arcane knowledge, their fortunes and fates intertwined with mystical practices.

Among the cobwebbed shelves, Redington uncovered a particularly compelling manuscript. It detailed an obscure 19th-century society that dabbled in alchemy and theosophy, hinting at connections to some of the city's most venerable families. The society, known as the "Aurelian Order," had been influential in shaping policy and thought in New York's formative years, though it later dissolved into the annals of obscurity following a scandal involving a prominent politician.

This discovery led Redington to realize the cyclical nature of these occult groups. Like the mythical phoenix, they seemed to rise from their ashes generation after generation, each time clothed in a new mantle, yet driven by similar esoteric goals. Their persistence through centuries suggested a deep-rooted ideological foundation that was both enthralling and alarming.

The implications of these findings were profound. The current occult activities in New York were not random or isolated incidents but were part of a larger, historical tapestry that had been woven into the city's very fabric. Redington's investigation revealed that today's cult had its genesis in the same ancient beliefs and practices that once captivated the city's forebearers.

Equipped with this newfound understanding, Redington began to piece together the cult's long-term objectives. The motives that once seemed elusive now started to form a coherent picture, suggesting a plan far more complex and historically entrenched than he had initially imagined. This perspective not only informed his strategy to combat the cult's resurgence but also provided him with a deeper appreciation for the city's rich, albeit shadowy, heritage.

As he left the archives, the weight of centuries-old secrets heavy on his shoulders, Redington felt a renewed determination to shed light on these dark corners of New York's past. The task was daunting, yet he was more resolved than ever to prevent history from repeating itself, armed with knowledge that was as much a weapon as it was a burden.

Chapter 42

The monks convened once again in the monastery's great hall, where the tranquil morning light filtered through high windows, casting serene patterns upon ancient stone walls. Today, Sophea prepared to explore another facet of Tobias' teachings, likening the complexities of life to a labyrinth.

"Tobias often contemplated the intricate and winding paths of life's challenges," Sophea began, her voice echoing softly in the quiet hall. "He compared these to a labyrinth, where one must navigate through a complex network of choices and consequences. He drew upon the example of Solomon, who navigated the intricate political landscape of his reign through strategic marriages and alliances" (1 Kings 3:1). "This, Tobias suggested, was akin to finding a path through a labyrinth—requiring wisdom, foresight, and careful decision-making."

Isabella, always eager to deepen her understanding, asked, "Sophea, how did Tobias believe we could apply this concept of navigating life's labyrinth in our personal journeys?"

"Tobias advised that just as one would carefully consider each turn within a labyrinth, we too should approach life's decisions with deliberation and prudence," Sophea replied. "He recommended developing a strategy based on our values and long-term goals, and constantly reassessing our path as circumstances evolve."

Kesia, reflecting on the practical aspects of this analogy, inquired, "What tools did Tobias suggest we use to help navigate these complexities effectively?"

"Tobias emphasized the importance of wisdom, gleaned from personal experience and the teachings of the wise, as our primary tool," Sophea explained. "He also highlighted the role of ethical judgment and spiritual guidance in making choices that not only lead us through the labyrinth but also enhance our growth and deepen our understanding."

Lexi, interested in overcoming challenges, asked, "How should we handle the inevitable dead ends and wrong turns we encounter in this labyrinth?"

"Tobias acknowledged that dead ends and wrong turns are part of the journey through any labyrinth," Sophea answered. "He encouraged viewing these setbacks as opportunities for learning and reflection rather than failures. Tobias taught that each mistake made, and each challenge encountered could refine our judgment and fortify our resilience."

Inspired by the discussion, Sophea led the monks in a reflective exercise. "Let us close our eyes and visualize ourselves in a vast labyrinth. As you walk through it, consider the choices you face in your own life. Reflect on how you can apply wisdom and ethical judgment to navigate these paths. Think about how you might use your experiences, both good and bad, as guides."

The monks engaged deeply in this meditation, each contemplating their personal labyrinths and the choices that lay before them.

Concluding the session, Sophea encouraged the monks, "Let us carry with us the image of the labyrinth as we go about our day. Remember, the complexity of life is not a barrier to our progress, but a series of lessons that, when navigated with wisdom and ethical judgment, lead to profound understanding and personal growth."

With renewed motivation, the monks dispersed, each determined to apply the wisdom of navigating life's labyrinth to their personal and communal challenges, guided by the teachings of Tobias and the wisdom of Solomon.

Chapter 43

In the deep quiet of the night, after a day filled
with reflections on navigating life's labyrinths,
Lexi drifted into sleep with her thoughts still
swirling with the imagery of mazes and intricate
pathways. In her dream, she found herself in a
celestial labyrinth unlike any earthly construct.
The walls were formed of shimmering light, and
the paths were lined with stars, creating a map of
radiant constellations under her feet.

As Lexi wandered through this luminous
maze, she sensed the presence of Archangel
Uriel beside her. His appearance was both awe-
inspiring and comforting, his wings subtly
reflecting the cosmic light surrounding them.

"Uriel," Lexi greeted him, her voice echoing
slightly in the vastness of the celestial space.

"Lexi," Uriel responded, his tone conveying a deep serenity. "Tonight, you walk the labyrinth of the heavens, where each turn and each decision mirrors the journeys you undertake in your waking life."

Lexi looked around, marveling at the beauty and complexity of the labyrinth. "It's overwhelming," she admitted. "In life, just like in this labyrinth, I often fear making wrong turns."

Uriel nodded, understanding her concerns. "The celestial labyrinth represents your journey through life. Like the labyrinth, life requires navigation through choices and challenges, some leading to dead ends, others to passages that open up to greater wisdom and deeper understandings."

As they walked together, Uriel guided Lexi to a viewpoint where they could see the entire labyrinth from above. From this perspective, Lexi could see that each path, each decision, no matter how seemingly trivial, contributed to the formation of a beautiful, intricate pattern.

"See how all paths form a whole," Uriel pointed out. "Each step you take, whether it seems right or wrong at the time, is part of a larger design. You are never truly lost; you are merely finding your way through the celestial pattern of your life."

"How can I navigate better?" Lexi asked, looking up at Uriel with a mix of awe and curiosity.

"Use the tools of wisdom, faith, and love," Uriel advised. "Wisdom to understand the lessons each path teaches you, faith to keep you moving forward even when the way is unclear, and love to guide your steps toward actions that bring light to you and those around you."

Uriel then handed Lexi a small, radiant orb of light. "This light represents your inner wisdom. Let it guide you as you make your choices. Remember, every challenge is an opportunity to illuminate your path and refine your soul."

With the orb in her hand, Lexi continued to navigate the labyrinth, feeling more confident with each step. The paths became clearer, and the choices felt more purposeful. The labyrinth no longer seemed a daunting puzzle but a journey of meaningful exploration.

As the dream began to fade with the approach of dawn, Lexi felt a profound peace settle over her. She awoke in her room, the first light of morning streaming through the window. Holding onto the feeling of guidance and clarity from her dream, she rose with a renewed sense of purpose, ready to navigate the day's challenges with wisdom, faith, and love, just as she had in the celestial labyrinth with Uriel.

Chapter 44

In the quiet of the early morning, the monks gathered in the monastery's great hall, where the ambiance of serenity and contemplation was palpable. Sophea was prepared to delve into the profound theme of forgiveness, using the imagery of a vault to illustrate its essential qualities.

"Tobias portrayed forgiveness as a vault—a secure place that protects valuable treasures," Sophea began, her voice conveying the depth and sanctity of the concept. "In his teachings, forgiveness was not just an act of letting go of grievances but a protective mechanism that preserves and fortifies the integrity of relationships, preventing the corrosive effects of bitterness and resentment."

She continued, drawing from biblical narratives, "Consider Solomon's reign, which, while marked by wisdom and prosperity, also faced its share of conflicts and missteps that required forgiveness. Tobias reflected on these moments, emphasizing how Solomon's ability to forgive, and be forgiven, played a crucial role in maintaining peace and stability within his kingdom."

Isabella, always keen to connect Tobias' teachings to practical applications, asked, "Sophea, how did Tobias suggest we cultivate a practice of forgiveness in our own lives?"

"Tobias advised that we view forgiveness as an essential safeguard for our emotional and spiritual well-being," Sophea replied. "He encouraged us to regularly examine our hearts for grudges or resentments we might be holding and to actively choose forgiveness as a way to release these burdens. Just as a vault is regularly checked and maintained to ensure its contents are safe, so too should we maintain our hearts to ensure they are free of bitterness."

Kesia, reflecting on the challenges of forgiveness, inquired, "What strategies did Tobias recommend for those finding it difficult to forgive?"

"Tobias recognized that forgiveness can be challenging, particularly when the hurt is deep," Sophea acknowledged. "He suggested starting with small steps—perhaps beginning with expressing a willingness to forgive, even if one is not yet ready to fully forgive. He also recommended seeking understanding of the offender's perspective, which can often lead to empathy and a greater readiness to forgive."

Lexi, interested in the broader implications, asked, "How does forgiveness impact community dynamics, according to Tobias?"

"Tobias believed that forgiveness is foundational to community health," Sophea explained. "By forgiving, we not only release our own hearts from anger but also enable relationships to heal and strengthen. This creates a ripple effect throughout the community, enhancing trust and cooperation among its members. Forgiveness, therefore, is not just personal; it is a communal strength that secures peace and prosperity."

Inspired by the discussion, Sophea guided the monks in a meditation. "Close your eyes and imagine yourself standing before a vault. Inside, place the memories or feelings you need to forgive. See yourself locking these away—not to ignore them, but to acknowledge and secure them in forgiveness. Reflect on how this act might free you to move forward."

As the monks engaged in this visualization, they felt the weight of old grievances lessen, experiencing the protective and liberating power of forgiveness.

Concluding the session, Sophea encouraged the monks, "Let us strive to keep the vault of our hearts well-guarded with forgiveness. In doing so, we not only protect ourselves but also nurture our communities. May the peace and freedom gained through forgiveness guide all our interactions."

With that, the monks rose, feeling refreshed and empowered, ready to practice forgiveness in a way that would protect and heal, both personally and within their community, inspired by the wisdom of Tobias.

Chapter 45

As the early morning sun covered the monastery's great hall in a gentle glow, the monks gathered quietly, eager to absorb another lesson from Tobias' profound teachings. Today, Sophea prepared to discuss the virtue of gratitude, beautifully likened by Tobias to a flourishing garden.

"Tobias often spoke of gratitude as a garden that needs constant tending," Sophea began, her voice reflective and warm. "He believed that just as a gardener nurtures plants to bloom and bear fruit, so too must we cultivate a spirit of thankfulness in our lives. This cultivation enriches our 'soil,' allowing us to grow in contentment and joy."

She continued, "Tobias drew inspiration from Solomon's dedication of the Temple, which was not only a significant religious event but also a grand expression of gratitude to God for the fulfillment of His promises" (1 Kings 8). "Solomon's act of gratitude demonstrated how acknowledging our blessings can lead to greater spiritual depth and community unity."

Isabella, always thoughtful, asked, "Sophea, how did Tobias suggest we cultivate gratitude in our daily lives?"

"Tobias recommended practical ways to nurture gratitude," Sophea replied. "He suggested starting each day by reflecting on things we are thankful for, no matter how small. He also encouraged keeping a gratitude journal to record these reflections, which can help us maintain a focus on the positive aspects of our lives, even during challenging times."

Kesia, reflecting on her own challenges with maintaining a grateful perspective, inquired, "What are the obstacles to cultivating gratitude, and how can we overcome them?"

"Tobias acknowledged that life's difficulties can sometimes overshadow our ability to feel grateful," Sophea explained. "He advised that in such times, we should make a conscious effort to recall past blessings and how we overcame previous challenges. This reminder of our resilience and the support we have received can reignite our sense of gratitude."

Lexi, interested in the broader impact of gratitude, asked, "How does fostering gratitude affect our interactions with others and our overall well-being?"

"Tobias taught that gratitude has a transformative effect on our interactions and our well-being," Sophea responded. "A grateful heart is more likely to act with kindness and generosity, seeing the good in others and extending goodwill. This creates a positive feedback loop in our relationships, enhancing our own well-being and that of our community."

Inspired by the discussion, Sophea guided the monks in a reflective exercise. "Close your eyes and envision your life as a garden. Think about the elements—sunlight, water, soil—that help it thrive. Now, think about how gratitude acts as sunlight, nurturing growth and bringing light to your garden. Reflect on what and who you are grateful for today."

As the monks meditated on these images, a sense of peace and appreciation filled the room. They visualized their personal gardens of gratitude, feeling the joy and contentment that this virtue can bring.

Concluding the session, Sophea encouraged the monks, "Let us strive to tend our gardens of gratitude daily. In doing so, we not only enrich our own lives but also bring joy and contentment to those around us. May your gardens flourish with the beauty of gratefulness."

With these inspiring words, the monks departed the hall, each carrying with them the resolve to cultivate gratitude actively, transforming their lives and their communities with the nurturing power of thankfulness, as taught by Tobias.

Chapter 46

As the monks assembled in the monastery's great hall, a serene light filtered through the windows, setting a reflective mood. Sophea prepared to discuss another vital virtue from Tobias' teachings—benevolence, depicted as a bridge that spans the divide between disparate shores, fostering connection and understanding.

"Tobias envisioned benevolence not just as a virtue but as a structural element in society, akin to a bridge that links people and communities together," Sophea began, her voice echoing the importance of connectivity in her words. "He admired how Solomon, despite the imperfections of his reign, demonstrated acts of benevolence that contributed significantly to the peace and prosperity of his kingdom" (1 Kings 4:34). "These acts, though sometimes overshadowed by his later failings, included policies that enhanced the lives of his subjects, showing the strength of kindness in governance."

Isabella, always keen to understand deeper applications, asked, "Sophea, how did Tobias suggest we incorporate benevolence into our own leadership and daily interactions?"

"Tobias believed that benevolence should be a cornerstone in both leadership and daily life," Sophea replied. "He advised that leaders, whether of nations, communities, or families, should act with a generous heart, always seeking to understand and address the needs of those they lead. For individual interactions, he recommended simple acts of kindness, such as offering support to those in distress or sharing resources with those in need, effectively building bridges of goodwill and support."

Kesia, reflecting on her own responsibilities, inquired, "What are the challenges of practicing benevolence, and how can we overcome them?"

"Tobias recognized that true benevolence often requires sacrifice and resilience," Sophea explained. "One challenge is the risk of being taken advantage of, which can lead to reluctance in continuing benevolent actions. Tobias advised maintaining a balance—being wise about whom, when, and how much to help, while keeping the heart open and compassionate."

Lexi, interested in the societal impact of benevolence, asked, "How does benevolence transform a community?"

"Benevolence acts like the pillars of a bridge, supporting and uplifting the community," Sophea elaborated. "It fosters an environment of trust and mutual support, where people are motivated to act kindly toward one another. This creates a positive cycle of generosity, reducing conflicts and enhancing the overall well-being of the community."

Inspired by the potential of benevolence to create lasting change, Sophea guided the monks in a visualization exercise. "Imagine you are building a bridge of benevolence from your own life to those around you. Consider the materials you would use—acts of kindness, words of support, gestures of understanding. Envision how this bridge can help someone today and how it might strengthen your community."

As the monks closed their eyes and contemplated, they visualized their actions weaving together to form sturdy, supportive bridges, connecting them more deeply with those around them.

Concluding the session, Sophea encouraged, "Let us each strive to be architects of benevolence, constructing bridges that connect and enrich our communities. Just as Solomon showed us through his acts, even flawed leaders can build legacies of kindness that resonate through generations."

With a renewed sense of purpose, the monks rose, ready to practice benevolence in their roles and interactions, inspired by the teachings of Tobias and the historical example of Solomon.

Chapter 47

After another insightful day of discussions on benevolence and the interconnectedness of community, Lexi retired to her small, austere room within the monastery. The discussions had stirred within her a deep contemplation about the nature of kindness and how it bridges human souls. As night enveloped the sky outside her window, she lay in her bed, her mind still buzzing with the day's teachings.

As sleep took her, Lexi found herself once again in the celestial realm, but this time, the setting was different. She was standing on a transparent platform suspended in the vastness of space, surrounded by an array of glowing planets and swirling nebulas. Beside her, Archangel Uriel appeared, his presence as calming as it was majestic.

"Welcome back, Lexi," Uriel greeted her with a gentle smile. "Tonight, we explore the universe not just as a creation but as a reflection of the interconnectedness you pondered today."

Uriel led her across the platform, which transformed into a bridge made of light extending into infinity. Below them, the cosmos whirled in a dance of creation, destruction, and rebirth.

"This bridge represents your journey through life and beyond," Uriel explained, his voice resonating with the hum of the stars. "It connects not only the physical places you will go but also the lives you touch and the spirits you connect with through acts of benevolence."

As they walked, images appeared around them like holograms—scenes of Lexi's past where she had acted with kindness and compassion. Lexi watched, moved by the memories of her own actions rippling outwards, affecting others in ways she had not realized at the moment.

"These are your bridges of light," Uriel said. "Every act of kindness, every word of support, every gesture of understanding you give, creates a pathway of light that extends far beyond the visible."

Lexi felt a profound sense of connection to everything around her, seeing her actions as part of a cosmic whole. "How can I create more of these bridges?" she asked, inspired by the visions.

"Continue to act with love and compassion," Uriel advised. "Look beyond the immediate response and toward the infinite impact of your benevolence. The universe thrives on interconnectedness, just as humanity does. Your benevolence is a powerful force, much like the gravity that holds these stars in place."

They reached the end of the light bridge, where a spectacular view of a glowing galaxy awaited them. Uriel handed Lexi a small crystal that pulsed with light.

"This crystal will remind you of the connections you forge through benevolence. Each facet reflects a life you've touched, a bridge you've built."

Holding the crystal, Lexi felt a warmth spread through her. It was a physical manifestation of her spiritual growth and the countless connections she had fostered through her actions.

As the vision began to fade, and the first light of dawn started to seep into her room, Lexi awoke. She held her hand open half-expecting to see the crystal, but instead, she felt its warmth in her heart. With a renewed sense of purpose, she rose from her bed, ready to face the day with a deeper understanding of how her acts of kindness could bridge worlds and souls, just as the stars are bridged by light in the vast cosmos.

Chapter 48

As Redington delved deeper into the investigation of the sinister cult that had infiltrated the city's underbelly, the case began to resonate with a disturbing intimacy. The tendrils of the cult's influence reached far and wide, touching even the upper echelons of the city's administration. Redington's latest discovery was a thread that, when pulled, unraveled a connection to a high-ranking official within the city administration—a figure who had always appeared beyond reproach.

The revelation sent shockwaves through Redington's core. The official, known for his polished demeanor and influential decisions, was someone Redington had respected, even admired. The thought of such a figure being entangled with the cult was not just disappointing; it was a betrayal of everything Redington stood for. Yet, the evidence was irrefutable, laid bare in covert communications and clandestine meetings detailed in the surveillance reports he had meticulously gathered.

Faced with this daunting reality, Redington knew the next steps would require more than just his skills as a detective; they demanded a strategic fine set to balance the pursuit of justice with the potential fallout. How he handled this situation could affect not just his career but also the integrity of his office. It was a delicate dance on a razor's edge, protecting the confidentiality and safety of his sources while rooting out corruption.

The confrontation with the official was inevitable. Redington arranged a discreet meeting under the guise of routine bureaucratic inquiry—an encounter that was anything but ordinary. As he sat across from the official in the dim light of a secluded office, the air was thick with tension. Redington's eyes, usually calm and discerning, now flashed with a steely resolve as he laid out the evidence before the official.

The official's initial reaction was a blend of shock and indignation. Veiled threats hung in the air, cloaked in the decorum of political jargon. "You do realize, Agent Redington, the implications of these accusations could extend far beyond my office, potentially destabilizing our city's governance?" the official warned, his voice a mix of threat and plea.

Redington remained unmoved, his voice steady. "And you must realize that ignoring the corruption festering under our noses could lead to far worse than political instability," he countered. "It's not just about your position or mine—it's about the city and its people."

The standoff continued, with each parry and thrust of words meticulously measured. Yet, it was Redington's unwavering commitment to justice and his clear moral compass that gradually wore down the official's defenses. Recognizing the futility of resistance and perhaps, struck by a remnant of conscience, the official capitulated.

"Alright, Redington, I'll cooperate. But I do this for the city, not for you," the official conceded, his face a mask of resignation mixed with relief.

This breakthrough was significant. With the official's cooperation, Redington gained valuable insights into the cult's logistical support and future plans. It was a critical pivot in the investigation, opening new avenues to accelerate the dismantling of the cult's network. The information provided could potentially lead to the identification and arrest of key cult members, striking at the heart of the organization.

As Redington left the meeting, the weight of the encounter lingered on his shoulders. The road ahead was still fraught with challenges, but with each step forward, he felt a renewed sense of purpose. The shadows within might have darkened the lines between friend and foe, but they also sharpened his focus on the fight for justice, illuminating the path ahead with the clear light of determination.

Chapter 49

The gentle morning light filled the monastery's great hall with a soft glow as the monks settled into their seats, eager for another session of learning and reflection with Sophea. Today's discussion promised to weave together the concepts of life, wisdom, and divine orchestration into a coherent symphony, drawing on the illustrious reign of King Solomon as a guiding example.

"Tobias often spoke of life and wisdom as a symphony," Sophea began, her voice reflecting the harmony and complexity of the metaphor. "In this symphony, each element—our thoughts, decisions, and actions—must synchronize not only with each other but with the divine will, creating a harmonious blend that resonates with the Creator's plan."

She continued, "Solomon's reign, particularly at its zenith as described in 1 Kings 10, illustrates this principle beautifully. Under his wise leadership, Israel experienced a period of unprecedented peace and prosperity. Solomon's ability to orchestrate these aspects of his kingdom serves as a vivid backdrop to understanding how personal actions and societal norms, when aligned with wisdom, can contribute to a golden age."

Isabella, intrigued by the application of this concept, asked, "Sophea, how did Tobias suggest we attune our lives to this symphony of synchronicity?"

"Tobias encouraged each individual to cultivate a deep connection with the divine through prayer, meditation, and the study of sacred texts," Sophea replied. "He believed that understanding the divine will is like learning the notes of a musical score—necessary before one can play them in harmony. He also stressed the importance of community, advising that just as musicians listen to each other to keep time and tune, so too should we be attentive to the needs and wisdom of our community."

Kesia, reflecting on her own leadership roles, inquired, "What specific actions can leaders take to promote this harmonious synchronization in their communities or organizations?"

"Tobias advocated for leaders to practice discernment and seek counsel, ensuring that their decisions are informed not only by their personal convictions but also by the collective wisdom of those they lead," Sophea explained. "He urged leaders to set examples of integrity and virtue, acting as conductors who guide and inspire their people to unite in achieving a common good."

Lexi, always keen to understand deeper spiritual implications, asked, "How does this symphonic approach help us deal with conflicts or challenges?"

"Sophea nodded thoughtfully before responding. "Tobias taught that in a symphony, not all notes are the same, yet each is crucial for the overall harmony. Similarly, he suggested that understanding and embracing diversity within our communities can help us address conflicts constructively. When challenges arise, viewing them as part of a larger composition allows us to find solutions that are in tune with our overall objectives and values."

Inspired by the session, Sophea led the monks in a short meditative exercise. "Close your eyes and imagine your life as part of a grand symphony. Think about how your actions, decisions, and interactions contribute to this music. Reflect on how you might adjust your parts to better harmonize with those around you and with the divine melody."

As the monks contemplated, they visualized their lives intertwining with others', each note playing a vital role in the divine composition.

Concluding the session, Sophea encouraged, "Let us go forth and live our lives as part of this divine symphony, ensuring that our actions and choices resonate beautifully with the Creator's plan. May our lives together create a symphony of synchronicity that brings peace and prosperity, as Solomon's did in his time."

With these words, the monks felt empowered and inspired to align their personal actions and societal roles with the harmonious will of the divine, carrying the lesson of life's symphony into their daily practices.

Chapter 50

As morning light spilled into the monastery's great hall, casting long shadows and illuminating the ancient walls, the monks gathered around Sophea. Today, she was set to delve into the virtue of resilience, vividly depicted by Tobias as a forge where metals are transformed under intense heat and pressure.

"Tobias likened resilience to the process of forging metal," Sophea began, her voice steady and compelling. "In the forge, metals are not merely heated; they are beaten and shaped, emerging stronger and more purposeful. He saw this transformative process as a powerful metaphor for the resilience required in life, particularly in leadership."

She continued, drawing from the scriptural account, "Solomon's early reign was marked by challenges that tested his resolve and fortitude.

He had to secure his kingdom against various adversaries and potential betrayals to establish his rule firmly" (1 Kings 2). "Tobias reflected on these actions as necessary, though harsh, demonstrating how Solomon used resilience to maintain stability and ensure the security of his nation."

Isabella, always eager to connect these teachings to practical life applications, asked, "Sophea, how did Tobias suggest we develop and harness such resilience in our own lives?"

"Tobias believed that resilience is built through facing challenges, not avoiding them," Sophea replied. "He advised that we should actively engage with our difficulties, using them as opportunities to learn and grow. He recommended practices like meditation and reflection to strengthen our inner resolve and prepare us for the inevitable hardships of life."

Kesia, reflecting on the metaphor of the forge, inquired, "What role does wisdom play in this process of resilience, according to Tobias?"

"Tobias taught that wisdom is crucial in guiding the forging process," Sophea explained. "It helps us understand which challenges are growth opportunities and which are merely destructive. Wisdom dictates when to stand firm and when flexibility might prevent unnecessary hardship. It also teaches us to recognize the lessons in each trial, allowing us to emerge not only stronger but also wiser."

Lexi, intrigued by the spiritual dimensions of resilience, asked, "How can we ensure that our spirit remains strong and does not break in the forge of life?"

"Tobias recognized that resilience is not about never breaking," Sophea responded. "Rather, it's about learning how to heal and rebuild when we do. He emphasized the importance of community, faith, and hope in maintaining our spiritual resilience. Community provides support, faith gives strength, and hope ensures that we always have a reason to rise again, even from the toughest of beatings."

Motivated by the depth of the discussion, Sophea led the monks in a visualization exercise. "Imagine yourself in a forge. Each trial you face is a hammer shaping you. Envision yourself being strengthened, not shattered, by each strike. Reflect on how each challenge refines and perfects your character."

As the monks meditated, they visualized themselves within the metaphorical forge, feeling the transformative power of their trials shaping them into stronger, more resilient individuals.

Concluding the session, Sophea encouraged, "Let us embrace the forge of life, allowing our challenges to strengthen and refine us. Remember, the resilience we develop is a testament not only to our survival but to our thriving. May we all emerge from our trials more resilient and wiser, ready to face the world with strength and grace."

With these empowering words, the monks felt fortified to face their personal and communal adversities, inspired by Tobias' teachings on resilience and the enduring metaphor of the forge.

Chapter 51

As the first rays of dawn crept into the monastery's great hall, casting a quiet glow on the assembled monks, Sophea prepared to delve into another of Tobias' rich metaphors—this time comparing discipline to intricate clockwork. The room hummed with the monks' focused attention, each eager to uncover how this virtue integrates into a life of spiritual and practical fulfillment.

"Tobias often spoke of discipline as being like the intricate clockwork in a timepiece," Sophea began, her voice mirroring the precision of the metaphor she described. "He illustrated how each component, or cog, must align and function in harmony for the clock to keep accurate time. Similarly, he saw discipline as essential in aligning our actions with our values and goals, ensuring that our lives run smoothly and efficiently."

She continued, drawing from the biblical narrative, "Tobias admired how Solomon demonstrated extraordinary discipline in managing his kingdom—a vast empire requiring meticulous organization and control. From daily provisions to the administration of twelve districts, Solomon's disciplined approach ensured stability and prosperity throughout his realm" (1 Kings 4:7-28).

Isabella, reflecting on the practical aspects, asked, "Sophea, how did Tobias suggest we cultivate such discipline in our own lives?"

"Tobias believed that discipline starts with setting clear priorities and establishing a routine that aligns with those priorities," Sophea replied. "He encouraged the practice of setting daily, weekly, and monthly goals, and systematically working toward them with consistency. Tobias also emphasized the importance of self-control in both small and large tasks, as this forms the foundation for a disciplined life."

Kesia, interested in overcoming personal struggles with discipline, inquired, "What strategies did Tobias recommend for those who find maintaining discipline challenging?"

"Tobias advised starting with small, manageable commitments and gradually building upon them," Sophea explained. "He recognized the role of accountability; suggesting that sharing goals with a community or a mentor can significantly enhance one's ability to stay on track. Furthermore, he advocated for regular self-reflection to evaluate progress and adjust strategies as needed."

Lexi, curious about the broader implications, asked, "How does discipline affect our ability to achieve long-term goals and maintain order in our lives?"

"Tobias taught that discipline is like the lubricant in the clockwork of our lives," Sophea elaborated. "It reduces friction and prevents the gears from grinding to a halt. With discipline, we can efficiently manage our time and resources, focus our energies on what truly matters, and more reliably achieve our long-term aspirations. This orderly approach not only helps us meet personal and spiritual goals but also contributes to the harmony and stability of our communities."

Inspired by the conversation, Sophea led the monks in a brief guided reflection. "Let us close our eyes and envision our lives as a series of gears and cogs, each representing different aspects of our daily routines and responsibilities. Reflect on how well these parts are aligned and moving. Consider areas where more discipline might be needed to improve functionality and efficiency."

As the monks visualized their personal 'clockworks,' they considered the adjustments necessary to enhance their discipline.

Concluding the session, Sophea encouraged, "Let us strive to refine the discipline within our lives, ensuring each action and decision meshes smoothly with our goals and values, just as cogs in a well-oiled clock. May the precision of your efforts bring you closer to achieving the harmony and order you seek."

With these motivating words, the monks left the hall, each renewed in their commitment to apply discipline in all aspects of their lives, inspired by Solomon's example and guided by Tobias' teachings on the clockwork of discipline.

Chapter 52

As the morning light cascaded through the stained-glass windows of the monastery's great hall, casting a spectrum of colors across the stone floor, the monks gathered around Sophea. Today's lesson from Tobias' teachings explored the concept of perspective, likened to a prism that reveals the hidden spectrum within white light.

"Tobias used the image of a prism to describe perspective," Sophea began, her voice as clear and illuminating as the light around them. "Just as a prism disperses white light to reveal a spectrum of colors, a wise perspective can unveil the hidden depths and varied complexities of life."

She continued, drawing on the biblical narrative, "Tobias often referred to Solomon's dream at Gibeon as a pivotal moment of enlightened perspective" (1 Kings 3:5-14). "When offered anything he desired by God, Solomon chose wisdom over riches, long life, or the death of his enemies. This choice reflected his deep understanding of his needs as a young king and his responsibilities toward his people."

Isabella, intrigued by the metaphor, asked, "Sophea, how did Tobias suggest we can use wisdom to broaden our perspective in everyday life?"

"Tobias believed that wisdom enhances perspective by allowing us to see beyond immediate appearances and understand deeper truths," Sophea replied. "He encouraged practices such as reflective meditation, engaging with diverse viewpoints, and studying sacred texts to cultivate a wise perspective. Tobias taught that these practices help us appreciate the complexities of situations and the motivations of others more fully."

Kesia, considering practical applications, inquired, "What are some ways we can develop a prism-like perspective that reveals more of life's spectrum?"

"Tobias recommended seeking out experiences and interactions outside of our usual environments," Sophea explained. "By stepping into different social, cultural, or spiritual contexts, we can challenge our preconceptions and expand our understanding. This approach, much like looking through a prism, allows us to see the many colors of human experience and gain a fuller appreciation of the world."

Lexi, interested in the challenges of maintaining such a perspective, asked, "How can we remain open to this broadened perspective without feeling overwhelmed by the complexities it reveals?"

"Tobias acknowledged that a wider perspective could indeed be overwhelming at times," Sophea responded. "He advised maintaining a grounding in our core values and beliefs while remaining flexible and open to new information. Balancing openness with grounding is key to managing the vast array of insights that a prism-like perspective can offer."

Inspired by the conversation, Sophea led the monks in a brief visualization exercise. "Imagine holding a prism in your hand, with light passing through it, revealing colors you hadn't noticed before. Think about how each color could represent different aspects or perspectives of a problem you are currently facing. Reflect on how this new view might influence your understanding and decisions."

As the monks contemplated this imagery, they felt their understanding deepen, appreciating the diverse facets of their challenges and experiences.

Concluding the session, Sophea encouraged them, "Let us each strive to use the prism of perspective wisely, allowing the light of wisdom to reveal the spectrum of life's complexities. May this enlightened view guide you in making decisions that are rich in understanding and compassion."

With these uplifting words, the monks dispersed, each carrying with them the image of the prism and the desire to see and appreciate the broader range of life's colors, guided by the wisdom of Solomon and the teachings of Tobias.

Chapter 53

As the day's teachings faded into the quiet solitude of evening, Lexi retired to her simple room, her mind swirling with the rich imagery of prisms and the spectrum of perspectives discussed by Sophea. The concept of using wisdom as a tool to uncover hidden depths of reality resonated deeply with her, echoing the spiritual journeys she had embarked on in her dreams.

That night, Lexi's sleep ushered her into a dream more vivid and profound than before. She found herself in a boundless, ethereal space where the darkness was punctuated by the brilliant light of distant stars. The tranquil silence was broken by the gentle arrival of Archangel Uriel, who appeared before her clad in an aura of soothing, radiant light.

"Lexi," Uriel greeted, his voice both a whisper and a clear, resonant tone, "tonight, we explore the celestial prism, where the light of divine wisdom reveals the spectrum of eternal truths."

Uriel extended his hand, and in his palm lay a crystal prism, larger and more luminous than any earthly counterpart. He raised the prism toward the starlight, and beams of pure white light passed through it, dispersing into an array of vibrant colors that danced and swirled around them.

"Each color you see represents different aspects of divine knowledge and human experience," Uriel explained as Lexi watched the colors weave through the space, illuminating the darkness with their beauty. "Just as the prism disperses light to reveal its hidden spectrum, so too can your wisdom reveal the complexities and depths of life."

Lexi, mesmerized by the display, felt a surge of understanding. "How can I use this celestial prism to gain wisdom in my daily life?" she asked, eager to apply this heavenly metaphor to her earthly challenges.

"To harness the wisdom of the celestial prism, you must remain open to the light of truth, much like this prism remains open to the light of the stars," Uriel advised. "Engage with the world around you, seek out diverse experiences, and reflect deeply on the truths they offer. This will allow you to perceive the varied colors of human experience and divine insight."

As they spoke, Uriel guided Lexi through the swirling colors, each hue revealing scenes from her past experiences and potential future paths. These visions were not just recollections but deeper revelations of the lessons each experience held.

"Remember, Lexi, that wisdom is not merely about accumulating knowledge," Uriel continued. "It is about understanding the greater context, the broader spectrum. It's about seeing the connections between seemingly disparate events and discerning the underlying truths that unite them."

Feeling empowered yet humbled by these revelations, Lexi looked at the prism with new appreciation. "And when the complexities seem overwhelming?" she inquired, her voice tinged with the weight of her burgeoning insights.

Uriel smiled gently, a reassuring presence amidst the cosmic spectacle. "Hold fast to your core values—the grounding facets of your prism. They will help you balance the vast spectrum of knowledge and keep you anchored in truth without being overwhelmed."

As the dream began to wane, Uriel placed the celestial prism in Lexi's hand. "Carry this with you in your heart," he said softly. "Let it remind you of the beauty and depth that wisdom can reveal."

Lexi awoke just as the first light of dawn crept into her room. Clutching the memory of the celestial prism, she felt a profound clarity and a renewed desire to apply the wisdom of her dream to her waking life. With a deep, calming breath, she prepared to meet the day, inspired to view each moment through the prism of enlightened perspective, just as she had been taught by both Sophea and the archangel Uriel.

Chapter 54

The soft morning light filled the monastery's great hall as the monks settled into their seats, the air filled with a sense of anticipation for the day's discourse. Sophea prepared to address the virtue of equity, using the metaphor of scales to symbolize balance and fairness, essential components of a just society.

"Tobias envisioned equity as a set of scales, perfectly balanced, each decision and action weighed carefully to maintain societal harmony," Sophea began, capturing the monks' attention with the gravity of the concept. "He used the famous judicial decision made by Solomon—the case of the two women claiming to be the mother of a child—as a prime example of how wisdom can be applied to achieve fairness" (1 Kings 3:16-28).

She continued, "Solomon's wise and somewhat unorthodox method of revealing the true mother by suggesting the baby be divided between the claimants demonstrated his deep understanding of human nature and his commitment to equity. His decision not only resolved the dispute but also restored peace and justice, reinforcing the role of wise leadership in maintaining order."

Isabella, always eager to delve deeper into the practical applications, asked, "Sophea, how did Tobias suggest we incorporate the principle of equity in our own leadership and daily interactions?"

"Tobias believed that true equity requires us to consider each situation individually, taking into account the unique circumstances and needs of all involved," Sophea replied. "He encouraged leaders to cultivate a deep sense of empathy and understanding, allowing them to see beyond surface appearances and make decisions that genuinely reflect fairness."

Kesia, reflecting on the challenges of implementing equity, inquired, "What strategies did Tobias recommend for those finding it difficult to maintain equity, especially in complex situations?"

"Tobias recommended seeking diverse perspectives before making decisions," Sophea explained. "He advised that consultation with a broad range of viewpoints can illuminate aspects of a situation that might not be immediately apparent, helping to ensure that decisions are well-rounded and equitable. Tobias also stressed the importance of self-awareness in recognizing one's own biases and working actively to mitigate them."

Lexi, interested in the broader implications, asked, "How does striving for equity impact a community or society as a whole?"

"Tobias taught that equity is fundamental to societal harmony and trust," Sophea elaborated. "When people believe that they are treated fairly and that their leaders make decisions with genuine fairness, it strengthens the social fabric and promotes peace. Equity, therefore, is not just about individual decisions but about fostering a culture where fairness is a foundational value."

Inspired by the depth of the discussion, Sophea led the monks in a brief reflection. "Close your eyes and imagine holding a set of scales in your hands. Reflect on a recent decision you made or a situation you encountered. Consider whether the scales were balanced or if adjustments could have been made for a fairer outcome. Think about how you can apply the principles of equity more effectively in the future."

As the monks meditated on these questions, they considered how they might act as instruments of equity in their community, weighing their decisions carefully like the scales of justice.

Concluding the session, Sophea encouraged them, "Let us each strive to be bearers of equity, balancing our scales with wisdom and empathy. In doing so, we not only resolve conflicts but also build a more just and harmonious world."

With these empowering words, the monks rose, each renewed in their commitment to fostering equity in every aspect of their lives, inspired by Solomon's example and guided by Tobias' teachings.

Chapter 55

After the morning's discourse on equity, Lexi felt a deeper sense of connection to the virtues that governed not only her own actions but also the fabric of the community within the monastery. The image of scales balancing justice and fairness resonated with her, prompting contemplation on her recent experiences and decisions.

Seeking further insight, Lexi joined Isabella and Kesia in the tranquil monastery garden, where the gentle rustle of leaves and the soft murmur of a nearby brook created an ideal setting for reflection and conversation.

"Today's lesson on equity has really made me think about how we apply fairness in complex situations," Lexi began, sharing her thoughts with her companions. "It's not just about finding a balance but truly understanding the depths of each situation."

Isabella nodded thoughtfully, her eyes reflecting a keen interest in delving deeper into the topic. "Yes, and I was particularly struck by how Tobias emphasized the importance of empathy in leadership. It's about seeing the heart of the matter, not just the facts as they appear."

Kesia, who was always keen on practical applications, added, "I think one of the biggest challenges is recognizing our own biases. It's easy to think we're being fair, but our perspectives can be so colored by our personal experiences and beliefs."

The three of them walked slowly along the garden paths, the fragrance of blooming flowers mingling with the fresh air, enhancing the contemplative mood.

"Have you ever found yourself in a situation where you realized your initial judgment was clouded by bias?" Lexi asked, genuinely curious about the experiences of her friends.

Isabella paused, considering the question. "There was a time when I had to mediate a dispute between two novices. Initially, I leaned toward the viewpoint of the one I knew better. But I caught myself and realized I needed to step back and consider both sides more objectively. It was a humbling reminder of how important it is to constantly check our assumptions."

Kesia chimed in with her own experience. "For me, it's about seeking those diverse perspectives Sophea mentioned. I try to consult with others who might see things differently. It's been crucial in helping me understand aspects of a situation that I wouldn't have considered otherwise."

As they reached a small bench, the three friends sat down, each lost in thought for a moment before Lexi spoke again. "These conversations, sharing our experiences and challenges, they're like our own way of balancing the scales, aren't they? We help each other see more of the whole picture."

Isabella smiled at that, her expression warm. "Exactly, Lexi. It's like having our own human prisms, helping to disperse the light of understanding in multiple directions."

Feeling inspired, Kesia suggested, "Why don't we make this a regular practice? A kind of equity circle where we can bring our dilemmas and decisions and help each other see them through different lenses?"

Both Lexi and Isabella agreed enthusiastically, excited by the prospect of not only supporting one another but also cultivating a deeper communal wisdom.

As the conversation drew to a close, the friends felt a renewed commitment to practicing equity in all aspects of their lives. With each shared story and each piece of advice exchanged, they understood more profoundly how interconnected their lives were and how each decision could tip the scales toward greater justice and harmony.

With hearts lightened by their mutual support and the beauty of their surroundings, Lexi, Isabella, and Kesia rose from the bench, their spirits buoyed by the knowledge that they were each integral threads in the tapestry of their community, each responsible for maintaining its balance and beauty.

Chapter 56

As the early morning sun cast a golden hue over the monastery's great hall, the monks gathered in their usual contemplative silence, ready to absorb the wisdom Sophea would share from Tobias' teachings. Today's lesson focused on leadership, likened to a beacon that guides through treacherous waters, drawing inspiration from the biblical reign of Solomon.

"Tobias often spoke of leadership as a beacon—a powerful light that not only warns of dangers but also illuminates the path forward," Sophea began, her voice resonating with the significance of the metaphor. "He referenced Solomon's expansive trade networks and his enhancements to military strength as examples of how a leader can extend their influence beyond borders and secure prosperity for their people" (1 Kings 10:22-26).

She continued, "Solomon's leadership ensured that his kingdom was not just internally stable but also respected and renowned internationally. This strategic expansion was akin to a beacon that not only guides ships safely to harbor but also signals a powerful presence on the international stage."

Isabella, always keen to connect historical insights to modern applications, asked, "Sophea, how did Tobias suggest we can embody such beacon-like leadership in our own roles today?"

"Tobias believed that wise leadership involves a clear vision and the courage to illuminate paths not just for oneself but for others as well," Sophea replied. "He encouraged leaders to cultivate deep understanding and foresight, making decisions that consider both the immediate needs and the long-term welfare of their followers. Tobias emphasized the importance of integrity and ethical consistency, which act like the light of a beacon, guiding and reassuring those who follow."

Kesia, considering the challenges leaders face, inquired, "What guidance did Tobias offer for leaders navigating through their own treacherous waters?"

"Tobias advised that leaders should seek wisdom through continuous learning and counsel from trusted advisors," Sophea explained. "He stressed that maintaining a network of support and gathering diverse perspectives can help leaders foresee potential challenges and navigate through them more effectively. Moreover, Tobias highlighted the importance of resilience and adaptability, qualities that enable leaders to adjust their strategies as circumstances evolve."

Lexi, interested in the broader impact of such leadership, asked, "How does beacon-like leadership influence the development of a community or organization?"

"Tobias taught that when leaders act as beacons, their actions create a ripple effect," Sophea elaborated. "Effective leadership fosters an environment where innovation, cooperation, and mutual respect flourish. It also sets a standard for future leaders, inspiring them to uphold these values and continue guiding others wisely."

Inspired by the discussion, Sophea led the monks in a short meditative practice. "Close your eyes and envision yourself as a lighthouse, standing firm on the coastline. Reflect on the light you emit and consider the ships you are guiding. Think about the ways you can shine brighter and reach further to ensure safe passage for all who depend on your light."

As the monks visualized themselves as beacons of leadership, they contemplated the areas in their lives where they could be more illuminating and guiding for others.

Concluding the session, Sophea encouraged them, "Let us strive to be beacons of leadership in all our endeavors. May your light guide those in darkness and lead them safely through their journeys, just as Solomon did through his wise rule."

With these motivating words, the monks rose, each renewed in their commitment to being leaders who not only guide but also inspire and protect, carrying the wisdom of Solomon and Tobias into their daily lives.

Chapter 57

In the serene morning light of the monastery's great hall, the monks gathered around Sophea, each carrying an air of eager anticipation for the wisdom to be shared. Today's discourse from Tobias' teachings focused on compassion, depicted as an everlasting wellspring that revitalizes and nurtures all who come into contact with it.

"Tobias often spoke of compassion not merely as an emotional response but as a vital force, akin to a wellspring that continuously nourishes and rejuvenates," Sophea began, her voice echoing the nurturing quality of the metaphor. "He drew upon Solomon's acts of generosity and care, particularly his thoughtful provisions for his household and his lavish gifts to the Queen of Sheba" (1 Kings 10:1-13). "These acts, though perhaps lesser known, underscore Solomon's use of compassion as a cornerstone of his wisdom and leadership."

She continued, "Tobias saw these gestures not just as obligations of a ruler but as manifestations of deep compassion, reflecting a leader's role in fostering a community's well-being through kindness and empathy."

Isabella, deeply moved by the concept, asked, "Sophea, how did Tobias suggest we cultivate such a wellspring of compassion in our own lives?"

"Tobias advocated for regular reflection on the needs of others and taking deliberate actions to address those needs," Sophea replied. "He believed that compassion, like a wellspring, should flow outward naturally and abundantly. Tobias encouraged practices such as volunteering, offering support to those in distress, and even simple acts of kindness, which collectively contribute to the vitality of this wellspring."

Kesia, reflecting on the challenges of consistently practicing compassion, inquired, "What did Tobias say about maintaining compassion even under difficult circumstances?"

"Tobias understood that maintaining compassion can be challenging, especially when faced with personal grievances or hardships," Sophea explained. "He recommended strengthening one's spiritual foundation through prayer and meditation, which can replenish our inner wellspring of compassion. Tobias also emphasized the importance of community support in sustaining our ability to give compassionately without depleting ourselves."

Lexi, curious about the impact of compassion on societal level, asked, "How does such a wellspring of compassion affect the broader community or society?"

"Tobias taught that compassion enriches communities by creating bonds of trust and mutual support," Sophea elaborated. "When leaders and individuals alike act compassionately, it sets a tone of empathy and cooperation that can transform social interactions. It encourages a culture where people are motivated to look out for one another, leading to a more cohesive and supportive society."

Inspired by the richness of the discussion, Sophea guided the monks in a visualization exercise. "Imagine yourself beside a flowing wellspring. Each act of compassion you perform adds to this stream. Visualize how this wellspring refreshes and supports your community. Think about the ways you can contribute to this flow today."

As the monks meditated on these images, they felt a renewed commitment to nurturing their personal and communal wellsprings of compassion.

Concluding the session, Sophea encouraged, "Let us each strive to be custodians of this wellspring of compassion, ensuring it never runs dry. May your acts of kindness continually rejuvenate those around you, just as Solomon's compassion enriched his kingdom."

With these empowering words, the monks rose, each inspired to infuse more compassion into their interactions, carrying forward the wisdom of Solomon and Tobias into their daily lives and communities.

Chapter 58

With a string of successful investigations behind him, Redington found himself at a crucial juncture as intelligence reports unveiled a major event that threatened to escalate the cult's influence dramatically. The upcoming ritual, dubbed "The Ritual of Shadows," was designed not only to solidify the cult's existing power but also to expand its reach across the region. The stakes were higher than ever, and the urgency of the situation demanded a swift and decisive response.

Redington meticulously planned a large-scale operation to disrupt the ritual. Gathering his most trusted agents, he detailed a strategy that involved multiple teams working in synchronized harmony to execute a raid on the cult's gathering. The location, a grand but secluded estate at the city's outskirts, offered the cult privacy and space to perform their rites undisturbed—or so they thought.

As dusk turned to evening, Redington's teams prepared for the operation. Each member was briefed thoroughly, understanding that timing and coordination were essential for success. They were equipped with the latest in tactical gear, prepared for any resistance they might encounter. The air was tense with anticipation as they awaited the go-signal, knowing the weight of what they were about to disrupt.

Under the cloak of night, the teams moved in. The estate, shrouded in darkness, was only lit by the eerie glow of torches that marked the perimeter of the ritual site. Redington led one of the main assault teams, his presence bolstering the resolve of his agents as they breached the estate's defenses.

The operation hit the ground running with precision. Surveillance teams had mapped out the layout of the estate, allowing the assault teams to navigate the sprawling grounds with confidence. As they closed in on the central courtyard, the sounds of the cult's incantations grew louder, a haunting melody that sent shivers down the spines of even the most seasoned agents.

The confrontation that ensued was intense and chaotic. Cult members, dressed in elaborate robes, turned in shock as Redington and his team disrupted the ceremony. The agents moved quickly to detain key figures, many of whom resisted fiercely, spurred on by fanaticism and desperation. Spells of confusion and fear seemed to hang thick in the air, a testament to the dark powers the cult had been tampering with.

Amidst the chaos, Redington remained a pillar of calm. His focus never wavered as he maneuvered through the melee, ensuring that his team maintained the upper hand. The tactical advantage was clearly with the FBI, trained for precisely such complex scenarios. The cultists, though fervent, were not prepared for such a well-executed strike.

As the operation wound down, the estate was secured, and the detained cult members were led away, the true extent of the cult's plans began to unravel. Documents and artifacts of great importance were recovered from the site, each shedding light on the cult's expansive network and their future intentions. The evidence was damning, a clear indicator of the threat they posed not just to the local community but potentially on a national scale.

The successful disruption of The Ritual of Shadows was a significant victory for Redington and his team. It not only curbed the immediate threat but also provided invaluable insights into the cult's hierarchy and operations. As dawn broke over the estate, now swarming with law enforcement, Redington watched as the last of the cult members were taken into custody. The relief was palpable among his team, but they all knew this was just one battle in a much larger war against darkness.

Chapter 59

The gentle morning light filtered through the monastery's stained-glass windows, casting colorful patterns on the stone floor as the monks assembled for their daily session with Sophea. Today's discourse focused on the virtue of integrity, which Tobias likened to a rich, unbroken tapestry, weaving a narrative that spanned the rise and challenges in Solomon's reign.

"Tobias envisioned integrity as a tapestry, complete and vibrant, each thread contributing to the strength and beauty of the whole," Sophea began, her voice imbued with the gravity of the concept. "He reflected on Solomon's early years, noting how his adherence to David's instructions and his commitment to God's statutes represented a tapestry of integrity at its finest" (1 Kings 3:3).

She continued, "However, as Solomon's reign progressed, this tapestry began to fray. His alliances and marriages with foreign nations, which led him to idolatry, marked significant tears in the fabric of his integrity" (1 Kings 11:1-8). "Tobias used these contrasting periods in Solomon's life to illustrate how vital it is to maintain integrity, lest the beauty and strength of one's character begin to unravel."

Isabella, deeply engaged, asked, "Sophea, how did Tobias suggest we preserve the integrity of our own tapestries throughout the challenges of life?"

"Tobias advocated for constant vigilance and regular self-assessment," Sophea replied. "He believed that just as a weaver checks for flaws or weaknesses in a tapestry, we must examine our actions and decisions to ensure they align with our core values and beliefs. Tobias also emphasized the importance of accountability, suggesting that we seek counsel and feedback from trusted peers to help maintain our course."

Kesia, considering her own experiences, inquired, "What strategies did Tobias recommend for repairing the tapestry when our integrity does falter?"

"Tobias recognized that even the most vigilant can sometimes stray from their principles," Sophea explained. "He recommended acts of restitution and reconciliation as ways to mend the fabric of our integrity. Returning to one's spiritual practices, seeking forgiveness from those harmed, and rededicating oneself to ethical living were all methods he endorsed for restoring integrity."

Lexi, interested in the broader implications, asked, "How does maintaining integrity impact our relationships and community interactions?"

"Tobias taught that integrity builds trust and fosters respect within a community," Sophea elaborated. "When individuals uphold their principles consistently, it strengthens not only their character but also the bonds within their community. A collective commitment to integrity creates a supportive and trustworthy environment where all members can thrive."

Inspired by the richness of the discussion, Sophea led the monks in a short reflective exercise. "Close your eyes and envision your life as a tapestry. Each thread represents a choice or action you have taken. Reflect on the pattern you are weaving. Are there any areas that need strengthening or repair? Consider how you can fortify these areas to ensure your tapestry reflects the integrity you aspire to."

As the monks meditated on these images, they considered the ongoing work required to maintain the integrity of their personal and communal tapestries.

Concluding the session, Sophea encouraged, "Let us each strive to weave our tapestries with diligent hands and pure hearts, ensuring that the beauty and strength of our integrity remain intact. May your actions consistently reflect the depth of your character, and may your integrity never fray."

With these motivating words, the monks rose, each renewed in their commitment to living lives of integrity, inspired by the lessons from Solomon's reign and Tobias' teachings.

Chapter 60

As the dawn light filled the monastery's great hall with a quiet luminescence, the monks gathered for their daily discourse with Sophea, eager to explore another profound virtue from Tobias' teachings. Today, she would discuss the virtue of contemplation, envisioned as an observatory from which one could gaze at the stars and ponder their place in the cosmos.

"Tobias likened contemplation to standing in an observatory, looking out at the vast expanse of the universe," Sophea began, her voice reflecting the depth and expansiveness of the metaphor. "He saw this practice as a means to gain a deeper understanding of both the divine and the mundane, using Solomon's extensive writings and proverbs as prime examples of how contemplation can lead to profound wisdom" (Proverbs and Ecclesiastes).

She continued, "Solomon's reflective writings, filled with observations on life, governance, and human nature, serve as testament to the benefits of deep contemplation. Through his proverbs and philosophical musings, Solomon shared insights that have guided countless generations in wisdom."

Isabella, intrigued by the concept, asked, "Sophea, how did Tobias suggest we practice contemplation to enrich our own wisdom?"

"Tobias advocated for setting aside dedicated times and spaces for contemplation," Sophea replied. "He believed in the power of solitude and silence, encouraging practices such as meditation, reading sacred texts, and observing nature. Tobias taught that these activities help quiet the mind, allowing deeper thoughts and insights to surface."

Kesia, reflecting on her own challenges with contemplation, inquired, "What obstacles might we face in cultivating a contemplative practice, and how can we overcome them?"

"Tobias recognized that the noise and distractions of daily life are major barriers to effective contemplation," Sophea explained. "He advised minimizing these distractions by creating a peaceful environment, perhaps a personal 'observatory,' where one can retreat to ponder life's deeper questions. He also suggested regularity in practice, to develop a habit of mindfulness and introspection."

Lexi, interested in the broader benefits, asked, "How does contemplation affect our relationships with others and our community?"

"Tobias taught that contemplation not only deepens our understanding of ourselves but also enhances our empathy toward others," Sophea elaborated. "By reflecting on our own experiences and the divine laws, we can better appreciate others' perspectives and struggles, leading to more compassionate interactions. This, in turn, strengthens the bonds within our community, as contemplation fosters a shared understanding and mutual respect."

Inspired by the discussion, Sophea led the monks in a contemplative exercise. "Let us close our eyes and imagine ourselves in an observatory, under a vast night sky. Reflect on your place in the universe and the interconnectedness of all things. Consider the divine and mundane aspects of your life and how they interweave."

As the monks engaged in this deep contemplation, they felt their minds broaden and their spirits uplift, gaining a clearer perspective on their personal and communal journeys.

Concluding the session, Sophea encouraged, "Let us strive to regularly visit our inner observatories, using the tool of contemplation to gain deeper insights and understanding. May your reflections enrich your wisdom and guide your actions toward greater compassion and harmony."

With these motivating words, the monks dispersed, each inspired to cultivate their contemplative practices, carrying with them the vision of their own observatories where they could continually seek and find wisdom.

Chapter 61

As the day's teachings about contemplation settled into the quiet corners of her mind, Lexi retired for the evening, feeling a deep yearning to explore the observatory of her own soul. That night, as she drifted into sleep, her subconscious mind carried her once more into the celestial realm where Archangel Uriel awaited her.

In this dream, Lexi found herself standing in a magnificent observatory that transcended any earthly structure. The walls and dome were transparent, composed of a crystalline material that shimmered with the light of countless stars. The observatory was perched upon a nebulous foundation, floating amidst the cosmos, galaxies swirling around it in a silent, majestic dance.

Uriel stood beside her, his presence both comforting and awe-inspiring. "Welcome, Lexi," he greeted her with a gentle nod. "Here, in this divine observatory, you can gaze not only upon the stars but also within the depths of your own spirit."

Lexi approached the telescope, which pointed toward the vast expanse of space. As she peered through it, the stars seemed to draw nearer, their light revealing patterns and secrets of the universe previously hidden from her eyes. Each constellation told a story of creation, destruction, and renewal—mirroring the cycles of her own life.

"Contemplation allows you to connect with the divine essence that permeates all existence," Uriel explained, his voice echoing the harmony of the spheres. "It is through this practice that you can understand the interconnectedness of all things, seeing beyond the surface to the profound truths that bind the cosmos."

Moved by the beauty and depth of the scene, Lexi turned from the telescope to Uriel. "How can I bring this celestial perspective into my everyday life? How can I use it to enhance my understanding and my relationships with others?"

Uriel smiled, a gesture that seemed to light up the surrounding cosmos. "Carry the stillness of this observatory within you," he advised. "Just as you have set aside this time to contemplate the stars, set aside moments in your life for deep reflection. These moments of inward looking will clarify your thoughts, emotions, and motivations, enhancing your interactions and helping you to act with compassion and wisdom."

He then handed her a small, luminous orb that seemed to pulse with the light of the stars they had been observing. "Let this orb remind you of the clarity and insight you gain from contemplation. When you feel overwhelmed by the mundane or disconnected from others, hold this light within you and remember the interconnectedness you've witnessed here."

As the dream began to dissolve, Lexi felt a profound sense of peace and a renewed desire to integrate the lessons of the observatory into her waking life. When she awoke the next morning, the memory of the stars and Uriel's words were still vivid in her mind. Filled with a sense of purpose, she rose to greet the day, committed to finding moments for contemplation amidst the busyness of her daily responsibilities.

With each moment of inward reflection, Lexi found herself more attuned to the rhythms of life around her, her relationships deepened, and her actions became more aligned with the harmony she had experienced in her celestial observatory. As she moved through her days, the wisdom gained from her dream guided her, fostering a life rich with understanding and compassion.

Chapter 62

As the morning sun filled the monastery's great hall in warm light, the monks assembled for their daily lesson with Sophea, who today would weave the theme of growth into the rich tapestry of Tobias' teachings. Using the metaphor of a garden, she aimed to elucidate how wisdom nurtures growth in various aspects of life.

"Tobias often spoke of growth using the image of a garden," Sophea began, her voice echoing the nurturing and patient tone of a seasoned gardener. "Just as each plant in a garden requires specific care and conditions to thrive, so too does every aspect of our lives—from personal development to societal progress—require the nurturing hand of wisdom."

She continued, focusing on a historical example, "Under Solomon's reign, Israel experienced tremendous growth, flourishing in economy, culture, and wisdom" (1 Kings 10). "This period of expansion was not merely a testament to Solomon's economic or administrative prowess, but also to his deep wisdom, which guided his decisions and helped establish a legacy of prosperity and knowledge."

Isabella, always eager to connect these teachings to practical applications, asked, "Sophea, how did Tobias suggest we apply the principles of wisdom to nurture our own growth?"

"Tobias encouraged the cultivation of wisdom through continuous learning, reflection, and openness to new experiences," Sophea replied. "He believed that by embracing wisdom in our daily decisions and interactions, we can foster personal growth and contribute positively to our communities. Wisdom helps us understand when to act, when to wait, what to embrace, and what to avoid, much like a gardener knows when to water, prune, or fertilize."

Kesia, reflecting on her personal journey of growth, inquired, "What are some specific practices Tobias recommended to facilitate personal and spiritual maturation?"

"Tobias emphasized the importance of meditation, prayer, and the study of sacred texts as foundational practices for spiritual growth," Sophea explained. "He also recommended engaging in community service and building meaningful relationships, which can challenge and refine our character, much like plants growing stronger through exposure to the elements."

Lexi, curious about overcoming growth obstacles, asked, "How should we deal with the inevitable challenges and setbacks that come with growth?"

"Tobias likened these challenges to the natural pests and diseases that can afflict a garden," Sophea responded. "He advised vigilance and resilience—recognizing problems early and addressing them directly. Tobias believed in resilience as a key component of growth, teaching that overcoming obstacles often leads to greater strength and wisdom, much as a plant might grow back stronger after being pruned."

Inspired by the richness of the discussion, Sophea led the monks in a short meditative exercise. "Close your eyes and envision yourself in a garden. Each plant represents an area of your life where you wish to see growth. Reflect on the nurturing each plant needs—be it more knowledge, deeper relationships, or greater challenges—and how you might provide it."

As the monks visualized their personal gardens, they contemplated the nurturing they required to foster their own growth in wisdom, spirituality, and community engagement.

Concluding the session, Sophea encouraged, "Let us each tend to our gardens with the wisdom and dedication of a mindful gardener.

May your efforts lead to abundant growth in every aspect of your lives, enriching not just yourselves but also those around you."

With these motivating words, the monks departed, each inspired to apply the principles of wisdom to nurture growth in their personal and communal lives, drawing from the profound legacy of Solomon and the teachings of Tobias.

Chapter 63

The city breathed a collective sigh of relief following the successful disruption of the Ritual of Shadows. The main architects of the dark assembly were now behind bars, their malignant intentions laid bare and thwarted by Redington and his team. The streets felt safer, the night less ominous, but the victory was bittersweet for Redington. He knew all too well that the roots of such evil ran deep, and dark tendrils could sprout anew if vigilance waned.

In the quiet aftermath, Redington found himself grappling with the weight of his responsibilities. The operation had taken a toll not just physically but spiritually. Seeking solace and a recharge of his moral compass, he turned his thoughts to the monastery in Nepal—a place where he had previously found profound peace and guidance. Though a physical visit was impossible due to his duties, he engaged in a meditation session where he could envision the monks, their serene faces and calming words a balm to his tumultuous thoughts.

As he focused on the monks, the tranquility of the monastery's halls, he was reminded of the times he had spent there, particularly with Lexi and the other dedicated souls. Their dedication to wisdom and inner peace contrasted sharply with the world he navigated daily. The thought of returning to that serene environment, to once again walk its peaceful grounds and reconnect with Lexi, Kesia, and Isabella, grew increasingly appealing. He considered planning a visit, craving the clarity and balance their perspectives always provided.

Just as Redington was about to check flights to Nepal, his phone rang. The caller ID displayed Professor Elena Mirov, a renowned scholar in criminology whose insights into criminal psychology had aided him in past investigations. He answered, his tone reflecting the weariness he felt.

"Elena, good to hear from you," Redington greeted.

"Redington, I hope I'm not calling at a bad time," Elena began, her voice carrying a warmth that hinted at an informal, friendly purpose. "I was wondering if you might be free this evening? I have some thoughts about your recent operation and some interesting theories I'd like to discuss. Perhaps over dinner?"

The invitation was timely. Elena's company and intellectual rigor could be just what he needed—a chance to unwind yet engage with a mind as sharp and as driven as his own. It might also provide a distraction from the darker reflections that the case had stirred within him.

"That sounds like a good idea, Elena. Dinner sounds perfect. Where were you thinking?" Redington replied, the prospect of an engaging evening rekindling a spark of energy in him.

"There's a new place I've been wanting to try, 'The Ivory Tusk.' It's quiet, the food is excellent, and I think it will be the perfect setting for our discussion," Elena suggested.

"Sounds great. I'll meet you there at 7?" Redington confirmed, already feeling a shift in his spirits.

"Perfect. See you then."

As he hung up the phone, Redington felt a renewed sense of purpose. The dinner with Elena would not only give him a chance to gain new insights into his work but also to momentarily step away from the looming shadows of his job. The battle against the dark forces within the city was far from over, but Redington was reminded once again that life also offered moments of connection and intellectual camaraderie, essential for keeping the shadows at bay within his own soul. The possibility of visiting the monastery remained in his thoughts, a beacon of peace he knew he would soon need to return to.

Chapter 64

As the monks assembled under the soft morning light that filtered through the monastery's high windows, casting serene patterns upon the old stone walls, Sophea prepared to share insights on the virtue of serenity, depicted as a sanctuary. This session promised to delve into how wisdom fosters serenity, using Solomon's construction of the Temple as a spiritual and historical backdrop.

"Serenity, according to Tobias, can be likened to a sanctuary—a sacred place where one can find refuge from the turmoil of the external world," Sophea began, her voice embodying the calm and peace the topic warranted. "Tobias often reflected on Solomon's efforts to build the Temple, which was not just an architectural feat but a spiritual endeavor to create a place of peace and connection with God" (1 Kings 6).

She continued, "This temple served as a physical and spiritual sanctuary where the Israelites could come to find solace and seek wisdom. Similarly, Tobias taught that serenity within ourselves acts as a sanctuary, offering us moments of peace and reflection amidst life's chaos."

Isabella, drawn to the practical application of these teachings, asked, "Sophea, how did Tobias suggest we build this sanctuary of serenity in our own lives?"

"Tobias emphasized the importance of cultivating inner peace through practices such as meditation, prayer, and contemplative reading," Sophea replied. "He believed that creating regular habits of stillness and reflection helps to build a personal sanctuary that can sustain us in times of stress and turmoil. Tobias also encouraged the nurturing of environments that promote peace, such as nature walks or creating peaceful spaces in our homes or workplaces."

Kesia, reflecting on the complexities of maintaining serenity in daily life, inquired, "What strategies did Tobias recommend for protecting our serenity when faced with external pressures and stresses?"

"Tobias acknowledged that maintaining serenity is a continuous challenge," Sophea explained. "He advised practicing detachment from the outcomes of our actions when possible, focusing instead on the integrity of the action itself. Tobias also recommended strengthening our connections with supportive community members who share our values and can help us maintain our peace."

Lexi, interested in the broader impact of serenity on community, asked, "How does personal serenity contribute to the overall harmony of a community?"

"Tobias taught that when individuals cultivate serenity, they are less likely to react impulsively or aggressively, leading to more thoughtful and compassionate interactions," Sophea elaborated. "This collective calm can significantly affect the community's atmosphere, promoting a culture of peace and mutual respect."

Inspired by the topic, Sophea guided the monks in a reflective exercise. "Close your eyes and imagine building your own sanctuary of serenity. Visualize its walls built from your daily practices of peace, its foundation laid in your deepest values. Reflect on how this sanctuary shields you from life's chaos and how you can invite others into this space of peace."

As the monks meditated, they visualized their personal sanctuaries, feeling the peace it brought into their hearts and minds.

Concluding the session, Sophea encouraged, "Let us each strive to fortify our sanctuaries of serenity. In doing so, we not only protect our own peace but also contribute to the serenity of our community. May your sanctuary be a place of refuge and wisdom, just as the Temple was for Solomon and his people."

With these profound thoughts, the monks dispersed, each carrying with them the vision and determination to cultivate their sanctuaries of serenity, inspired by Solomon's temple and the teachings of Tobias.

Chapter 65

As evening draped its velvet cloak over the city, Redington arrived at "The Ivory Tusk," a restaurant known for its discreet ambiance and exquisite cuisine. The place was an oasis of calm in the bustling city, with soft lighting and a décor that blended modern chic with touches of antique elegance.

He spotted Professor Elena Mirov already seated at a secluded table. She was dressed stunningly in a sleek, emerald-green dress that complemented her keen eyes and sharp features. Redington couldn't help but notice how the color accentuated her vibrant personality, something that had always intrigued him during their professional interactions. Tonight, however, there was an air of casual sophistication about her that he hadn't seen before.

"Elena, you look... amazing," Redington greeted, his words carrying a hint of genuine admiration.

"Thank you, Raymond," Elena responded with a smile that reached her eyes, adding a playful note, "I thought it might be nice to dress up a bit for a change from our usual academic drab."

They ordered their meals, and as they waited, the conversation swiftly moved from casual catch-ups to the intricacies of their respective fields. Elena was particularly interested in discussing the psychological profiles of the cult leaders Redington had apprehended, probing for details on their motivations and the dynamics within the cult.

"As fascinating as it is disturbing," Elena mused, swirling her wine thoughtfully. "The charismatic leader, the indoctrinated followers— it's like a textbook case of cult psychology, but every instance reveals something new, doesn't it?"

"Exactly," Redington agreed, appreciating the depth of the conversation. "Each case provides its own set of puzzles. It's not just about catching the bad guys; it's about understanding the why, which is where your insights come in handy."

As the evening progressed, their discussion deepened, touching on theories of criminal behavior and justice. Elena's insights were sharp and her questions probing, pushing Redington to think about his cases from angles he hadn't considered before.

The chemistry between them was palpable, and throughout dinner, Elena's demeanor was playfully flirtatious. Redington found himself drawn into the ease of their interaction, the intellectual stimulation adding a layer of excitement to the evening.

After dessert, as they stepped out of the restaurant into the cool night air, Elena turned to Redington with a spontaneous suggestion. "Would you like to come over for a nightcap? I have a rare scotch I've been saving for a special occasion, and tonight's discussion definitely qualifies."

Redington, caught slightly off guard by the invitation but intrigued by the prospect of continuing their engaging conversation, nodded. "I'd like that," he said, his tone reflecting both his anticipation and the slight tension of stepping into a more personal realm with Elena.

They walked to her place, which was not far from the restaurant. As they entered her elegantly appointed apartment, Redington felt a blend of curiosity and excitement. The evening had taken a turn toward the personal, and he was keen to see where this engaging and unexpected encounter would lead.

Chapter 66

Elena's apartment reflected her personality—
sophisticated and tastefully adorned with art that
likely had fascinating stories behind them, much
like the subjects she studied. She led Redington
to a cozy sitting area and poured two glasses of
scotch, handing one to him with a smile that
suggested she was as pleased with the evening as
he was.

"To new insights and good company," Elena
toasted, raising her glass.

"To both," Redington replied, clinking his
glass gently against hers.

As they settled into the comfortable sofas, the
conversation shifted from the professional to the
personal. Elena shared anecdotes from her
travels and research, each story showcasing her
passion for understanding human behavior.
Redington, in turn, found himself opening up
about his own experiences in the field, the

challenges and the rare, rewarding moments that defined his career.

The scotch was smooth, and the warmth it spread was matched by the warmth of the interaction. Elena's presence was captivating, her intellect and charm intermingling to create an atmosphere charged with an unexpected intimacy.

As the night deepened, Elena moved a little closer, her hand brushing against Redington's as she laughed at a joke he had just made. The contact sent a subtle spark through him, and he noticed the fragrance of her perfume, a complex blend that seemed to draw him in closer.

There was a pause in the conversation as they both acknowledged the shift in their dynamics. Elena looked at Redington with an expression that was both inviting and questioning, as if she were seeking his consent to breach the professional boundary they had always maintained.

Redington felt the tension, a mix of anticipation and hesitation. It was then that Lexi's image flashed through his mind—their deep conversations, her earnest quest for wisdom, and the spiritual connection they shared. The thought was fleeting but poignant, leaving him momentarily divided.

However, the moment passed, and the compelling allure of the present, with Elena's engaging eyes locked onto his, drew him back.

He leaned in, his decision made in the silence that spoke volumes, and kissed her. It was a gentle kiss, one that spoke of new possibilities and mutual respect, tinged with the excitement of exploring what had so far been uncharted territory between them.

Elena responded with equal measure, her hands reaching up to touch his face, deepening the kiss for a brief moment before they both pulled back, a little breathless.

"That was..." Elena started, her voice a soft murmur.

"Unexpected," Redington finished for her, but with a smile. "But not unwelcome."

They both laughed lightly, the sound mingling with the clink of their glasses as they settled back into the cushions, the scotch forgotten for a moment.

The night stretched on, filled with more talk, laughter, and shared confidences. When it was time for Redington to leave, they both knew something had changed, perhaps irrevocably. Yet, there was an unspoken agreement that whatever this was or could be, it would not disrupt the respect and camaraderie they had for each other.

As Redington stepped out into the cool night air, his thoughts were a blend of contemplation and contentment. The kiss had been a surprising turn of events, one that might or might not lead somewhere. Regardless, he felt a renewed sense of connection—not just to Elena, but to his own emotions and desires, which he often kept guarded.

The night had offered him more than just a distraction; it had opened up a new chapter, one that he was now curious to explore, even as the memory of Lexi remained a gentle echo in the back of his mind.

Chapter 67

As night enveloped the monastery, Lexi retired to her chamber, the discussions of the day and the teachings of contemplation still echoing in her mind. As she settled into the quiet darkness, she prepared herself for another potential visitation in her dreams from Archangel Uriel, whose guidance had always illuminated her path and deepened her understanding.

However, as sleep claimed her, the dream that unfolded was starkly different from what she had anticipated. Instead of the celestial landscapes and the comforting presence of Uriel, her dream wove into the fabric of a more personal and unexpected scenario. She found herself walking along a moonlit path in a garden she didn't recognize, the air filled with the scent of jasmine and the rustle of leaves in a gentle breeze.

As Lexi followed the winding path, she saw a figure standing in the shadows ahead—a figure that, as she approached, resolved into Redington. In the dream, he was dressed in casual attire, a stark contrast to the usual formal or tactical wear she associated with him. His presence was both surprising and strangely fitting within the dream's serene landscape.

Redington turned to her with a smile that seemed to light up the surroundings, his eyes reflecting an emotion she hadn't seen in him before—an openness, a vulnerability that he seldom showed in waking life. Lexi felt her heart quicken as she stepped closer, the distance between them charged with an unspoken connection.

Without a word, Redington reached for her hand, pulling her gently toward him. Lexi's intuition, usually so attuned to the spiritual and ethereal, gave way to a more human, more immediate instinct. She found herself drawn in by the moment, by the look in his eyes that beckoned her closer with a silent invitation.

As they stood face to face, Redington leaned in, and Lexi met him halfway, their lips meeting in a kiss that was tender and questioning, as if exploring the possibilities of a new, uncharted relationship. The kiss deepened, stirring feelings within Lexi that she had only fleetingly acknowledged in her waking hours—feelings of affection and perhaps something more, something deeper, tied to the complex layers of their interactions.

Suddenly, the scene shifted, and the dream took on a vivid clarity—Lexi could feel the cool night air, smell the subtle fragrance of Redington's cologne, feel the slight pressure of his hands on her back. It was as real as any waking moment, and it left her breathless.

Then, just as suddenly as it had begun, the dream dissolved, and Lexi awoke in her room at the monastery, the echo of the kiss lingering on her lips, the emotional residue clinging to her like a second skin. She lay in the dark, her heart still racing, her mind reeling from the dream's intensity.

Why had her subconscious brought her such a vision, especially now? Was it merely a reflection of her own suppressed thoughts and feelings, or was it something more, a sign or a premonition? Lexi was unsettled yet undeniably intrigued by the dream's implications.

As dawn crept through her window, Lexi rose to meet the day, the image of the dream still vivid in her mind. She knew she would need time to ponder its meaning, to understand what her heart and soul were trying to tell her about Redington, about herself, and about the potential paths her life could take. The dream had opened a door she had long tried to keep closed, and now, she wondered if she was ready to step through it.

Chapter 68

In the serene morning light that filled the monastery's great hall, the monks gathered around Sophea, each prepared to delve into the teachings of Tobias on the virtue of patience. The tranquility of the setting contrasted sharply with the turmoil in Lexi's mind as she struggled to focus on Sophea's words. Her dream about Redington from the night before lingered vividly in her thoughts, casting a shadow of distraction over her usually clear focus.

"Tobias depicted patience as a loom, on which the threads of time, effort, and perseverance are interwoven to create something enduring and valuable," Sophea began, her voice resonating with the depth of the metaphor. She spoke of the construction of Solomon's Temple, which took seven years to complete—a testament to sustained commitment and patience.

As Sophea elaborated on the virtues of long-term dedication, Lexi found her thoughts drifting back to the dream, to the unexpected intimacy and the emotions it stirred within her. The metaphor of the loom, meant to symbolize patience, ironically mirrored the complex tangle of feelings and decisions Lexi now faced in her own life.

Isabella, always keen on practical application, pulled Lexi back from her reverie with a question. "Sophea, how did Tobias suggest we cultivate the patience needed to manage our own 'long-term construction' projects?"

Sophea's answer, focusing on setting clear goals and breaking tasks into smaller parts, floated through Lexi's distracted consciousness. She recognized the parallel in her need to process her feelings in stages, to acknowledge the impact of her dream and what it might mean for her future.

Kesia's inquiry about managing fraying patience resonated even more with Lexi. "What advice did Tobias give for those moments when our patience begins to fray?"

Sophea's advice to return to one's spiritual practices to realign with inner calm seemed directly aimed at Lexi. She felt a gentle nudge from within to consider this approach, to use meditation or prayer to sift through her emotions and regain her spiritual equilibrium.

Lexi, gathering a semblance of focus, contributed her own question, aligning with her current inner conflict. "How does cultivating patience influence our relationships and community interactions?"

Sophea's response highlighted patience as a cornerstone of strong relationships, fostering understanding and empathy. "In a community, patience helps create a more harmonious environment, as individuals are more likely to approach conflicts with a willingness to listen and resolve issues gradually."

The visualization exercise Sophea led next invited the monks to imagine themselves weaving on a loom, where each thread represented a day's efforts. Lexi participated, visualizing her own tapestry of emotions and decisions slowly forming. This exercise brought her a measure of peace, offering a metaphorical framework through which to view her dilemma.

As the session concluded and the monks dispersed, Lexi remained seated, her mind a blend of calm and confusion. The teachings on patience had unexpectedly provided her with a lens to view her feelings for Redington—a project of the heart that would require careful and patient handling, just like the threads on a loom.

Determined to find clarity, Lexi decided to spend more time in meditation, hoping to weave her own tapestry of understanding that would integrate her spiritual journey with the personal revelations that had recently surfaced. The dream had opened a door, and now, with patience as her guide, she was ready to explore what lay beyond.

Chapter 69

The monastery's nightfall brought a deep silence that enveloped the ancient stones and the hearts of those dwelling within. As Lexi retired to her modest chamber, her mind was fraught with the echoes of her recent dream of Redington and the lingering emotions it stirred. Seeking guidance, she hoped for a visit from Archangel Uriel in her dreams, a presence that always seemed to bring clarity and comfort.

As she drifted into sleep, the celestial realm unfolded before her, revealing Uriel waiting amidst a backdrop of shimmering stars and nebulous clouds. His countenance was serene, his eyes reflecting a wisdom that transcended time and earthly concerns.

"Uriel," Lexi began, her voice tinged with the vulnerability of her human emotions, "I find myself at a crossroads, where the heart's inclinations seem to challenge the path I believed was my calling. How does love shift a person's perspective, and can it distract us from our chosen path?"

Uriel listened with a compassionate gaze, understanding the depth of her turmoil. "Lexi, love is a powerful force, one that can indeed transform your perspective. It opens you to new possibilities, new understandings, and even new challenges. Love can make you see the world differently, aligning you closer to the essence of what it means to be truly alive and connected."

He continued, "However, love can also be a distraction if it pulls you away from your values or your divine purpose. It is not the feeling of love itself that distracts, but rather the choices made in its name. Like any powerful tool, it must be wielded wisely and with a heart aligned to your spiritual truths."

Lexi pondered Uriel's words, relating them to the teachings of Tobias she had learned. "Tobias spoke of patience on a loom, weaving together threads to create something enduring. Is love then a thread that can be woven into the fabric of our spiritual journey without causing it to unravel?"

Uriel nodded, his expression softening with approval. "Precisely, Lexi. Consider love as one of the many threads in the tapestry of your life. It is essential, vibrant, and transformative, but it must be balanced with other threads—duty, compassion, truth, and growth. Together, these threads form a complete picture that reflects not only who you are but who you aspire to be."

Encouraged by Uriel's metaphor, Lexi asked, "How can I ensure that this thread enriches rather than entangles my path?"

"The key," Uriel advised, "Is to remain grounded in your spiritual practice and true to your inner self. Allow love to be a light that enhances your vision, not a fog that clouds it. Reflect on your feelings and decisions through meditation and prayer. Seek wisdom in moments of stillness, and you will find the balance to integrate love harmoniously into your journey."

As the dream began to fade, Uriel's figure dissolving into the celestial landscape, Lexi felt a renewed sense of purpose and understanding. She awoke the next morning with a clearer mind, ready to explore how the thread of love might be woven into her life's tapestry. Her conversation with Uriel had provided not just comfort but a profound directive on how to harmonize her spiritual and emotional worlds.

With a quiet resolve, Lexi prepared for the day, inspired to continue her path with both the wisdom of Tobias and the celestial guidance of Uriel shaping her steps. The love that had once seemed a distraction now appeared as a crucial part of her spiritual evolution, a testament to the dynamic and multifaceted nature of her journey.

Chapter 70

The soft morning light illuminated the monastery's great hall as the monks gathered, their faces reflecting a sense of purpose and readiness to delve into today's lesson from Tobias' teachings. Today, Sophea would discuss the concept of virtue as a compass, an essential tool for navigating the moral landscapes of life.

"Tobias likened virtue to a compass, an instrument that guides us through life's ethical and moral decisions," Sophea began, setting the tone with her calm and clear delivery. "He used Solomon's diplomatic negotiations and treaties as examples of how a strong moral compass is essential for maintaining peace and prosperity" (1 Kings 5:12).

She continued, "Solomon's ability to form and sustain fruitful alliances without compromising his kingdom's principles showcased his moral orientation. Tobias saw this as a testament to the guiding power of wisdom in navigating complex ethical scenarios."

Isabella, intrigued by the practical implications, asked, "Sophea, how did Tobias suggest we develop and maintain this moral compass in our own lives?"

"Tobias advocated for constant engagement with sacred teachings and reflective practices that reinforce one's moral and ethical values," Sophea replied. "He encouraged seeking counsel from wise and experienced individuals who exemplify virtue in their lives. Additionally, Tobias emphasized the importance of self-awareness and regular moral self-assessment to ensure that one's actions align with their core ethical beliefs."

Kesia, reflecting on the complexities of modern ethical dilemmas, inquired, "What guidance did Tobias offer for applying this moral compass to today's diverse and often conflicting ethical landscapes?"

"Tobias acknowledged that today's ethical landscapes are fraught with complexities that Solomon himself might not have encountered," Sophea explained. "However, he believed that the principles of wisdom and virtue are timeless. Tobias advised that in situations where ethical paths are not clear, one should lean on the foundational virtues of honesty, justice, and compassion. He also suggested that maintaining open dialogues within one's community can provide multiple perspectives, which aid in making balanced decisions."

Lexi, considering the impact of such guidance, asked, "How does following a moral compass influence our relationships and community interactions?"

"Tobias taught that a well-maintained moral compass not only guides individual actions but also fosters trust and respect within a community," Sophea elaborated. "When community members observe consistent, virtuous behavior in their leaders and peers, it creates a culture of ethical integrity. This trust enhances cooperation and collective well-being, as individuals feel secure in a community where ethical guidelines are respected and upheld."

Inspired by the conversation, Sophea led the monks in a brief meditative exercise. "Close your eyes and imagine holding a compass in your hand. Each direction it points represents a virtue guiding you. Reflect on how this compass influences your daily decisions and interactions. Consider moments when this guidance was crucial and how it might direct you in future scenarios."

As the monks engaged in deep contemplation, they visualized their personal ethical compasses, feeling empowered by the clarity it brought to their decision-making processes.

Concluding the session, Sophea encouraged, "Let us each strive to hone our compasses of virtue, allowing them to guide us faithfully through life's moral landscapes. May your paths be guided by the wisdom and integrity that Solomon aspired to, and may your actions reflect the noblest of your convictions."

With these inspiring words, the monks departed, each committed to refining and following their moral compasses, enriched by the teachings of Tobias and the historical wisdom of Solomon.

Chapter 71

The calm of the early morning enveloped the monastery's great hall as the monks gathered for their daily discourse with Sophea. Today's discussion would explore the virtue of modesty, depicted by Tobias as an anchor that provides stability and keeps one grounded in the face of life's temptations and excesses.

"Tobias envisioned modesty as an anchor, essential for maintaining one's balance and humility, regardless of the wealth, power, or praise one might accumulate," Sophea began, her voice echoing the depth and importance of the virtue. "He drew upon the later years of Solomon's reign as a cautionary tale. Despite his wisdom, Solomon's indulgence in wealth and power ultimately led him astray, demonstrating the dangers of losing one's modesty" (1 Kings 11:1-6).

She continued, "This part of Solomon's story serves to remind us that wisdom includes the modesty to recognize our limits and to resist the temptations that come with excess."

Isabella, intrigued by the practical implications, asked, "Sophea, how did Tobias suggest we cultivate and maintain modesty in our own lives?"

"Tobias recommended regular self-reflection and accountability as key practices for cultivating modesty," Sophea replied. "He advised setting boundaries for oneself and adhering to them, regardless of external circumstances. Tobias also stressed the importance of surrounding oneself with peers and mentors who are not afraid to speak truthfully and provide necessary critiques."

Kesia, pondering the challenges of maintaining humility, inquired, "What strategies did Tobias recommend for those who struggle with the allure of excess and the loss of modesty?"

"Tobias understood that the human heart is often drawn to excess," Sophea explained. "He suggested focusing on spiritual practices that enhance contentment and satisfaction with what one has. Tobias also advocated for community engagement and service to others, which can shift the focus from self-aggrandizement to the welfare of those around us, reinforcing the value of modesty."

Lexi, interested in the broader impact of modesty, asked, "How does maintaining modesty affect our relationships and societal roles?"

"Tobias taught that modesty strengthens relationships by fostering respect and genuine interactions," Sophea elaborated. "In societal roles, modesty prevents the abuse of power and promotes fair leadership. When leaders exhibit modesty, they are more likely to be empathetic and equitable, enhancing trust and cooperation within the community."

Inspired by the depth of the discussion, Sophea guided the monks in a visualization exercise. "Close your eyes and imagine modesty as an anchor that holds you steady in turbulent waters. Reflect on areas of your life where this anchor is particularly needed. Consider how maintaining this anchor can help you stay true to your values and avoid the pitfalls of excess."

As the monks meditated on this imagery, they contemplated their personal challenges with modesty and excess, recognizing areas where they could strengthen their anchors.

Concluding the session, Sophea encouraged, "Let us each strive to keep our anchors of modesty firmly planted, allowing us to remain stable and grounded no matter the societal pressures or riches we encounter. May your modesty be a testament to your wisdom and a guide to living a balanced and ethical life."

With these motivating words, the monks rose, each committed to cultivating deeper modesty in their lives, inspired by the teachings of Tobias and the sobering example of Solomon's later years.

Chapter 72

As the monks assembled in the monastery's great hall, bathed in the gentle light of dawn, they prepared for another insightful session with Sophea. Today's discourse would explore the virtue of strategy, likened by Tobias to a quiver filled with arrows, each representing a different tactical approach to life's myriad challenges.

"Tobias described strategy as a quiver stocked with various arrows, emphasizing the importance of having multiple approaches at one's disposal," Sophea began, her voice steady and clear. "He often referred to Solomon's strategic prowess, not only in governance but also in military expansions and building projects" (1 Kings 9:15). "Solomon's ability to choose the appropriate strategy for each challenge was a testament to his wisdom and foresight."

She continued, "Just as an archer selects the right arrow based on the target and wind conditions, wise leaders and individuals select the most suitable strategy based on the nuances of each situation."

Isabella, always keen to understand practical applications, asked, "Sophea, how did Tobias suggest we develop and refine our strategic thinking?"

"Tobias advocated for continuous learning and the study of past successes and failures, both personal and historical," Sophea replied. "He encouraged engaging with diverse fields of knowledge and seeking counsel from experienced advisors to fill one's quiver with a broad array of strategic options. Tobias also emphasized the importance of scenario planning—thinking through potential challenges and rehearsing various responses."

Kesia, reflecting on the complexities of decision-making, inquired, "What guidance did Tobias offer for choosing the right strategy from our quiver in complex situations?"

"Tobias recognized that selecting the right strategy involves both wisdom and discernment," Sophea explained. "He advised careful analysis of the situation at hand, considering all variables and potential outcomes. Tobias also suggested that intuition, honed by experience and ethical considerations, plays a crucial role in this selection process."

Lexi, interested in the ethical dimensions of strategic choices, asked, "How does Tobias suggest we balance strategic thinking with ethical considerations?"

"Tobias taught that strategy should never be divorced from ethics," Sophea elaborated. "He believed that the most effective strategies are those that not only achieve goals but do so in a way that is just and honorable. Tobias stressed the importance of integrating ethical considerations into every strategic decision, ensuring that actions align with one's moral values and the greater good."

Inspired by the discussion, Sophea led the monks in a brief meditative exercise. "Close your eyes and imagine holding a quiver full of arrows. Each arrow represents a different strategy you've learned or developed. Reflect on a current challenge and visualize selecting the most appropriate arrow. Consider how this choice aligns with both your objectives and your ethical principles."

As the monks visualized this process, they considered how they could apply their strategic and ethical insights to various aspects of their lives.

Concluding the session, Sophea encouraged, "Let us each strive to fill our quivers with a diverse array of strategic options, preparing ourselves to face life's challenges with wisdom and integrity. May your choices always reflect the depth of your strategic thinking and the strength of your ethical convictions."

With these motivating words, the monks rose, each more prepared to approach life's challenges with a strategic mindset, guided by the wisdom of Solomon and the teachings of Tobias.

Chapter 73

The weeks following the successful operation against the cult had been a mix of professional highs and personal exploration for Redington. His relationship with Elena Mirov had evolved from intellectual camaraderie to something deeper, something more intimate. Their dinners had become more frequent, and their conversations had started to weave in personal dreams and vulnerabilities alongside professional insights. Elena, with her sharp intellect and surprising warmth, had started to occupy a significant place in Redington's thoughts.

However, as their relationship began to crystallize into something more serious, Redington found himself wrestling with unexpected emotions and doubts, triggered by a vivid dream.

One night, after a particularly pleasant evening out with Elena, Redington returned home feeling content yet unsettled. As he drifted off to sleep, his mind replayed the evening's laughter and the easy silence they shared. But deep in the night, his subconscious took him elsewhere.

In his dream, Redington found himself back in Nepal, at the monastery he had visited virtually a few weeks prior. The serene, snow-capped mountains and the peaceful ambiance of the monastery provided a stark contrast to his life in New York. As he walked through the monastery's tranquil corridors, he saw Lexi, her face calm and introspective, turning toward him with a soft smile.

The dream shifted, and suddenly he and Lexi were walking through the monastery gardens, discussing life's profound questions and personal journeys. Lexi's presence in the dream was not just comforting but also evoked a sense of peace and clarity he hadn't realized he was missing. Just as they were about to speak something significant, Redington awoke, her words fading away, leaving a poignant sense of loss.

The residual feelings from the dream lingered throughout the morning, casting a shadow of doubt over his feelings for Elena. Why had Lexi appeared in his dream so vividly now, just as his relationship with Elena was deepening? Was his subconscious trying to tell him something he was deliberately ignoring in his waking life?

Redington found himself contemplating the nature of his attachment to Elena. Was it truly rooted in a deep emotional connection, or was it the comfort and excitement of finding someone who understood the demands of his profession? Lexi, on the other hand, represented a different kind of connection—one that touched on spiritual and existential matters, areas of his life that Elena, for all her understanding and companionship, didn't quite reach.

The confusion led Redington to seek solitude, hoping to clear his mind and gain some perspective. He decided to go for a long walk in the city park, a place where the natural beauty provided a temporary escape from the urban chaos and his tumultuous thoughts.

As he walked, he weighed his feelings and the implications of his dream. How should he interpret these emotional signals? Could he pursue a future with Elena while a part of him still responded so strongly to Lexi, even if just in a dream?

The more Redington thought, the more he realized that he needed to resolve these inner conflicts before making any further commitments to Elena. He valued honesty, not just in his professional life but also in his personal relationships. It was clear he needed to understand the depth of his feelings for both Elena and Lexi to ensure that his actions and choices would not lead to regrets or hurt those he cared about.

Determined to find clarity, Redington decided that the next step would be a conversation with both women, though in very different contexts. With Elena, he needed an open and honest discussion about his current state of mind. With Lexi, it would be a deeper exploration of the feelings she evoked in him—a conversation that he hoped would help him understand the path his heart truly wanted to follow.

Chapter 74

In the tranquil early hours, as the first light filtered through the monastery's chapel windows, the monks gathered around Sophea, ready to absorb the teachings on self-reflection, depicted by Tobias as a mirror revealing the true self. Today's discussion promised to delve deep into the introspective aspect of wisdom, using Solomon's reflective writings as a guide.

"Tobias likened self-reflection to looking into a mirror, not to see our outer appearance, but to view the depths of our inner selves," Sophea began, her voice imbued with the solemnity appropriate to such introspective discussion. "He pointed to Solomon's proverbs and his philosophical explorations in Ecclesiastes as exemplary texts that demonstrate the power and necessity of self-reflection for anyone seeking wisdom."

She continued, "These writings encourage us to contemplate our actions, our motivations, and the transient nature of worldly pursuits, urging us to focus on what truly enriches our spirits."

Isabella, always keen to apply these teachings to her personal development, asked, "Sophea, how did Tobias suggest we practice self-reflection effectively?"

"Tobias recommended daily periods of quiet contemplation, where we might review our actions and their motivations," Sophea replied. "He advocated for the use of journals to record thoughts and feelings, as writing can often help clarify the reflections seen in our 'mirrors.' Tobias also stressed the importance of seeking feedback from trusted friends or mentors, as they can help us see aspects of ourselves that we might overlook or avoid."

Kesia, pondering the challenges of honest self-assessment, inquired, "What did Tobias say about facing the uncomfortable truths that this mirror might reveal?"

"Tobias acknowledged that true self-reflection is often challenging, as it can reveal flaws and weaknesses," Sophea explained. "He advised embracing these discoveries with grace, viewing them as opportunities for growth rather than reasons for self-reproach. Tobias emphasized the need for humility and the willingness to change, which are essential for transforming insights into action."

Lexi, interested in the broader implications, asked, "How does this practice of self-reflection contribute to greater wisdom and spiritual integrity?"

"Tobias taught that self-reflection deepens our understanding of ourselves and our place in the world," Sophea elaborated. "It allows us to align our actions with our deeper values and ensures that we live authentically and ethically. This alignment fosters spiritual integrity and wisdom, as we become more adept at navigating life's complexities with moral clarity and a strong sense of purpose."

Inspired by the depth of the discussion, Sophea led the monks in a short meditative exercise. "Close your eyes and imagine yourself before a mirror that reflects not your face but your soul. Contemplate what you see—your strengths, your struggles, your growth areas. Think about how you might address what you see, enhancing your strengths and working on your weaknesses."

As the monks engaged in this reflective practice, they considered the insights gained and how they could apply them to foster personal growth and spiritual integrity.

Concluding the session, Sophea encouraged, "Let us each strive to use the mirror of self-reflection regularly, ensuring that our lives are true reflections of our highest selves. May your reflections guide you to deeper wisdom and greater inner peace."

With these thoughtful words, the monks dispersed, each committed to the practice of self-reflection, inspired by the teachings of Tobias and the introspective legacy of Solomon.

Chapter 75

As the morning sun streamed into the monastery's great hall, casting a warm glow across the attentive faces of the monks, Sophea prepared to unfold another lesson from Tobias' teachings. Today, she would explore the virtue of generosity, likened to a well-balanced scale, essential for a fulfilling and harmonious life.

"Tobias depicted generosity as a scale, emphasizing the importance of balance between giving and receiving," Sophea began, her voice resonant with the wisdom of the metaphor. "He pointed to Solomon's reign as an exemplar of this principle, highlighting how Solomon's generosity, both to his workers and in his diplomatic exchanges, contributed significantly to his kingdom's prosperity and his own personal fulfillment" (1 Kings 10:13).

She continued, "This balanced approach not only enriched his relationships with other nations but also solidified his reputation as a wise and benevolent king."

Isabella, intrigued by the practical aspects, asked, "Sophea, how did Tobias suggest we cultivate such generosity in our own lives?"

"Tobias encouraged seeing generosity not merely as an act of giving but as a state of openness to sharing one's resources, time, and abilities," Sophea replied. "He recommended starting small, with acts of kindness within one's immediate community, and gradually expanding the scope of one's generosity. Tobias also emphasized the joy and satisfaction that come from giving, which often serve as their own reward."

Kesia, considering her experiences with generosity, inquired, "What did Tobias say about the challenges of being generous without feeling depleted or taken advantage of?"

"Tobias recognized that true generosity should not lead to depletion," Sophea explained. "He advised setting wise boundaries and practicing discernment in giving. Tobias believed that generosity should be sustainable, coming from a place of abundance and goodwill, not from a sense of obligation or pressure."

Lexi, curious about the broader impacts, asked, "How does practicing generosity affect our relationships and community dynamics?"

"Tobias taught that generosity fosters trust and strengthens bonds within a community," Sophea elaborated. "When people observe acts of generosity, they are often inspired to act similarly, creating a cycle of giving that enhances the overall well-being of the community. Generosity can transform societal interactions, promoting a culture of mutual support and empathy."

Inspired by the discussion, Sophea guided the monks in a visualization exercise. "Close your eyes and imagine your life as a scale. On one side, place your acts of generosity. On the other, consider what you receive in return, not only materially but also in terms of affection, respect, and gratitude. Reflect on how you might balance this scale more evenly."

As the monks meditated, they considered their own practices of generosity, recognizing areas where they could give more freely or where they might need to balance their giving with self-care.

Concluding the session, Sophea encouraged, "Let us each strive to balance our scales of generosity, giving freely as we are able, and receiving with gratitude. May your generous actions enrich your lives and those around you, creating a lasting impact on your community."

With these inspiring words, the monks departed, each determined to implement and maintain a balanced approach to generosity, guided by the wisdom of Solomon and the teachings of Tobias.

Chapter 76

That night, after absorbing the day's lessons on generosity and the balance of giving and receiving, Lexi retired to her room, her mind filled with thoughts of how to apply these teachings in her own life. As she drifted into sleep, she hoped for another visit from Archangel Uriel, seeking his celestial wisdom on the virtue that had so deeply resonated with her during the day's discourse.

In her dream, Lexi found herself in a serene, celestial landscape, the stars twinkling above like countless eyes watching over the universe. The air around her was crisp and clear, carrying a sense of peace and boundless possibility. Uriel appeared beside her, his presence comforting and his aura bright under the cosmic light.

"Uriel," Lexi greeted him, her voice echoing softly in the ethereal space. "Today we learned about generosity as a scale, balancing giving and receiving. How does this concept play out on a spiritual level? How can I ensure that my own scales are balanced?"

Uriel smiled, his eyes reflecting the starlight, and gestured for Lexi to follow him to a nearby overlook. Below them spread a vast landscape, showing various scenes of people giving and receiving—kindness, help, love, and wisdom flowed between them like streams of light.

"Generosity, Lexi, is more than a transaction; it is an expression of the abundant love that flows from the Creator," Uriel began. "In the divine perspective, generosity is about channeling this love through your actions and interactions. It is about filling your heart so fully with divine love that it overflows naturally to those around you."

He paused, allowing the scenes below to sink in. "You ask about balance. It is achieved not by measuring and calculating each act of giving against what you receive, but by aligning your heart with divine intentions. When you give from a place of true generosity, you become a conduit for love's infinite flow, and this very act of giving fills you as well."

Lexi watched the scenes of generosity unfold below, seeing the joy and light in both the givers and the receivers. "And what of taking too much, or giving too much?" she asked, her voice tinged with the concern of overextending oneself.

"True generosity is self-sustaining when it comes from a place of divine alignment," Uriel explained. "It does not deplete you because it is powered by an endless source. However, in human form, maintaining balance does require you to listen to your heart and recognize when your physical or emotional resources demand replenishment. This is where the wisdom of discernment comes into play, allowing you to give without losing yourself."

Uriel handed Lexi a small, luminous orb that seemed to pulse with light. "Hold this as a reminder of the balance within generosity. Let it guide you to know when to give, how much to give, and when to replenish."

As the dream began to fade, Lexi felt a profound sense of clarity and peace envelop her. She awoke the next morning with a renewed understanding of how to live out the virtue of generosity in a way that enriched both her life and the lives of those around her.

Carrying the wisdom from her dream into her daily life, Lexi felt more connected to the divine flow of generosity, confident in her ability to balance giving and receiving in a way that nurtured her soul and served her community. She was grateful for Uriel's guidance, feeling ever more equipped to walk her path with grace and wisdom.

Chapter 77

The day was brisk, the kind that hinted at change—not just in weather but perhaps in life's very trajectory. Redington paced the departure lounge, his mind a tumult of emotions and plans. Today, he was bound for Nepal, not on a case or an operation, but a personal quest that might redefine his entire future. He had resolved to confront and perhaps reconcile the profound feelings he harbored for Lexi, feelings that had surfaced unmistakably in his recent dreams and during quiet moments of reflection.

He boarded the flight with a sense of purpose, the weight of his impending confession lending a gravity to each step he took down the jetway. Settling into his seat, he rehearsed the words he might say to Lexi, each phrase carefully sculpted to convey the depth of his emotions without overwhelming her. His heart raced at the thought of their impending conversation, one that could either forge a new beginning or mark a painful, albeit necessary, closure.

As the plane ascended, Redington gazed out the window, watching the familiar sights of the city shrink away. His thoughts drifted to Lexi—her intelligent eyes, her serene demeanor, the way she seemed to exist so effortlessly in tune with the spiritual rhythms he struggled to perceive. The more he thought about her, the more he realized how much he needed to not just express his feelings but also hear her own, whatever they might be.

However, fate had a different script in mind. Midway through the flight, a sudden commotion broke his reverie. Shouts echoed through the cabin, and within moments, the situation became chillingly clear: the plane was being hijacked. A group of hijackers, armed and determined, moved swiftly to take control of the aircraft, their motives unclear but their intentions undeniably serious.

As trained as he was for critical situations, Redington instinctively assessed his environment for any advantage or means to intervene. Yet, with the safety of all passengers at stake, he knew that any misstep could lead to disaster. The hijackers directed the pilot to divert the plane to an undisclosed location, far from the intended destination of Nepal.

The aircraft eventually landed on a remote airstrip, surrounded by arid terrain that offered no clue as to their whereabouts. The hijackers herded the passengers into a makeshift holding area—a barren, windowless building adjacent to the airstrip. Redington, along with his fellow passengers, was left to grapple with the uncertainty and fear of their predicament.

Amidst the chaos, Redington's thoughts returned to Lexi. The irony of his journey—a quest to confess deep feelings only to be thwarted by a hijacking—was not lost on him. He felt a profound sense of frustration, mixed with a renewed concern for what the future held. The hijacking not only endangered lives but also suspended his personal quest in an agonizing limbo.

As hours turned into days, Redington used his skills to keep calm, helping to maintain a semblance of order among the hostages. His training as an FBI agent provided him with the tools to negotiate and manage stress, both his own and others', in the direst situations.

Yet, even as he navigated this unexpected crisis, his thoughts lingered on Lexi, on what he had hoped to share, and the responses he had hoped to hear. This delay, this diversion, was yet another test of the patience and resilience he had learned from his own tumultuous life—a reminder that the path to resolution, whether personal or professional, is seldom straight.

Chapter 78

As daylight filled the monastery's great hall, the monks gathered around Sophea, eager for another session exploring the deep wisdom imparted through Tobias' teachings. Today's focus was on knowledge, envisioned as a vast library filled with endless shelves of books, and the discernment required to navigate such extensive information effectively.

"Tobias likened the pursuit of knowledge to exploring a vast library," Sophea began, her voice resonating with the reverence appropriate to such an expansive metaphor. "He frequently cited Solomon's example, who not only sought after knowledge but also compiled significant works of proverbs, songs, and scientific observations" (1 Kings 4:32). "Solomon's example illustrates that true wisdom involves not just the accumulation of information but understanding how to apply that knowledge in ways that are meaningful and beneficial."

She continued, "This ability to discern the useful from the merely interesting, the essential from the extraneous, is what marks the wise."

Isabella, intrigued by the application of this concept, asked, "Sophea, how did Tobias suggest we cultivate the ability to discern and apply knowledge effectively in our own lives?"

"Tobias encouraged the development of critical thinking and reflection," Sophea replied. "He advised that one should not only absorb information but also contemplate its implications and applications. Tobias recommended engaging with diverse fields of study and seeking perspectives from others to enhance understanding and avoid the narrowness of thought that often accompanies isolated learning."

Kesia, reflecting on her experiences with information overload, inquired, "What strategies did Tobias recommend for managing the vast amounts of information we encounter, particularly in our digital age?"

"Tobias recognized the challenges posed by the modern deluge of data and information," Sophea explained. "He suggested establishing priorities based on one's values and goals to guide what information to seek out and retain. He also advocated for regular 'information fasts,' periods during which one abstains from consuming new information to process and apply what has already been learned."

Lexi, curious about the broader implications, asked, "How does effectively managing our knowledge impact our personal growth and our contributions to society?"

"Tobias taught that when we manage our knowledge well, we not only enhance our personal wisdom but also contribute more effectively to our communities," Sophea elaborated. "Knowledge, when thoughtfully applied, can solve problems, improve lives, and enlighten not just the individual but also those around them. It turns information into insight and wisdom into action."

Inspired by the depth of the discussion, Sophea led the monks in a reflective exercise. "Close your eyes and imagine yourself in a library filled with books. Each book represents a piece of knowledge you have acquired. Reflect on how you can organize this library to best serve your purposes and those of your community. Consider what books you would place in prominent positions, and which might be archived."

As the monks engaged in this visualization, they contemplated their personal 'libraries of knowledge,' considering how to curate and apply their learning more effectively.

Concluding the session, Sophea encouraged, "Let us each strive to build and navigate our libraries of knowledge with discernment and wisdom. May your studies enrich your life and those of others, guided by the thoughtful application of what you learn."

With these motivating words, the monks rose, each committed to refining their approach to the vast world of knowledge, inspired by Solomon's example and guided by Tobias' teachings.

Chapter 79

The morning light cast a gentle glow in the monastery's great hall as the monks assembled for their daily teachings with Sophea. Today, she was poised to discuss the concept of timeliness, using the metaphor of a sundial to illustrate the precision and necessity of acting at the right moment.

"Tobias likened timeliness in our actions to a sundial, which meticulously measures the passing of time and indicates the most appropriate moments to act," Sophea began, capturing the monks' attention with her vivid depiction. "He often cited Solomon's achievements, notably the timely completion of the Temple and his own royal palace" (1 Kings 6:1, 7:1). "These accomplishments were not only feats of engineering and artistry but also exemplars of executing plans at the right times, ensuring their success and lasting impact."

She continued, "This precision in timing is a critical aspect of wisdom, allowing one to synchronize their actions with the rhythms of opportunity and necessity."

Isabella, intrigued by how to apply this principle, asked, "Sophea, how did Tobias suggest we can develop the ability to recognize and act according to the right timing in our own lives?"

"Tobias recommended cultivating a keen awareness of our environment and the flow of events around us," Sophea replied. "He encouraged the practice of mindful observation and active listening, which can help us better understand when and how to act most effectively. Tobias also emphasized the importance of patience and preparation, so that when the right moment arrives, we are ready to seize it."

Kesia, pondering the practical challenges of timeliness, inquired, "What guidance did Tobias offer for situations where it's difficult to discern the right timing?"

"Tobias acknowledged that discerning the optimal time to act can often be challenging," Sophea explained. "He advised seeking advice from more experienced individuals who have navigated similar situations. Additionally, Tobias suggested prayer and meditation as means to gain clarity and insight, which can align our actions with a deeper sense of timing and purpose."

Lexi, curious about the broader impacts, asked, "How does acting with timeliness affect our relationships and community engagements?"

"Tobias taught that timeliness enhances respect and trust within relationships and communities," Sophea elaborated. "When actions are well-timed, they are more likely to be received positively and to have the intended effect. This can lead to more effective collaboration and stronger, more cohesive community bonds."

Inspired by the conversation, Sophea guided the monks in a reflective exercise. "Close your eyes and imagine a sundial in a quiet garden. Think about a decision or action you are considering. Reflect on the shadow of the sundial—where it points—and let this guide you in understanding the right timing for your action."

As the monks meditated, they visualized the sundial, considering how its guidance could apply to their current decisions and plans.

Concluding the session, Sophea encouraged, "Let us each strive to be as precise and mindful as a sundial in our decisions and actions. By aligning our actions with the optimal timing, we enhance not only the effectiveness of what we do but also contribute positively to the rhythms of our communities."

With these motivating words, the monks rose, each more committed to applying the principle of timeliness in their lives, inspired by the wisdom of Solomon and the teachings of Tobias.

Chapter 80

Trapped within the confines of the austere building on the remote airstrip, Redington, along with the other passengers, faced the grim reality of their situation. The hijackers, a group of methodically organized individuals with unclear objectives, kept a tight control over their hostages, their motives shrouded in mystery, adding to the tension and fear that permeated the air.

Redington, ever the analyst, observed the hijackers closely, trying to discern any patterns or weaknesses in their behavior. He noted how they communicated with each other, the shifts they took, and the security lapses that occasionally emerged during their exchanges. Each piece of information was a potential key to understanding their intentions and perhaps finding a way out.

As hours turned into days, the initial shock of the hijacking began to give way to a strained routine. Meals were brought in at irregular intervals, and bathroom breaks were closely monitored. Despite the harsh conditions, Redington's training allowed him to maintain a calm demeanor, helping to stabilize the morale of his fellow hostages. He became a makeshift leader, a source of strength for those around him.

One afternoon, as tensions ran particularly high following a heated exchange between a hostage and one of the hijackers, Redington saw an opportunity to initiate a dialogue with the hijackers. Using his experience in crisis negotiation, he approached one of the less confrontational hijackers during a quieter moment.

"My name is Redington," he began, his voice steady and authoritative yet non-threatening. "I understand you have your reasons for doing this, and while I can't agree with your methods, I'm here to talk if you think there's a way we can resolve this situation peacefully."

The hijacker, taken aback by Redington's direct but composed approach, hesitated before responding. After a brief, silent exchange with another hijacker, he nodded slightly, signaling Redington to continue.

"We have women and children here, people who are scared and need medical attention,"

Redington continued, gesturing subtly toward a young mother comforting her child. "Let's work together to ensure their safety. What do you need from us to make that happen?"

Negotiations were tense, with the hijackers wary of any tricks. However, Redington's sincere concern for the hostages and his professional demeanor slowly began to wear down their initial mistrust. Over several discreet conversations, he managed to establish a fragile line of communication, gathering vital information about their demands and the reasons behind the hijacking.

Meanwhile, back at FBI headquarters, efforts were underway to locate and rescue the hostages. Using satellite imagery and intelligence reports, a rescue operation was being planned. Unaware of these developments, Redington continued his delicate negotiations, hoping to buy enough time for a peaceful resolution or an external intervention.

As Redington navigated this precarious balance, his thoughts occasionally drifted to Lexi and the conversation that never happened. The irony of his current predicament —being a hostage negotiator in his own crisis—was not lost on him. He wondered about the different kinds of captivity, both physical and emotional, and how his feelings for Lexi had, in a way, held him captive in their own right.

Chapter 81

In the tranquil ambiance of the monastery's great hall, with morning light filtering softly through the high windows, the monks gathered around Sophea for their daily teaching. Today's lesson from Tobias focused on the virtue of decisiveness, likened to a helm that guides a ship through treacherous waters, ensuring it stays on course.

"Tobias depicted decisiveness as a helm, an essential tool for steering not just a ship but also the ship of state or the course of one's personal life," Sophea began, her voice steady and authoritative. "He drew upon Solomon's early actions upon ascending the throne—decisive acts that secured his kingdom's stability and asserted his leadership" (1 Kings 2). "These decisions, though tough, were necessary to prevent chaos and ensure the prosperity of his realm."

She continued, "This ability to make firm, timely decisions is a critical component of wisdom, as it prevents stagnation and resolves uncertainties that could hinder progress."

Isabella, reflecting on her own decision-making challenges, asked, "Sophea, how did Tobias suggest we cultivate decisiveness in our own lives?"

"Tobias recommended developing a clear set of values and priorities, which can provide a strong foundation for making decisions," Sophea replied. "He also emphasized the importance of gathering sufficient information and seeking counsel when necessary, but cautioned against over-analyzing to the point of paralysis. Finally, Tobias stressed the need for practice—like any skill, decisiveness improves with regular use."

Kesia, interested in the practical aspects, inquired, "What strategies did Tobias offer for overcoming the fear of making wrong decisions?"

"Tobias acknowledged that fear of error is a common obstacle to decisiveness," Sophea explained. "He advised focusing on the process of decision-making rather than obsessing over potential outcomes. Tobias suggested embracing the possibility of making mistakes as part of the learning process and emphasized the importance of being adaptable and ready to correct course as needed."

Lexi, curious about the impact of decisiveness on leadership, asked, "How does being decisive affect one's ability to lead effectively?"

"Tobias taught that decisiveness is crucial for leadership because it inspires confidence and trust among followers," Sophea elaborated. "A decisive leader can guide their team with clarity, reducing confusion and aligning efforts toward common goals. This not only enhances team performance but also builds respect and loyalty, as team members feel secure under a leader who acts with conviction and purpose."

Inspired by the discussion, Sophea led the monks in a brief meditative exercise. "Close your eyes and imagine you are at the helm of a ship. The sea represents the challenges you face. Visualize making decisive turns at the helm, steering confidently through the waters. Reflect on how each decision helps you navigate closer to your goals."

As the monks visualized themselves steering their ships, they contemplated the decisions looming in their own lives and how they might apply decisiveness more effectively.

Concluding the session, Sophea encouraged, "Let us each strive to grasp the helm of decisiveness firmly, making informed and timely decisions that keep our lives on a steady course. May your actions reflect the courage and clarity of a wise and effective leader."

With these empowering words, the monks rose, each feeling more prepared to tackle the decisions in their lives with decisiveness, inspired by Solomon's example and guided by the teachings of Tobias.

Chapter 82

As night fell on the third day of captivity, the atmosphere inside the makeshift holding area grew increasingly tense. The hijackers, visibly anxious about the prolonged situation and the growing international attention, began to show signs of strain. Redington, alert to every subtle shift in their demeanor, sensed an opportunity to push for more substantial concessions.

His ongoing negotiations, marked by a careful balance of empathy and assertiveness, had slowly built a rapport with one of the hijackers, whom he discerned to be less ideologically driven and more concerned with the safety of his own group. Leveraging this connection, Redington proposed a bold move: the release of all hostages in exchange for safe passage and medical supplies for the hijackers.

The proposal was a gamble, and as Redington presented it, he could feel the weight of every gaze upon him—both from his fellow hostages, whose hope he carried, and the hijackers, whose decision could pivot on a knife-edge. The air was thick with anticipation, every breath held as they awaited the response.

After a long, tension-filled pause, the lead hijacker called Redington aside. Under the dim light of a solitary bulb, they spoke in hushed tones. The hijacker's face, usually stern and unreadable, showed signs of fatigue and worry. The negotiations were taxing for both sides, each grappling with the potential outcomes of their decisions.

"We need guarantees," the lead hijacker stated firmly, his voice low. "Guarantees for safe exit and no pursuit for twelve hours. We leave the hostages; you let us leave."

Redington nodded, understanding the stakes. "I'll communicate your terms to my contacts. They can ensure your safe exit, but you must release all the hostages first. It's the only way to ensure everyone's safety."

With the hijacker's agreement tentatively in place, Redington used a satellite phone provided by the hijackers under strict supervision to contact his FBI colleagues. He relayed the terms of the agreement, emphasizing the critical nature of the situation and the hijackers' demand for a no-pursuit window.

Back at FBI headquarters, the response was immediate and carefully calculated. The negotiation team, while not fully agreeing to the terms, prepared a strategy that would allow the safe release of the hostages while planning a covert operation to apprehend the hijackers once the hostages were secure.

The tension among the hostages grew as they awaited the outcome of Redington's negotiations. Every minute seemed to stretch into an hour, each small noise a reason to startle. Yet, amidst the uncertainty, Redington's presence provided a pillar of calm strength.

Finally, after hours that felt like days, the hijackers began releasing the hostages. One by one, families, elders, and children were freed, their expressions a mix of relief and disbelief as they were escorted out of the holding area by a small team of international peacekeepers who had arrived to oversee the release.

As the last of the hostages walked free, Redington was among the final few to leave. He took a moment to look back at the hijackers, understanding the complexity of human motives and the depths of despair that could drive such actions. His heart was heavy with the burden of the ordeal, yet lightened by the successful resolution.

Upon his safe return to New York City, Redington's thoughts immediately turned to Lexi. The entire ordeal had sharpened his feelings and his need for resolution in his personal life. He felt an urgent need to speak with her, to share not just his recent harrowing experience but also the revelations about his feelings that had become clear during the crisis.

As Redington navigated the bustling corridors of JFK International Airport, the stark contrast between his recent captivity and the chaotic vibrancy of the terminal was palpable. It felt as though he was transitioning from one world to another, stepping out of the shadows of his ordeal into the bright, noisy thrum of life moving all around him. This shift underscored his readiness to bridge the experiences of his past with a future he hoped would deeply involve Lexi. The path ahead remained shrouded in uncertainty, yet for the first time in many months, Redington approached it with an open heart and a mind cleared of doubts, fully prepared to embrace whatever challenges and changes lay before him.

Chapter 83

As dawn's gentle light spilled across the monastery's great hall, illuminating the attentive faces of the gathered monks, Sophea prepared to impart another profound lesson from Tobias' teachings. Today, she would explore the virtue of empathy, envisioned as a lush garden where understanding and compassion flourish under the nurture of wisdom.

"Tobias often spoke of empathy as a garden, a place where the seeds of understanding and compassion are carefully planted and tended," Sophea began, her voice resonant with the nurturing nature of the metaphor. "He reflected on Solomon's early reign, noting how the king's ability to understand and respond to his people's needs and emotions was crucial to his success and popularity" (1 Kings 3:16-28). "Solomon's empathetic decisions, particularly his wise judgment in the case of the two mothers, demonstrated his deep connection with the hearts of his subjects."

She continued, "This capacity to truly empathize with others is a key aspect of wisdom, as it enables one to forge deeper, more meaningful relationships and build a supportive community."

Isabella, intrigued by the application of empathy in daily interactions, asked, "Sophea, how did Tobias suggest we cultivate such empathy in our own lives?"

"Tobias encouraged active listening and genuine engagement with others' experiences as foundational practices for cultivating empathy," Sophea replied. "He recommended spending time with different community members, sharing in their joys and struggles, and actively seeking to see situations from their perspectives. Tobias also stressed the importance of reflection and prayer to deepen one's capacity for compassion and understanding."

Kesia, considering the challenges of empathy, inquired, "What did Tobias say about dealing with emotional fatigue that can come from deep empathy?"

"Tobias recognized that while empathy is enriching, it can also be emotionally taxing," Sophea explained. "He advised maintaining a balance between caring for others and self-care. Tobias recommended setting aside time for personal rejuvenation and spiritual renewal to ensure that one's own emotional and spiritual reserves are replenished."

Lexi, curious about the broader implications, asked, "How does cultivating a garden of empathy impact a community?"

"Tobias taught that a community where empathy is valued and practiced is a community that thrives," Sophea elaborated. "Empathy promotes understanding and reduces conflicts, as community members are more inclined to approach disputes with compassion rather than judgment. It fosters an environment where individuals feel valued and supported, which in turn strengthens the collective resilience and harmony of the group."

Inspired by the depth of the discussion, Sophea guided the monks in a visualization exercise. "Close your eyes and imagine walking through a lush garden, where each plant represents an act of empathy you have shown. Reflect on how these plants grow and interact, creating a harmonious and beautiful space. Think about new plants you might add, representing future acts of empathy."

As the monks meditated on their empathetic gardens, they contemplated how they could cultivate more understanding and compassion in their interactions.

Concluding the session, Sophea encouraged, "Let us each strive to nurture our gardens of empathy with as much dedication as we would any garden. May your understanding and compassion bloom abundantly, enriching not just your own lives but also those around you."

With these inspiring words, the monks rose, each more committed to fostering empathy within themselves and their community, guided by the wisdom of Solomon and the teachings of Tobias.

Chapter 84

The monks gathered in the serene light of morning, filling the monastery's great hall with an air of thoughtful anticipation. Today, Sophea would explore the virtue of temperance, depicted by Tobias as a reservoir that carefully controls and moderates the flow of life's resources.

"Tobias described temperance as a reservoir, essential for regulating the use of resources and maintaining balance," Sophea began, her voice reflecting the calm and measured approach that temperance requires. "He pointed to Solomon's early wisdom in managing the kingdom's wealth and resources as an exemplary demonstration of this virtue" (1 Kings 4:20-28). "During this period, Solomon's judicious use of resources contributed greatly to the prosperity and stability of his realm."

She continued, "This prudent management is a cornerstone of temperance, which involves not only controlling one's own desires and impulses but also ensuring that resources—whether personal or communal—are used wisely and sustainably."

Isabella, keen to understand practical applications, asked, "Sophea, how did Tobias suggest we cultivate temperance in our own lives?"

"Tobias recommended practicing self-control in all aspects of life, from financial expenditures to personal habits," Sophea replied. "He emphasized the importance of setting clear, realistic goals for resource use and sticking to them. Tobias also suggested creating systems of accountability, such as budgeting or planning tools, which can help maintain discipline in managing both time and material assets."

Kesia, reflecting on her own struggles with impulsivity, inquired, "What strategies did Tobias offer for those who find it difficult to maintain temperance, especially in the face of temptation or excess?"

"Tobias understood that maintaining temperance can be challenging," Sophea explained. "He advised strengthening one's willpower through small, consistent acts of self-discipline, which can build resilience over time. Tobias also recommended surrounding oneself with a supportive community that values and practices temperance, as peer influence can greatly reinforce personal efforts."

Lexi, curious about the broader impacts, asked, "How does temperance affect our relationships and our ability to lead effectively?"

"Tobias taught that temperance builds respect and trust, as it demonstrates to others that one can manage responsibilities and resources wisely," Sophea elaborated. "In leadership, temperance ensures that decisions are not made on whims or personal bias but are thoughtfully considered and aimed at the common good. This not only enhances personal integrity but also fosters a culture of responsibility and trustworthiness within any group or community."

Inspired by the discussion, Sophea guided the monks in a visualization exercise. "Close your eyes and imagine a reservoir filled with water. Each stream entering the reservoir represents a resource or impulse you manage. Visualize controlling the flow of these streams, adjusting them to ensure a balanced and sustainable use. Reflect on how this moderation improves your life and relationships."

As the monks engaged in this meditative practice, they considered how they might better regulate their own resources and impulses, embodying the virtue of temperance.

Concluding the session, Sophea encouraged, "Let us strive to be like wise stewards of a reservoir, carefully moderating our resources and impulses. May your practice of temperance lead to a balanced, prosperous, and sustainable life."

With these motivating words, the monks departed, each more committed to practicing temperance in their daily lives, inspired by Solomon's example and guided by the teachings of Tobias.

Chapter 85

As the first light of dawn filled the monastery's great hall, casting a serene glow across the gathered monks, Sophea prepared to delve into the virtue of loyalty, envisioned by Tobias as a fortress that safeguards and strengthens relationships.

"Tobias often spoke of loyalty as a fortress, providing protection and security to those within its walls," Sophea began, her voice imbued with the gravity of the concept. "He reflected on the relationship between David and Solomon, highlighting how Solomon's loyalty to his father's advice and his steadfast adherence to God's statutes were fundamental in establishing the stability and prosperity of his reign" (1 Kings 2:3).

She continued, "This loyalty, deeply rooted in wisdom, helped Solomon maintain the integrity of his kingdom and his personal relationships, illustrating how loyalty acts as a strong foundation for trust and mutual respect."

Isabella, intrigued by the application of this virtue, asked, "Sophea, how did Tobias suggest we cultivate and maintain loyalty in our own lives?"

"Tobias recommended fostering loyalty through consistent, honorable actions and open, honest communication," Sophea replied. "He emphasized the importance of commitments and the need to honor them, suggesting that reliability is the cornerstone of loyalty. Tobias also encouraged understanding and empathy, which help in appreciating others' perspectives and strengthening bonds."

Kesia, reflecting on her experiences in communal living, inquired, "What did Tobias say about dealing with conflicts that might challenge our loyalty?"

"Tobias recognized that conflicts are inevitable in any relationship," Sophea explained. "He advised approaching such challenges with a mindset of resolution and reconciliation. Tobias believed that maintaining loyalty involves working through disagreements with patience and integrity, ensuring that actions taken in difficult times do not breach the trust that forms the core of loyalty."

Lexi, curious about the broader impacts, asked, "How does cultivating a fortress of loyalty impact our leadership and community dynamics?"

"Tobias taught that loyalty within leadership and community roles builds a strong sense of unity and commitment," Sophea elaborated. "Leaders who exhibit loyalty inspire similar behavior in others, creating a more cohesive and supportive environment. This trust fosters cooperation and collective resilience, enhancing the group's ability to achieve common goals."

Inspired by the depth of the discussion, Sophea guided the monks in a visualization exercise. "Close your eyes and imagine yourself within a fortress, surrounded by those to whom you have pledged your loyalty. Visualize how you protect and support each other, and reflect on the strength this loyalty adds to your relationships. Consider any areas where this fortress might need strengthening and how you might fortify it."

As the monks engaged in this reflective practice, they considered how to enhance the loyalty in their personal and professional relationships, recognizing its value as a protective and unifying force.

Concluding the session, Sophea encouraged, "Let us strive to build and maintain the fortresses of loyalty in all areas of our lives. May your loyalty be as steadfast as a fortress, providing security and strength to your relationships and endeavors."

With these motivating words, the monks dispersed, each resolved to uphold and nurture the fortresses of loyalty in their lives, inspired by the teachings of Tobias and the biblical example of Solomon's reign.

Chapter 86

The flight to Nepal was a mixture of anticipation and introspection for Redington. Each mile that brought him closer to Lexi also drew him further from the familiar confines of his daily life and recent turmoil. He was about to bridge two worlds that, until now, had remained distinct—the relentless pace of his career in law enforcement and the tranquil spirituality of the monastery where Lexi had found her peace.

As the plane descended into the lush landscapes of Nepal, the towering Himalayas in the distance seemed to echo his inner quest for elevation—not just of location but of spirit. Redington felt a surge of clarity. Whatever uncertainties had clouded his thoughts, the decision to come here felt unequivocally right.

Upon landing, Redington made his way to the monastery. The journey from the bustling streets of Kathmandu to the serene isolation of the mountainside retreat was reflective and calming. With each passing mile, the noise of the world fell away, replaced by the whispering winds and the occasional distant bell of a temple.

He arrived at the monastery in the late morning. The air was crisp, carrying the scent of pine and earth, grounding him further into his purpose. He paused for a moment before entering, taking in the profound tranquility of the place that Lexi called her spiritual home.

Redington was directed to the great hall where Sophea was leading a session with the monks, including Lexi. He hesitated at the entrance, not wanting to disrupt the lesson, but as he caught sight of Lexi among the monks, everything else seemed to fade into the background. She was deeply engrossed in the lesson, her expression one of intense focus and calm.

Taking a deep breath, Redington stepped into the hall. His presence was soon noticed, and a gentle murmur of curiosity spread among the monks. Sophea paused her teaching, her eyes questioning as she looked toward him. Lexi turned, and upon seeing Redington, her expression transformed with surprise and a flicker of something deeper, more personal.

Redington approached, his steps measured and respectful of the sanctity of the hall. "I'm sorry to interrupt," he began, addressing both Sophea and the assembly with a respectful nod. "I need to speak with Lexi. It's important."

Lexi rose, her movements fluid, a mirror of the peace that the monastery instilled in its denizens, yet her eyes were filled with questions. Sophea gave a slight nod, an acknowledgment of the necessity of the moment, and gestured for Lexi to go ahead.

As Lexi walked toward Redington, the monks watched, a silent respect hanging in the air for whatever reunion this might herald. Once they stepped outside, the door closing softly behind them, Lexi turned to Redington with an openness he hadn't seen before.

"What brings you here, Redington? Is everything okay?" Lexi asked, her voice a mix of concern and a faint, underlying joy at seeing him.

Redington looked into her eyes, those deep wells of calm and strength that had haunted his dreams. "I came here for you, Lexi. There are things I need to say, feelings I need to share," he confessed, his voice steady but laden with the weight of his emotions.

They found a quiet spot in the monastery's gardens, overlooked by the majestic mountains, and there, under the watchful gaze of the ancient peaks, Redington laid bare his heart. He spoke of his recent ordeal, his reflections, and how each event had inexorably drawn him closer to understanding his feelings for her—feelings that were deep, complicated, and undeniably real.

As the conversation unfolded, Lexi listened, her heart open and her mind clear. This was a moment of truth, a juncture in their lives where the past and the future could weave together, forming a new tapestry of possibilities.

Chapter 87

Under the expansive sky, framed by the towering Himalayas, Lexi listened intently to Redington's heartfelt revelations. Each word resonated within her, stirring emotions she had compartmentalized amidst her spiritual pursuits. The contrast between her life at the monastery—devoted to inner peace and understanding—and the possibility of a life with Redington, filled with the complexities of love and companionship, left her profoundly divided.

"I need time," Lexi finally said, her voice reflecting the turmoil within. "I am deeply moved by what you've shared, and I feel a connection with you that's hard to ignore. But I'm also committed to my path here, to the learning and growth I've found in this place. It's not easy to step away from a journey that has shaped so much of who I am now."

Redington nodded, his expression one of understanding and patience. "I wouldn't ask you to make a decision lightly, Lexi. I know what this place means to you. I see the peace it brings you, and that matters to me." His voice was sincere, each word underpinned by the respect he had for her and her choices. "I just wanted you to know how I feel, to consider what life might be like if we explored this… together."

Lexi's heart ached with the weight of her decision. The serene environment of the monastery, which had always offered clarity, now seemed to echo her inner conflict. "I care for you too, Redington, more than I expected," she admitted, her gaze wandering across the verdant gardens, seeking anchor. "But I can't leave just yet. Not until I'm certain it's the right step—not just for me, but for us."

Redington reached out, taking her hand gently. "Then take your time, Lexi. I don't want to rush you into a decision. I'm here for now, and no matter what you decide, I'll respect your choice." His assurance was a balm, easing the sharp edge of her dilemma.

"Let's just take it one day at a time," he suggested. "I'll stay for a while, here, close to you. We can see how things feel without any pressure. Would that work for you?"

Lexi nodded, feeling a mixture of relief and joy at his proposal. "I'd like that," she said softly. The possibility of exploring their feelings gradually, without the immediate need for life-altering decisions, felt like the breathing space she needed.

Over the following days, Redington joined Lexi in various monastery activities. He participated in meditative sessions, engaged with the monks, and delved into discussions about philosophy and spirituality. This new routine brought them closer, allowing them to discover each other in a space that was deeply significant to Lexi.

Each shared moment, each conversation, whether light-hearted or profound, helped Lexi see the potential of a life where her spiritual growth and personal love could coexist. Yet, the decision to leave the sanctuary that had become her home was not one she could make hastily. The monastery had been her refuge, a place of transformation and discovery, and stepping away, if she chose to, had to be a transition marked with the same thoughtfulness that had guided her spiritual journey.

As Redington's temporary stay extended, the connection between them deepened, weaving a new layer into Lexi's life tapestry. Though the future remained uncertain, the present moments were rich with potential and understanding, offering both Lexi and Redington a glimpse into a life that could be both nurturing and challenging, anchored in love and mutual respect.

Chapter 88

As the morning sun immersed the monastery's great hall in a soft, golden light, the monks—including Redington, who had grown more familiar with these sessions—settled into their seats, ready for another enlightening discourse from Sophea. Today's focus on the virtue of insight seemed particularly relevant to Redington, given the complex decisions looming over him regarding his feelings for Lexi and his life in New York.

"Tobias described insight as standing in an observatory, looking out over vast distances to see beyond the superficial and grasp the essence of matters," Sophea began, her words echoing the expansiveness of the metaphor. She recounted the biblical story of Solomon's discernment in identifying the true mother of a child, illustrating the power of deep insight in uncovering hidden truths.

As Sophea spoke, Redington found the metaphor of the observatory strikingly apt. His recent experiences had forced him to look beyond the immediate crises and consider the wider implications of his personal and professional choices.

Isabella, always keen to understand practical applications, asked, "Sophea, how did Tobias suggest we develop such insight in our own decision-making?"

Sophea explained the importance of contemplation and empathy in understanding different perspectives, which can dramatically broaden one's vision. She also emphasized the role of prayer and meditation in connecting with the divine, enhancing intuitive understanding.

Kesia, pondering the complexities of applying insight, questioned, "What strategies did Tobias recommend for situations where the right course of action isn't clear?"

"Tobias advised gathering as much information as possible, then stepping back to view the situation holistically," Sophea replied. She highlighted the need to balance logical analysis with intuitive judgment, ensuring decisions are well-rounded and informed.

Lexi, reflecting on her own journey and the insights she had gained, asked about the broader impacts of possessing such insight. "How does possessing such insight affect our relationships and our roles within the community?"

Sophea noted that insightful individuals are often seen as wise and trustworthy, qualities that enhance leadership and interpersonal relationships. Insight allows for deeper empathy and understanding, fostering stronger community bonds.

Inspired by the discussion, Sophea led the monks in a visualization exercise. "Close your eyes and imagine yourself in an observatory, high above the world. Consider a current challenge or decision you face. Visualize seeing beyond the immediate details to the broader implications."

As Redington engaged in the exercise, he visualized himself and Lexi, contemplating the vast landscape of their potential future together. The observatory of his mind allowed him to see beyond the complexities of their situation, considering not just the emotional implications but also how their union could enrich both their lives.

The session concluded with Sophea's encouraging words, urging everyone to maintain their observatories of insight and continually seek the higher perspective that wisdom provides.

Redington left the hall feeling a renewed sense of clarity. The teachings had not only provided him with a metaphor for his internal deliberations but had also reaffirmed the value of taking a step back to gain a broader perspective. As he walked through the peaceful monastery grounds, he felt more prepared to face the decisions ahead, armed with a deeper insight that would guide him not only in his personal life with Lexi but in all his future endeavors.

Chapter 89

The early morning sun painted the monastery's great hall with hues of gold and amber, the monks assembled for their daily learning session. Today, Sophea planned to explore the concept of community through the teachings of Tobias, drawing parallels with the historical efforts of King Solomon to unite and strengthen his kingdom through inclusivity and cooperation.

"Tobias depicted the community as a tapestry," Sophea began, her voice enveloping the room with warmth. "Each thread in this tapestry represents an individual, each color a different background, belief, or perspective. Through Solomon's leadership, we see a practical application of this metaphor. His building projects, for instance, were not just about constructing temples and palaces but were also efforts to weave the diverse threads of Israel into a unified fabric" (1 Kings 5:13-14).

Her explanation set the stage for a rich discussion on the strength derived from diversity within a community. "This approach didn't just strengthen the physical infrastructure of the kingdom," she continued, "but also reinforced the social fabric, fostering a sense of belonging and mutual respect among the people."

Isabella, intrigued by the application of these ancient principles to modern challenges, raised a question that resonated with many in the room. "Sophea, in our diverse and often divided world, how did Tobias suggest we foster a sense of community?"

"Tobias advocated for the active pursuit of understanding and appreciation for each community member's unique contributions," Sophea answered. "He recommended creating opportunities for collaboration where different perspectives are valued and can synergize to achieve shared objectives. Celebrating both individual and collective achievements enhances unity and pride within the community."

Kesia, thoughtful about the practical challenges of community building, asked, "What strategies did Tobias offer for dealing with conflicts that arise from diversity?"

Sophea nodded, acknowledging the importance of the question. "Tobias recognized that diversity could lead to conflicts if not managed wisely. He advised addressing these conflicts through open and honest dialogue, sometimes facilitated by impartial mediators. He also emphasized the need for patience and empathy, encouraging leaders to exemplify these virtues as they navigate through difficult discussions."

Lexi, reflecting on her experiences and the discussions, wondered about the broader impacts. "How does building such a community affect its members' sense of identity and belonging?"

"A well-integrated community," Sophea explained, "strengthens each member's identity by affirming their individual contributions while also fostering a strong collective identity. This balance leads to greater personal satisfaction and a cohesive community where members feel valued and understood."

Inspired by the depth of the discussion, Sophea guided the monks in a reflective visualization exercise. "Close your eyes and imagine the community as a tapestry being woven around you. Reflect on your own thread—its color, its strength. Think about how it intertwines with others, forming a complex yet beautiful pattern. Consider ways you can strengthen those connections."

As the monks engaged in the exercise, they visualized their individual roles within the community's tapestry, contemplating how they could contribute more effectively to its richness and cohesion.

Concluding the session, Sophea encouraged everyone to weave their threads into the community tapestry with care and respect. "Let us each strive to create a vibrant, inclusive, and supportive community, reflecting the wisdom and unity that Solomon sought for his people."

With these motivating words, the monks dispersed, each feeling a renewed commitment to fostering a sense of community within their environments, inspired by the teachings of Tobias and the example set by Solomon's integrative efforts.

Chapter 90

The gentle morning light spilled across the monastery's great hall, touching the faces of the monks gathered for their daily discourse with Sophea. Today, she would discuss the concept of community, likened by Tobias to a richly woven tapestry, made vibrant and strong by the diversity of its threads.

"Tobias depicted the community as a tapestry, each thread representing a different individual, each color a different background, belief, or perspective," Sophea began, her voice warm and inclusive. "He drew on Solomon's efforts to unify his kingdom through inclusive policies and collaborative projects. Notably, Solomon's building projects, which employed men from all tribes of Israel, demonstrated a practical application of integrating diverse talents and strengths for a common goal" (1 Kings 5:13-14).

She continued, "This approach not only strengthened the physical infrastructure of the kingdom but also reinforced the social fabric, promoting a sense of belonging and mutual respect among the people."

Isabella, always eager to understand how ancient wisdom can be applied today, asked, "Sophea, how did Tobias suggest we can foster a sense of community in our diverse and often divided world?"

"Tobias recommended actively seeking to understand and appreciate the unique contributions of each community member," Sophea replied. "He advocated for creating opportunities for collaboration, where different perspectives can come together to achieve shared objectives. Tobias also emphasized the importance of celebrating both individual and collective achievements, which can enhance the sense of unity and pride within the community."

Kesia, thinking about the challenges of community building, inquired, "What strategies did Tobias offer for dealing with conflicts that arise from diversity within the community?"

"Tobias recognized that diversity can lead to conflicts when not managed wisely," Sophea explained. "He advised addressing these conflicts through open and honest dialogue, facilitated by impartial mediators if necessary. Tobias also stressed the need for patience and empathy, encouraging community leaders to model these virtues as they guide their communities through challenging discussions."

Lexi, interested in the broader impacts, asked, "How does building such a community affect its members' sense of identity and belonging?"

"Tobias taught that a well-integrated community strengthens each member's sense of identity by affirming their individual contributions while fostering a strong collective identity," Sophea elaborated. "This dual sense of belonging can lead to greater personal satisfaction and a more cohesive community, where members feel valued and understood."

Inspired by the depth of the discussion, Sophea guided the monks in a reflective exercise. "Close your eyes and imagine the community as a tapestry being woven around you. Consider your own thread—its color, its strength. Reflect on how it intertwines with others, forming a complex yet beautiful pattern. Think about ways you can strengthen those connections."

As the monks visualized their place within the tapestry of their community, they contemplated their roles and how they might contribute more effectively to its richness and cohesion.

Concluding the session, Sophea encouraged, "Let us each strive to weave our threads into the tapestry of our community with care and respect. May your efforts help to create a vibrant, inclusive, and supportive community, reflecting the wisdom and unity that Solomon sought for his people."

With these inspiring words, the monks dispersed, each more committed to fostering a sense of community within their environments, inspired by the teachings of Tobias and the integrative efforts of Solomon.

Chapter 91

That night, after the profound discourse on the community as a tapestry, Lexi found herself deeply reflective as she prepared for sleep. The ideas about the interwoven nature of community, each thread vital to the whole, resonated with her not only in the spiritual sense but also personally, as she considered her connections and potential future with Redington.

As she drifted into sleep, Lexi's mind conjured the celestial presence of Archangel Uriel, who had guided her in dreams before. Tonight, she found herself in a vast, starlit space, where the fabric of the universe stretched out around her, shimmering like a cosmic tapestry.

Uriel appeared beside her, his presence calm and reassuring. "Lexi," he began, his voice echoing softly in the vast expanse, "You seek understanding about the paths before you, about how the threads of your life might weave together with another's."

"Yes, Uriel," Lexi responded, her voice tinged with uncertainty. "I'm struggling with how my personal desires for love and partnership fit into the broader tapestry of my spiritual journey. How can I align these threads without losing the essence of either?"

Uriel gestured toward the stars, where patterns of light spun and shifted, forming images of Lexi's life at the monastery interwoven with flashes of her times with Redington. "Each life is a tapestry, woven from threads of many colors and strengths. Your journey with Redington can be a harmonious part of your spiritual path, not apart from it, if you choose to weave this thread with intention and care."

He continued, "Consider the balance of your own tapestry, how the inclusion of Redington might add to its design. True love and partnership can enhance your spiritual growth, bringing new colors and strengths to your life's fabric."

Lexi watched as the celestial tapestry before her showed potential futures—some where the threads blended seamlessly, creating beautiful patterns, and others where the threads clashed or overwhelmed.

"How do I ensure that the pattern remains beautiful and true to my essence?" Lexi asked, her eyes fixed on the shifting lights.

"By maintaining your commitment to your core values and by fostering open, honest communication about your needs and visions for the future," Uriel advised. "Your partnership must be woven with threads of mutual respect, support, and genuine understanding. Just as in a community, diversity in unity enriches the tapestry, so too in relationships, differing strengths can support and enhance each other."

Comforted yet contemplative, Lexi felt a newfound appreciation for the complexity and potential beauty of weaving Redington into her life. "Thank you, Uriel. I need to reflect on how best to integrate these aspects of my life without losing my spiritual focus or the depth of my personal commitments."

As the dream faded, Lexi awoke in the quiet of her room, the first light of dawn peeking through her window. She felt a clarity beginning to emerge—an understanding that her love for Redington could be a strength, adding a rich, vibrant thread to the tapestry of her life.

Today, she would walk the monastery grounds, pondering her next steps, ready to explore how the threads of love and spiritual growth might intertwine in the beautiful, complex pattern of her life's tapestry.

Chapter 92

The light spilled over the monastery, casting long shadows and bathing the tranquil gardens in warmth, Lexi walked slowly along the stone paths, her thoughts as intertwined as the vines climbing the ancient walls. The dream with Uriel had left her with a profound sense of possibility—and an acute awareness of the careful deliberation required to align her spiritual journey with her personal desires.

Her morning walk was introspective, each step a meditation on her potential futures. Lexi considered not just the romantic possibilities with Redington but also the impact of this choice on her spiritual commitments and her role within the monastery community. How could she ensure that these aspects of her life not only coexisted but also enhanced each other?

The peaceful environment of the monastery, with its murmurs of nature and soft chants in the distance, provided a perfect backdrop for such reflections. Lexi stopped by a small, serene pond, watching as the water reflected the clear blue of the sky. It was here, amidst the simple beauty of nature, that Lexi felt a sense of clarity beginning to crystallize.

She realized that her relationship with Redington could be like the water in the pond—reflective, deep, and capable of supporting diverse forms of life. Just as the pond thrived with every rain and sustained the life within it, so too could her relationship with Redington bring new energies and inspirations into her life, enriching her spiritual journey rather than detracting from it.

However, Lexi knew that such a relationship required mutual understanding and support. It would need to be a partnership where both their spiritual and worldly ambitions were respected and nurtured. This realization led her to decide to open up a dialogue with Redington, one where they would lay out their visions for the future and see how they might weave them together into a shared tapestry.

Later that day, Lexi sought out Redington, who had been spending his time engaging with the monks and participating in the daily activities of the monastery. She found him in the library, engrossed in a book about Eastern philosophies and their intersections with Western thought.

"Redington," Lexi began, her voice calm yet carrying an undercurrent of decisive emotion. "Can we talk about us, about how we see our paths intersecting? I've been doing a lot of thinking, and I feel it's time we understand each other's visions more clearly."

Redington looked up, his expression shifting from concentration to attentiveness. "Of course, Lexi. I've been hoping we'd have this conversation. I think it's crucial we're on the same page about what we want and need, not just individually but together."

They chose a quiet corner of the monastery gardens, a space where the late afternoon light created a tapestry of shadows and light on the ground. There, they began a conversation that would stretch into the evening.

Lexi and Redington discussed their hopes and fears, their commitments, and their love. They explored how their different lives could possibly converge, considering practical steps to blend their paths without losing the core of what made each of them unique. They talked about potential challenges and how they might address them, always returning to the mutual respect and admiration that had brought them to this point.

As the stars began to appear in the twilight sky, Lexi felt a weight lifting from her shoulders. The conversation had not solved every issue, nor had it charted a definitive course for the future. But it had opened a door to new possibilities and confirmed that the journey, however uncertain, was one they were both willing to explore together.

With hearts lighter and minds at ease, Lexi and Redington walked back to the monastery together, their steps in sync, both understanding that the tapestry of their lives was still being woven, one careful, thoughtful thread at a time.

Chapter 93

The early morning quiet of the monastery was filled with a sense of anticipation as the monks gathered around Sophea in the great hall. Today, she would delve into the virtue of justice, described by Tobias as a carefully kept ledger that demands accuracy and fairness in all entries. This lesson would explore how wisdom informs and directs the administration of justice, using Solomon's renowned judicial capabilities as a focal point.

"Tobias likened the concept of justice to a ledger that must be meticulously maintained to ensure fairness and accuracy," Sophea began, her voice steady and commanding respect. "He often referred to Solomon's wisdom in judicial matters, highlighting the king's ability to make informed and fair decisions, as seen in his famous judgment involving two women claiming to be the mother of a child" (1 Kings

3:28). "This example not only demonstrated Solomon's discernment but also his commitment to justice, which was integral to his wise rule."

She continued, "Such wisdom is crucial in ensuring that justice is not just a concept but a lived reality within governance and everyday interactions."

Isabella, deeply engaged, asked, "Sophea, how did Tobias suggest we cultivate the ability to administer justice wisely in our roles and responsibilities?"

"Tobias advocated for a deep understanding of the principles of justice, which include impartiality, fairness, and the protection of the vulnerable," Sophea replied. "He recommended studying historical and contemporary examples of just leadership and engaging with philosophical and legal texts to ground oneself in these principles. Tobias also emphasized the importance of empathy, which enables one to consider the perspectives and needs of all parties involved."

Kesia, reflecting on the complexities of just decision-making, inquired, "What strategies did Tobias offer for those who struggle with the challenges of maintaining justice, especially under pressure?"

"Tobias acknowledged that administering justice can be daunting, particularly when faced with complex or high-stakes situations," Sophea explained. "He suggested seeking counsel from wise and experienced advisors to aid in the decision-making process. Moreover, Tobias emphasized the need for self-awareness and regular reflection on one's biases and motivations, to ensure that decisions are not swayed by personal interests."

Lexi, curious about the broader implications, asked, "How does a commitment to justice affect the larger community?"

"Tobias taught that a steadfast commitment to justice builds trust and stability within a community," Sophea elaborated. "When leaders and individuals consistently act justly, it establishes a foundation of fairness that can permeate all aspects of community life. This not only enhances social harmony but also encourages active participation in governance, as community members feel confident that their rights and voices are respected."

Inspired by the topic, Sophea led the monks in a brief meditation. "Close your eyes and imagine yourself holding the scales of justice. Reflect on the decisions you face in your daily life. Consider how you can apply the principles of justice to ensure fairness and accuracy in your judgments, just as you would maintain a precise ledger."

As the monks engaged in this contemplative practice, they considered how to integrate justice more fully into their decisions and actions.

Concluding the session, Sophea encouraged, "Let us each strive to uphold the ledger of justice with diligence and integrity. May your decisions reflect the wisdom and fairness that Solomon aspired to, ensuring that justice is not only administered but also embodied in all your interactions."

With these inspiring words, the monks rose, each more determined to embody justice in their roles, inspired by Solomon's example and guided by the teachings of Tobias.

Chapter 94

As the kaleidoscopic morning light streamed through the monastery's stained-glass windows, the monks, including Redington, settled around Sophea for today's lesson on integrity. Redington, now a familiar presence in the monastery, appreciated these sessions for their depth and relevance not only to his personal life but also to his professional decisions. Today's discussion on integrity seemed particularly pertinent as he navigated the complexities of his relationship with Lexi and his career commitments.

Sophea began, "Tobias often described integrity as a compass, an essential tool that guides us through ethical dilemmas and ensures we remain true to our moral convictions." She recounted the story of Solomon's dealings with Hiram, emphasizing how integrity underpinned successful and respectful leadership that led to enduring accomplishments and alliances.

Redington listened intently, reflecting on his own experiences where integrity had played a crucial role in maintaining trust and respect in his professional life, and now, these principles seemed all the more significant as he considered his future with Lexi.

Isabella, always keen on applying the lessons practically, asked, "Sophea, how did Tobias suggest we cultivate and maintain integrity in our daily lives?"

"Tobias advocated for living in accordance with one's deepest values and principles," Sophea responded. "He highlighted the importance of regular self-reflection to ensure one's actions consistently align with their ethical standards and the necessity of transparency in all interactions."

Redington found the advice on regular self-reflection particularly resonant. He had been considering his decisions and their alignment with his values, especially in how he managed his relationships—both personal and professional. The discussion reminded him that maintaining integrity often meant making difficult choices that might not always be immediately gratifying but were correct in the long term.

Kesia, pondering the difficulties of ethical consistency, asked about managing integrity under external pressures. Sophea's advice to seek counsel from wise, morally grounded individuals reminded Redington of his own reliance on mentors throughout his career and now, on figures like Sophea in his personal growth.

As Lexi asked about the impact of integrity on relationships and the community, Redington felt a deep affirmation about his decision to be open and honest with Lexi about his feelings and his future intentions. Sophea's words that "integrity builds trust and fosters respect" echoed his belief that a strong foundation of trust and mutual respect was essential for their relationship to flourish.

Inspired by the session, Sophea led a visualization exercise, inviting everyone to imagine their integrity as a compass guiding their decisions. Redington closed his eyes and visualized his moral compass, considering recent times when it had guided him well and moments when he faced challenges. He thought about his ongoing journey with Lexi, how vital it was to navigate this new relationship with the same commitment to integrity that he applied in his professional life.

Concluding the session, Sophea's words resonated deeply with Redington. "Let us each strive to uphold the compass of integrity, ensuring it points unwaveringly to our true north."

As the monks dispersed, Redington felt strengthened in his resolve to continue his path with Lexi with integrity at the forefront. He was reminded that maintaining this moral compass would not only guide him personally but would also set an example for those around him, just as Solomon's example had resonated through history. With these principles in mind, Redington was ready to face the complexities of blending his life with Lexi's, ensuring that every step they took together was marked by honesty, respect, and true commitment.

Chapter 95

Dawn's early light painted vibrant hues through the stained-glass windows of the monastery's great hall, the monks gathered around Sophea, each ready to delve into the teachings of Tobias. Today's discussion on adaptability seemed particularly relevant to Redington, who sat among the monks, increasingly drawn into the philosophical foundations that supported Lexi's spiritual journey.

Sophea started the session by drawing a parallel between adaptability and a wheel that adjusts to the terrain. "Tobias likened adaptability to a wheel, essential for navigating the varied and often unexpected terrains of life," she explained. She cited Solomon's strategic governance adjustments, which showcased his capacity to respond to the needs of an expanding

kingdom, as a prime example of effective
adaptability.

Redington found the analogy enlightening,
especially as he considered his own need to
adapt to the new realities of his relationship with
Lexi and his ongoing role in law enforcement.
The concept of adaptability as a wheel made it
clear that smooth navigation through life's
complexities often required changes in approach
without losing direction.

Isabella, intrigued by practical applications,
asked how one could cultivate adaptability in
daily life. Sophea's response emphasized
embracing change as a natural part of existence
and adopting a mindset that views challenges as
opportunities for growth. She suggested staying
informed and flexible, allowing for the
adjustment of plans as situations evolve.

Kesia brought up a crucial point about
balancing adaptability with core principles.
Sophea addressed this by highlighting the
importance of defining and adhering to
fundamental values, which should guide all
adaptations. "True wisdom," Sophea noted, "lies
in knowing when to be flexible and when to
remain steadfast, ensuring our adjustments do
not compromise our foundational beliefs."

Lexi's question on adaptability's impact on
leadership and relationships resonated deeply
with Redington. Sophea explained that
adaptability fosters resilience and promotes a

collaborative environment. In relationships, it enhances understanding and cooperation, while in leadership, it is crucial for dynamically responding to the needs of teams or communities.

Inspired by the discussion, Sophea led a reflective exercise that involved visualizing oneself navigating various terrains with a flexible wheel. This visualization helped the monks, including Redington, think about areas in their lives where increased adaptability could lead to more effective outcomes.

Redington considered his efforts to integrate more seamlessly into Lexi's world and how adopting an adaptable mindset might improve not just his personal relationships but also his professional engagements. The need to balance flexibility with his core principles of justice and integrity was a poignant takeaway from the session.

As the monks concluded their morning discourse, Redington felt equipped with new insights into managing the complexities of his evolving life. The lesson on adaptability reinforced his determination to approach his relationship with Lexi with both flexibility and steadfastness, ensuring that his actions were always aligned with his deepest values.

With a renewed sense of purpose, Redington left the session alongside Lexi, both appreciative of the philosophical teachings that not only guided their spiritual growth but also offered practical insights into managing life's ever-changing landscapes. Together, they walked back through the monastery grounds, their conversation a reflection of their mutual commitment to adapt and grow together, guided by wisdom and unwavering principles.

Chapter 96

The first rays of morning sunlight streamed through the high windows of the monastery's great hall, the monks gathered around Sophea, each carrying a sense of anticipation for the day's discourse on hope, a virtue seen as a beacon in the teachings of Tobias. Redington, seated beside Lexi, felt a particular resonance with the topic, considering the recent trials and decisions that had cast both shadow and light on his path.

"Tobias spoke of hope as a beacon, a powerful light that guides us through uncertainty and darkness," Sophea began, her voice comforting and resonant. "During Solomon's golden age, his hopeful outlook and wise leadership fostered an era of peace and prosperity, proving how a leader's hopeful vision can inspire and shape a nation's future," she cited from the book of Kings.

Redington listened intently, drawing parallels between the hopeful leadership of Solomon and the leadership required in his own line of work, where maintaining hope often meant the difference between success and failure in missions fraught with peril.

Isabella, always keen on practical applications, asked about ways to cultivate hope in daily life. Sophea's response highlighted nurturing hope through engagement with inspirational teachings and the support of a community, reinforcing the belief that collective support and shared visions significantly strengthen hope.

Kesia, reflecting on personal struggles, wondered about sustaining hope during difficult times. Sophea suggested focusing on small, achievable goals and practicing gratitude, emphasizing that appreciating the positive aspects of one's life could renew hope and bolster spirits.

Lexi, thinking about the implications for leadership, asked about hope's influence on decision-making and community dynamics. Sophea's explanation—that hopeful leaders inspire confidence and optimism, enhancing community morale and fostering innovative solutions—struck a chord with Redington. It reinforced his understanding of the role optimism played in his professional life and the potential impact of his and Lexi's relationship on their respective communities.

Inspired by the rich discussion, Sophea led the monks in a visualization exercise. "Close your eyes and imagine holding a lantern—the beacon of hope—in your hands. Visualize its light spreading, illuminating paths in dark woods. Reflect on how you can carry this beacon for yourself and for others, lighting the way through challenges."

As Redington engaged in the exercise, he visualized himself and Lexi together, each holding their lanterns, their combined light weaving through the complexities of their lives, guiding them through personal and professional landscapes.

Concluding the session, Sophea encouraged the monks to embrace their role as carriers of hope, using their wisdom to light paths and guide those around them toward peace and prosperity. "May your beacon of hope shine brightly," she concluded, "bringing light to dark places and guiding your journey."

As the monks dispersed, Redington felt a renewed sense of purpose and clarity. The session had not only deepened his understanding of the spiritual underpinnings of hope but had also reinforced his resolve to integrate these teachings into his relationship with Lexi. Together, they could become beacons of hope, not only within the confines of the monastery but also in the wider world.

With these thoughts, Redington and Lexi walked together through the monastery gardens, their conversation turning to ways they could integrate the day's lessons into their ongoing journey, committed to being sources of light and hope for each other and for those they served.

Chapter 97

As night descended upon the monastery, the stillness of the surroundings enveloped everything, a stark contrast to the day's discussions on hope and leadership. Lexi, her mind swirling with the ideas shared, found herself wrestling with the convergence of her spiritual path and her deepening relationship with Redington. Seeking clarity, she retired to her room, hoping for a restful night but instead found herself walking the corridors of her subconscious in a vivid dream.

In her dream, Lexi found herself in a lush, verdant garden that seemed to stretch infinitely. The garden was bathed in a gentle, ethereal light, and at its center stood Archangel Uriel, his presence as comforting and majestic as ever. He was surrounded by a soft radiance that seemed to pulse with wisdom and serenity.

"Uriel," Lexi greeted him, her voice echoing slightly in the vast expanse of the dream.

"Lexi," Uriel responded, his tone imbued with warmth. "You seek guidance at the crossroads of your journey. What burdens your heart?"

Lexi took a moment, gathering her thoughts. "I'm at a pivotal point, Uriel. I am deeply committed to my spiritual growth here at the monastery, yet my heart is also with Redington. I fear that choosing one path might mean losing something precious on the other."

Uriel listened intently, nodding slightly as Lexi spoke. He gestured toward the garden around them, where the paths branched in numerous directions, each lined with different flowers and trees.

"Consider this garden, Lexi. It is full of different paths, each leading to its unique beauty. Your journey can also embrace more than one path—your spiritual growth and your relationship with Redington do not have to be mutually exclusive."

Uriel walked with Lexi along one of the garden's paths, the plants around them seeming to glow subtly. "Hope, like the light illuminating this garden, does not diminish when it splits among various paths. Instead, it expands, reaching further and enlightening more," Uriel explained. "Your love and your spiritual pursuits can enhance and illuminate each other, provided you navigate with intention and wisdom."

Lexi felt a sense of relief, her fears beginning to dissipate like mist in the morning sun. "How can I ensure I walk this combined path without losing my way?" she asked.

"Keep your values as your compass, and let love and faith be the lights guiding you through the garden of life," Uriel advised. "Communicate openly with Redington about your hopes and fears. Share your spiritual journey with him, just as you share your heart. Together, you can find a way to intertwine your paths without losing the essence of either."

As the dream began to fade, Uriel's figure shimmering with a departing glow, Lexi found herself back in her room, the first light of dawn peeking through her window. She awoke refreshed and renewed, filled with a newfound confidence in the possibility of harmonizing her spiritual path with her personal life.

That morning, Lexi sought out Redington, ready to discuss her insights and feelings. As they met in the tranquility of the monastery's dawn-lit gardens, Lexi shared her dream and Uriel's counsel. Together, they began to explore how they might weave their paths into a shared journey, each enriching the other, guided by hope, love, and the wisdom of their shared experiences.

Chapter 98

In the serene ambiance of the monastery garden, where the air was crisp and the light of dawn cast a gentle glow on the dew-speckled foliage, Lexi shared her dream with Redington. She described the ethereal garden, Uriel's presence, and the profound counsel she received about harmonizing their paths.

Redington listened intently, his eyes reflecting both the depth of his affection and his respect for her spiritual journey. "Your dream... it sounds like a vision of how we could really make this work," he responded thoughtfully. "I've always believed that our paths, while different, have potential points of convergence. Maybe it's not about choosing one life over another, but about blending them in a way that enriches both."

Encouraged by Lexi's recount of Uriel's advice, they discussed practical steps to integrate their lives without compromising Lexi's commitments to her spiritual growth or Redington's responsibilities. They explored ideas like Redington participating in community projects at the monastery, which would allow him to better understand Lexi's world while contributing his own skills and experience.

"Perhaps I could also learn more about your work," Lexi suggested, a spark of excitement in her voice. "Not just the details, but the values and decisions that guide you. It would help me see the parts of your life that resonate with what I learn and live here."

Redington agreed enthusiastically, pleased at the prospect of sharing more of his life with Lexi. "And I think there's a lot about the discipline and perspective I've gained from being around you and the monastery that could benefit my team back home," he admitted. "There's a depth to the peace I find here that I want to carry with me, maybe even share with my colleagues."

As they walked together through the garden, discussing these ideas, they felt a renewed sense of connection. It was as if the conversation itself was a manifestation of the intertwining paths Uriel had described—distinct yet mutually supportive, leading them toward a shared horizon.

Their talk soon turned to more immediate plans. Redington would extend his stay at the monastery, taking part in various activities and immersing himself in the community life that was so integral to Lexi's development. They planned visits to places significant to both their spiritual and professional lives, aiming to deepen their understanding of each other's worlds.

In the following weeks, Redington's integration into the monastery community deepened. He joined discussions, participated in meditation sessions, and contributed to community projects, his presence becoming a familiar sight to the monks and visitors alike. Lexi, in turn, took an active interest in learning about the principles of justice and integrity that guided Redington's actions in his work.

The monks, initially curious about Redington's frequent presence, came to respect his sincere engagement with their practices and his genuine interest in their teachings. His questions were thoughtful, his demeanor respectful, and his willingness to learn and participate endeared him to many.

One evening, as they sat watching the sunset from a hill overlooking the monastery, Redington turned to Lexi with a reflective look. "This place, these weeks with you—they've changed me," he confessed. "I used to think my life back in New York was all I wanted, but now I see there's so much more to live for. And whatever this is, this journey we're on together, I want to keep exploring it, with you."

Lexi smiled, her hand finding his. "I feel the same, Redington. There's a harmony in our lives coming together—a melody that's just beginning to play. And I'm eager to hear how it unfolds."

Their shared smile in the fading light was a silent vow, a mutual commitment to continue weaving their paths together, guided by the wisdom they had learned and the love they had grown. Their journey was not without challenges, but with each step, they were crafting a life uniquely their own, enriched by the convergence of their diverse worlds.

Chapter 99

As the early light of dawn softly illuminated the monastery's great hall, the monks, including Redington, assembled around Sophea for the morning lesson on the virtue of peace. Redington, now more integrated into the monastery's life, found these sessions increasingly resonant, as each lesson seemed to weave seamlessly into the fabric of his evolving relationship with Lexi and his personal transformation.

Sophea began by describing peace as a sanctuary, invoking the image of Solomon's Temple as a profound symbol of divine peace and a center for communal harmony. "Solomon's dedication of the Temple and his prayers for peace exemplify the profound role peace plays not only as a personal refuge but also as a cornerstone of community welfare," she explained.

The idea of peace as both a personal and communal sanctuary resonated deeply with Redington, particularly as he considered the conflicts and challenges he faced in his professional life back in New York. The lesson reminded him of the importance of creating and maintaining peace within oneself as a precursor to fostering peace in one's environment.

Isabella, curious about practical application, asked how to cultivate peace within and extend it outward. Sophea's response emphasized the significance of personal spiritual practices like meditation and reflection, and the impact of kindness and understanding in strengthening community bonds.

Kesia raised a question about maintaining peace in times of conflict or stress. Sophea's advice on looking for long-term solutions and promoting forgiveness highlighted strategies that Redington found applicable not only in personal relationships but also in negotiating and resolving conflicts in his role as an FBI agent.

Lexi, reflecting on the broader implications, inquired about the influence of a peaceful sanctuary on leadership and community dynamics. "A leader who embodies peace and fosters peaceful environments commands respect and trust, facilitating more effective crisis management and community leadership," Sophea elaborated.

Inspired by the depth of the discussion, Sophea led the monks in a meditative exercise, asking them to visualize themselves in a peaceful sanctuary. As Redington closed his eyes and envisioned a tranquil garden, he felt a profound sense of peace enveloping him, a stark contrast to the chaos and noise of his usual urban environment. He imagined bringing this sense of calm back to his team, wondering how he might incorporate these practices into his leadership style to foster a more harmonious and productive workplace.

As the session concluded, Sophea encouraged the monks to nurture their inner sanctuaries of peace and to radiate this tranquility outward, enhancing their community interactions. "May your inner calm bring solace and harmony to your communities, guided by the wisdom of Solomon and the teachings of Tobias," she said.

The monks dispersed, each more committed to being a beacon of peace. Redington felt a renewed commitment to his path, both in his personal life with Lexi and in his professional role. He was beginning to see how the lessons from the monastery could not only enrich his relationship but also enhance his effectiveness as a leader.

As he walked with Lexi through the quiet monastery grounds, discussing their thoughts on the lesson, they shared how each could bring these insights into their daily lives. For

Redington, the concept of peace as a sanctuary offered a transformative perspective on managing stress and conflict, while for Lexi, it reaffirmed her commitment to fostering a peaceful community within and beyond the monastery walls. Together, they envisioned a future where their individual sanctuaries of peace would merge, creating a shared haven of tranquility and strength.

Chapter 100

As the monks gathered in the monastery's great hall, the morning light filtered softly through the stained-glass windows, casting a mosaic of colors across the stone floor. Today marked a special session with Sophea, one dedicated to reflecting on the collective wisdom imparted through Tobias' teachings over the past months. Redington and Lexi, both deeply integrated into the life of the monastery now, were particularly eager for today's comprehensive recap, hoping to further internalize the lessons that had resonated so strongly with them.

Sophea began with a gentle smile, acknowledging the journey they had all undertaken together. "Today, we will revisit the teachings of Tobias, reflecting on the virtues we have explored and contemplating how each connects to form a holistic spiritual path," she announced, her voice echoing softly in the tranquil space.

The Virtue of Good Counsel: "We started with the virtue of good counsel," Sophea reminded the monks. "Tobias likened this to a forest rich with diverse trees, each offering shade and protection. Just as a forest thrives with a variety of species, so too does our understanding grow from a multitude of perspectives."

The Virtue of Charity: "Tobias then guided us through the virtue of charity, envisioned as a garden where acts of giving bloom into beauty and joy across the community. This teaching emphasized the transformative power of generosity, not only in giving materially but also in offering time, attention, and compassion."

The Virtue of Wisdom: "Wisdom was portrayed as a celestial harmony, a divine symphony that aligns the heavens with the earth," Sophea continued. "This lesson highlighted how integrating our virtues, like notes in a symphony, creates a balanced and harmonious life."

The Virtue of Meekness: "Our discussion on meekness presented it as a meadow—soft, inviting, and resilient. Tobias taught us that meekness is not weakness; rather, it is strength in gentleness, allowing one to inherit the earth through humility and patience."

The Virtue of Hope: "Hope was described as a beacon, a light guiding us through darkness,"

Sophea recalled. "Through the example of Solomon's reign, Tobias showed us how a hopeful vision and wise leadership can foster peace and prosperity."

The Virtue of Peace: "Finally, we explored peace as a sanctuary, a place of refuge from the world's chaos. Here, Tobias emphasized the importance of creating inner sanctuaries of peace to extend tranquility outwardly, enhancing our community interactions and personal well-being."

After reviewing each virtue, Sophea invited the monks to share their reflections. "Think about how these teachings have influenced your thoughts and actions," she suggested. "Consider how you might continue to weave these virtues into the fabric of your daily lives."

As the monks shared, Redington reflected on how each lesson had not only deepened his understanding of spiritual principles but also provided practical insights applicable to his relationship with Lexi and his professional responsibilities. Lexi, on her part, felt a renewed appreciation for the depth of Tobias' teachings and their relevance to her spiritual and relational goals.

Chapter 101

The session moved into its final phase, Sophea invited everyone to settle into a comfortable position for a guided meditation. The room quieted, and the soft rustle of robes subsided as each monk, including Redington and Lexi, closed their eyes and focused on their breathing. The air was filled with a serene stillness, punctuated only by the distant sound of leaves rustling outside the great hall.

"Let's begin by taking a deep breath in," Sophea instructed in a gentle, soothing tone. "And let it out slowly. With each breath, feel your body relax, your mind clear, and your heart open."

As the monks' breathing deepened, Sophea continued, "Now, in your mind's eye, visualize a vast, blank tapestry before you. This tapestry represents your life, your community, your spiritual journey. It is woven from many threads, each thread symbolizing a virtue we have explored together."

"Imagine the thread of good counsel," she said, her voice a calm whisper through the hall. "See its vibrant color, perhaps a rich green, weaving through the tapestry, intersecting with other threads, strengthening the fabric of your relationships by offering diverse perspectives and wisdom."

"Next, add the thread of charity," Sophea guided. "This might be a warm gold, spreading across the tapestry, bringing brightness where it touches, representing your acts of kindness and compassion that enrich the lives of those around you."

"Now, introduce the thread of wisdom," she continued. "Visualize it as a deep blue, running through the tapestry, harmonizing with the other colors, its celestial harmony guiding your decisions and actions with balance and insight."

"Bring in the thread of meekness," Sophea suggested. "See it as a gentle pink, soft but strong, weaving through your tapestry, offering a path of humility and strength, allowing you to inherit the wisdom of the earth."

"Add the thread of hope," she said. "Imagine it as a bright light, a beacon within your tapestry, cutting through darker colors, guiding you through challenges with its unwavering light and promise."

"Finally, weave in the thread of peace," Sophea instructed. "This might be a serene lavender, creating a space of tranquility and refuge, enveloping your tapestry in calm and making it a sanctuary for yourself and others."

"As you see each thread intertwine with the others, observe how they strengthen and support the whole, creating a resilient and beautiful tapestry. Each virtue supports the others, their colors and strengths blending to form a complete picture of your spiritual and communal life."

"Take a few moments to reflect on this tapestry," Sophea concluded. "Think about how these virtues appear in your daily life. How can you strengthen these threads? How can they guide you in your relationships, your leadership, and your personal growth?"

The room remained silent as each monk, deeply immersed in the visualization, considered their own tapestry. Redington found the meditation particularly profound, seeing not just his individual growth but also his intertwined path with Lexi as integral parts of this tapestry.

After several minutes of reflective silence, Sophea gently called everyone back. "When you're ready, open your eyes and bring the peace and strength from your tapestry back with you."

As the monks slowly opened their eyes, there was a shared sense of renewal and commitment. They felt better equipped to weave the virtues discussed into the fabric of their everyday lives, each understanding the importance of these teachings in creating a harmonious and fulfilling existence. Redington and Lexi shared a look, a silent acknowledgment of the shared vision and mutual support they had found in each other through these teachings.

Chapter 102

The next day, as the morning light once again filled the great hall of the monastery, Sophea gathered the monks for a session dedicated to sharing and reflecting on the meditation experience from the previous day. The atmosphere was contemplative, with each participant pondering the intricate tapestry of virtues they had visualized and how these ideals resonated in their personal and spiritual lives.

Sophea, sensing the depth of reflection the exercise had inspired, decided to open the floor for individual reflections. "Yesterday, we visualized our lives as tapestries woven from the threads of virtues we have discussed over the past weeks," she began. "I would like to hear about your experiences with this meditation. How did the imagery of the tapestry manifest for you? How do you feel these virtues are woven into your life?"

Turning to Lexi first, who had been particularly thoughtful since the session, Sophea invited her to share her insights. "Lexi, would you start us off? How did this meditation speak to you?"

Lexi took a moment to collect her thoughts before responding, her voice calm and reflective. "Thank you, Sophea. The meditation was quite profound for me," she began, her gaze introspective. "Visualizing the tapestry helped me see the interconnectedness of the virtues in a very tangible way. Each thread—each virtue—felt like a vital part of a whole, and it made me realize how interdependent they are."

She continued, "The thread of hope stood out particularly for me. In the tapestry, it was like a golden beam of light, cutting through darker shades, representing challenges I've faced. It reminded me of the times when maintaining hope has kept me grounded and focused, especially during times of uncertainty with my path here and my relationship with Redington."

Lexi paused, looking toward Redington briefly, who offered a supportive smile. "The thread of peace also resonated deeply with me. I visualized it as a soft, encompassing glow, providing a calm base for all other colors. It symbolized the sanctuary I've found here in the monastery and the peace I strive to carry into every aspect of my life."

"Seeing all these virtues woven together reinforced my understanding that each action, each decision I make, contributes to this ongoing creation of my life's tapestry. It has given me a clearer vision of how I wish to proceed, intertwining my spiritual growth with my personal relationships, ensuring that each thread strengthens and supports the others."

Sophea nodded appreciatively, touched by the depth of Lexi's reflection. "Thank you, Lexi, for such a heartfelt share. It's inspiring to hear how the visualization helped you see the integral role these virtues play in your life and how you envision integrating them moving forward."

The room filled with a warm sense of community and understanding as others prepared to share their reflections, each person's experience adding another layer to the collective insight. Lexi's openness set a thoughtful tone for the discussions that would follow, as each monk, including Redington, prepared to delve into their personal reflections on the tapestry of virtues.

Chapter 103

As the sharing continued, Sophea turned her attention to Kesia, who had been listening intently to Lexi's reflections. "Kesia, would you like to share your experiences with the meditation?"

Kesia nodded, her expression thoughtful as she gathered her thoughts. "Certainly, Sophea. The meditation was particularly impactful for me," she began, her voice steady and clear. "Visualizing the tapestry allowed me to see how each virtue not only stands alone but also complements and supports the others, much like the threads in a fabric."

She continued, focusing on the virtue of adaptability, which had been a significant theme in her personal journey. "The thread of adaptability was very vivid for me. I visualized it as a flexible, vibrant thread, weaving through the tapestry, adjusting its course as it encountered other threads. It reminded me of the many times I've had to adapt my approach, both in my personal life and in my interactions within the community here."

Kesia's eyes lit up with a spark of realization. "This adaptability hasn't always been easy for me. I've struggled at times with the balance between maintaining my core values and adapting to new challenges. Seeing this thread interwoven with the threads of integrity and wisdom in the tapestry helped me understand that adaptability doesn't mean compromising my values but rather applying them in ways that are responsive to changing circumstances."

She paused for a moment, reflecting on the broader implications of her insights. "In terms of community, the thread of adaptability has shown me that being flexible can lead to greater harmony and understanding. It's about finding common ground, even when it seems like our differences might pull us apart."

Turning her thoughts to the communal impact, Kesia addressed how adaptability influences leadership. "As a part of this community, I've seen how adaptability in leadership fosters trust and encourages a more dynamic and supportive environment. It's about leading by example, showing that it's possible to embrace change while staying true to our principles."

Concluding her reflection, Kesia expressed gratitude for the visualization exercise. "This meditation has reinforced my commitment to being both a steadfast and flexible member of our community. I'm inspired to continue weaving these virtues into my daily actions, ensuring that the tapestry of our community remains strong and cohesive."

Sophea nodded in appreciation, pleased with the depth of insight Kesia brought to the discussion. "Thank you, Kesia, for such a comprehensive reflection. Your ability to integrate adaptability with your core values is a testament to your growth and your important role in our community."

The monks, inspired by Kesia's articulation of her experience, felt encouraged to think about how they too could better weave the virtues discussed into their own lives, enhancing their personal growth and their collective contribution to the monastery's ethos.

Chapter 104

After Kesia's thoughtful reflections, Sophea turned her attention to Isabella, whose keen interest in applying the lessons practically had always enriched the discussions. "Isabella, we'd love to hear your thoughts on the meditation and how it resonated with your experiences."

Isabella nodded, her eyes reflecting a deep engagement with the topic. "Thank you, Sophea. The meditation on the tapestry of virtues was incredibly illuminating for me," she began, her voice carrying a mix of enthusiasm and introspection. "Visualizing the intertwining threads helped me see my life's journey not just as a series of events, but as a cohesive narrative woven from these profound teachings."

Isabella focused particularly on the virtue of peace, which had struck a chord with her during the session. "In the tapestry, I visualized the thread of peace as a serene blue that ran through the entire fabric, touching and influencing all the other threads. It reminded me of the pervasive nature of peace—it doesn't just exist on its own but is integral to the structure and strength of the whole."

She continued, reflecting on her personal application of the lesson. "On a personal level, maintaining peace within myself has sometimes been challenging, especially when facing personal and professional pressures. The meditation reinforced the importance of nurturing inner peace as the foundation for extending peace to others around me."

Isabella then shared how she applies these insights in her interactions. "In our community, I've tried to be a mediator and a peacemaker, drawing on the calmness and resilience that comes from this inner sanctuary of peace. Seeing this role reflected in the tapestry helped validate my efforts and inspired me to continue strengthening these bonds."

Regarding the broader impacts, Isabella spoke about the role of peace in leadership. "As someone who often takes on leadership roles, I've learned that a leader imbued with peace can diffuse tensions and inspire confidence. This tapestry visualization has deepened my commitment to be such a leader, one who can guide with tranquility and clarity, even in turbulent times."

Concluding her reflections, Isabella expressed a renewed commitment to her personal and community goals. "This exercise has motivated me to further cultivate peace within myself and actively promote it within our community. I'm inspired to continue weaving this thread into the tapestry of my daily life, ensuring it strengthens not only myself but also those around me."

Sophea smiled appreciatively at Isabella's insights. "Thank you, Isabella, for sharing such powerful reflections. Your dedication to embodying and spreading peace is a wonderful example of how these virtues can be lived out in meaningful ways."

Isabella's contributions sparked further conversation among the monks, encouraging them to consider how their individual virtues contribute not only to their personal growth but also to the fabric of their communal life. As each monk shared, the collective understanding deepened, drawing them closer in their spiritual and communal journey.

Chapter 105

After Isabella's insightful reflections, the group's attention turned to Redington, whose integration into the monastery's community had been observed with interest by all. Sophea, recognizing the unique perspective he brought as someone deeply rooted in a world outside their spiritual enclave, was particularly keen to hear his thoughts. "Redington," she began, her tone inviting, "we would very much appreciate hearing about your experience with the meditation. How did the visualization of the tapestry resonate with you?"

Redington took a moment to collect his thoughts, aware of the attentive eyes of the monks on him. He was accustomed to analytical discussions but sharing personal reflections in this spiritual setting offered a new kind of challenge and growth.

"Thank you, Sophea," Redington started, his voice steady but infused with a deeper openness than usual. "The meditation was a profound experience for me, quite different from the analytical exercises I'm used to in my line of work. Visualizing the tapestry allowed me to see the virtues not just as abstract concepts but as interconnected threads that are actively part of my life."

He paused, reflecting on the specific virtues that had struck a chord. "The threads of hope and peace were particularly vivid for me," he continued. "In the tapestry, I saw the thread of hope as a bright beacon, guiding through darker patches, which reminded me of challenging times when hope was what I clung to. It's what kept me moving forward, especially in my career where outcomes can often be uncertain and stakes are high."

Redington shifted slightly, his focus turning inward. "Peace, on the other hand, was like a quiet, strong undercurrent that steadied the other threads. It's something I've had to learn to cultivate actively. Working in law enforcement, where chaos is part of the everyday, finding and maintaining inner peace has been essential not just for personal resilience but for making balanced decisions."

He looked around at the monks, his gaze settling on Lexi for a moment with a gentle acknowledgment of her influence on his journey. "Being here, engaging with these teachings, I've started to understand how these virtues interlace not just in my personal growth but also professionally. Integrating what I've learned here about peace and hope into my leadership style is something I'm keen to explore further."

Redington concluded, "This exercise has helped me visualize how I can weave these virtues more consciously into the fabric of my life. It's given me a framework to think about my actions and decisions in a more holistic way."

Sophea nodded appreciatively, pleased with Redington's candid sharing. "Thank you, Redington. Your reflections bring valuable insight into how these teachings transcend the boundaries of our immediate community and apply in various life contexts, including your professional world."

The monks, moved by Redington's sharing, felt a deeper connection with him, seeing how the monastery's teachings could impact lives beyond their immediate spiritual practices. Redington's reflections not only enriched his personal and professional life but also bridged the gap between his world and theirs, highlighting the universal relevance and applicability of the virtues they all strived to live by.

As the session ended, the monks dispersed with a renewed sense of community and understanding, each carrying with them the images of their own tapestries and how they might continue to enrich the broader fabric of their lives. Redington and Lexi shared a quiet moment of connection, each grateful for the journey they were on together, weaving their individual threads into a shared pattern of growth and understanding.

Chapter 106

As the monks gathered once again in the peaceful sanctuary of the monastery's great hall, the morning light cast a serene glow over the assembly. Following the rich discussions of the previous sessions, Kesia felt a deep curiosity about how the teachings of Tobias linked to broader spiritual concepts, particularly the gift of knowledge.

After the initial meditations and prayers of the morning, Kesia raised her hand, her expression thoughtful and earnest. "Sophea," she began, "over these past sessions, we've deeply explored the virtues Tobias taught. I've been reflecting on these discussions and wondering, how do all these teachings relate to the broader spiritual gift of knowledge? How does understanding these virtues enhance our spiritual wisdom?"

Sophea, always appreciative of thoughtful inquiries, nodded approvingly at Kesia's question. "That's a wonderful question, Kesia," she responded, her voice infused with encouragement. "The gift of knowledge, in a spiritual sense, isn't merely about accumulating facts or information. It's about deepening our understanding of divine truths and how they apply to our lives."

Sophea paused to gather her thoughts, ensuring her explanation would resonate clearly with her attentive audience. "Tobias' teachings on virtues such as hope, peace, charity, and wisdom are all facets of this greater gift of knowledge. Each virtue helps us peel back layers of superficial understanding to reveal deeper spiritual insights."

She continued, "For instance, when we meditate on the virtue of peace, we're not just learning how to be calm; we're accessing a deeper knowledge about the nature of tranquility and its source. We learn how peace isn't just the absence of conflict, but a profound positive state that influences all around us."

Sophea walked slowly among the monks, her presence calm and commanding. "Similarly, understanding hope as more than just wishful thinking, but as a dynamic force that propels us forward, enhances our spiritual knowledge by connecting us with the nature of divine providence and the reality that we are guided and supported in our journeys."

She looked around, making eye contact with several monks, including Kesia and Redington. "Each virtue you learn about and integrate into your life enriches your spiritual tapestry, adding depth and color to your understanding. This is the essence of the gift of knowledge—it allows us to see beyond the surface and appreciate the spiritual dimensions of our experiences."

Sophea suggested that integrating these virtues was a lifelong journey, one that continually expanded the monks' spiritual horizons. "The gift of knowledge is dynamic," she explained. "It grows as you grow, deepening as you deepen your commitment to living out these virtues. Each day, with each decision to act with integrity, wisdom, or compassion, you are not just acting; you are learning and embodying the divine qualities that shape a spiritually enlightened life."

Encouraged by Sophea's explanation, Kesia felt a renewed sense of purpose. The discussion had not only answered her question but had also provided a clearer framework for how to continue her spiritual development in a practical, daily context.

The session concluded with a collective meditation focused on absorbing the divine knowledge through the lens of Tobias' teachings, each monk reflecting on how to consciously apply this deeper understanding to their personal spiritual practices. As they dispersed, there was a shared sense of enlightenment and gratitude for the journey of learning they were on together, guided by the wisdom of Sophea and the ancient teachings of Tobias.

Chapter 107

$\mathcal{I}$n the serene ambiance of the next gathering, the monks convened with a palpable sense of deep contemplation, spurred by recent discussions about the gift of knowledge and its integration into their spiritual practices. As the session began, Kesia, reflecting on the profound insights shared by Sophea about knowledge, felt a new curiosity about another profound spiritual gift—wisdom.

After the morning rituals concluded and Sophea invited questions, Kesia raised her hand, her demeanor reflecting her earnest desire for deeper understanding. "Sophea," she began, her voice carrying a mix of reverence and inquiry, "you have beautifully explained how the teachings of Tobias and our understanding of various virtues contribute to our spiritual knowledge. Could you now elaborate on how all this relates to the gift of wisdom? How does wisdom differ from knowledge in our spiritual journey?"

Sophea, pleased with Kesia's thoughtful progression from knowledge to wisdom, responded with a gentle smile. "Thank you for such an insightful question, Kesia," she said warmly. "While knowledge and wisdom are closely related, they are distinct in their essence and application. If we consider knowledge as the understanding of facts, principles, and truths, wisdom is the ability to apply these truths appropriately in our decisions and life practices."

Sophea paced slowly in front of the monks, her steps measured, as she deepened the explanation. "Wisdom, therefore, can be seen as the practical application of knowledge. It involves judgment, discernment, and the insight to know the right course of action in a given situation. It's about making choices that not only serve us but also serve the greater good."

She continued, linking back to the teachings of Tobias, "When Tobias teaches us about virtues such as peace, charity, or meekness, he is not merely expanding our knowledge of these concepts; he is guiding us toward wisdom. Each virtue we explore is an opportunity to cultivate wise actions that reflect our deeper understanding."

"To give a specific example," Sophea elaborated, "consider the virtue of peace. Knowledge of peace teaches us what it is and why it is valuable. Wisdom guides us in creating peace in challenging situations, influencing not just our actions but also the actions of others around us. It's about embodying peace in a way that transforms environments and relationships."

Sophea then addressed how these teachings prepare the monks for leadership and communal living. "Wisdom is particularly crucial for leadership because it empowers us to guide others not just with command, but with compassion and foresight. It's about seeing beyond the immediate to the potential outcomes of our choices."

Encouraged by Sophea's insights, Kesia nodded thoughtfully, clearly processing the depth of the distinction between knowledge and wisdom. Sophea suggested a practice to deepen this understanding. "I encourage each of you to reflect on situations from your past where you've applied your spiritual knowledge. Consider how you might have used wisdom—or could use wisdom in the future—to guide your actions more effectively."

Concluding the session, Sophea led the monks in a meditative practice focused on visualizing themselves in scenarios where they could apply wisdom, imagining the outcomes of wise versus unwise choices. "Visualize the paths your actions could take, and see where wisdom leads," she guided.

As the monks left the hall, each carried with them a renewed commitment to not only understand the virtues they discussed but also to apply them wisely in their lives. Kesia felt particularly inspired, seeing a clear path to integrating wisdom into her daily interactions and decisions, enhancing her growth as a member of the community and a spiritual seeker.

Chapter 108

As night enveloped the monastery, Lexi found herself restless, her mind grappling with the recent discussions on wisdom and its application. Seeking clarity and insight, she hoped for guidance in her dreams—a medium through which she often found profound understanding.

That night, as Lexi drifted into sleep, she once again entered a dream vivid with symbolism and presence. She found herself in a vast, ancient library, its shelves stretching endlessly, filled with scrolls and books. The air was imbued with a sense of timelessness and knowledge. It was here that Archangel Uriel appeared to her, his presence both awe-inspiring and comforting.

"Uriel," Lexi greeted him, her voice echoing slightly in the grand space.

"Lexi," Uriel responded, his tone filled with warmth. "You seek understanding about the essence of wisdom. Let us explore this together."

Uriel led Lexi through the library, their steps silent on the stone floor. He paused before a large, ornate book laid open on a reading stand. The pages glowed faintly, illuminating the words written in elegant script.

"Wisdom," Uriel began, "is more than just the accumulation of knowledge. It is the judicious application of that knowledge in ways that transcend the immediate and address the foundational truths of existence. It involves seeing beyond the surface, understanding the deeper patterns that connect events, decisions, and emotions."

He gestured toward the glowing book. "Consider this text as a metaphor for the universe's wisdom. Each page, each line represents different aspects of knowledge and experience. Wisdom is the ability to read between the lines, to integrate these aspects into a cohesive understanding that guides not only your actions but also nourishes your soul."

Uriel turned to Lexi, his gaze piercing yet gentle. "Wisdom is knowing when to act and when to be still, when to speak and when to listen. It embodies patience, compassion, and discernment. It's about making choices that align with the greater good, that consider the well-being of others as well as your own."

He continued, "In your life, wisdom manifests each time you make decisions that are rooted in love and understanding rather than fear or haste. It grows each time you pause to reflect on your experiences, learning from them, and applying those lessons in future interactions."

Uriel then invited Lexi to visualize herself applying wisdom in her daily life. "Imagine each interaction as an opportunity to practice wisdom. Visualize yourself responding to challenges with a calm mind and a compassionate heart, guided by the lessons you have learned."

As Lexi engaged in this visualization, she felt a profound sense of peace and clarity. She saw herself navigating complex situations with grace and insight, her actions thoughtful and her impact positive.

"Carry this understanding back into your waking life," Uriel advised as the dream began to fade. "Let wisdom light your path and guide you in nurturing relationships, making decisions, and fulfilling your purpose. Remember, true wisdom is a light that never dims, shining through the darkest times."

As Lexi awoke, the first light of dawn was breaking over the horizon. She lay in bed for a few moments, reflecting on her dream. Uriel's teachings felt like a beacon, illuminating her path forward. With a renewed sense of purpose and understanding, Lexi rose from her bed, ready to apply the wisdom of her dream to her daily life at the monastery and beyond.

Chapter 109

As the monks gathered in the monastery's great hall, bathed in the soft morning light, a palpable sense of anticipation filled the air. Sophea's discussions on faith promised not only to conclude their current series of teachings but also to seamlessly bridge to their next spiritual exploration, focused on "the faith of a soul."

Sophea began by invoking the image of a crucible, a powerful metaphor for faith as described by Tobias. "Faith, much like a crucible, is where our deepest beliefs are tested by the trials of life, refined and strengthened through each challenge," she stated, setting the tone for the lesson. Her description of Solomon's dedication of the Temple illustrated how profound acts of faith could anchor and deepen one's spiritual life.

Isabella, always eager to connect teachings to practical applications, asked about ways to strengthen faith amidst trials. Sophea's response highlighted the importance of regular spiritual practices and the supportive role of the community, emphasizing that enduring faith was cultivated not in isolation but in communion with others.

Kesia, reflecting on her personal spiritual uncertainties, sought advice for moments when faith wavers. Sophea reassured her that such fluctuations were natural and advised revisiting the foundational experiences that shape one's beliefs, promoting a reflective approach to faith that embraces questioning as a pathway to deeper understanding.

Lexi, interested in the broader impacts of faith, questioned its role in leadership and community service. Sophea articulated that a leader fortified by strong faith serves as a guiding light, inspiring ethical behavior and a commitment to justice, thereby enhancing the well-being and cohesion of the community.

Inspired by these discussions, Sophea guided the monks through a meditation exercise. She invited them to visualize themselves within a crucible, surrounded by the flames of their personal challenges, and reflect on how these experiences were refining their faith. This visualization helped them see their trials as opportunities for spiritual growth and renewal.

As the session concluded, Sophea's parting words resonated deeply with the monks: "Let us each embrace the crucible of faith with courage and openness. May your trials refine and affirm your beliefs, enabling you to navigate life's challenges with wisdom and integrity." These words not only summarized the day's teachings but also set the stage for their next spiritual exploration.

The monks left the hall feeling fortified, with a renewed commitment to view their life's challenges as catalysts for strengthening their faith. For Lexi and Redington, the lesson had a profound personal significance, reinforcing their belief in the shared path they were carving out together, one that balanced personal love with spiritual growth.

As they prepared for the upcoming series on "the faith of a soul," each monk, including Lexi and Redington, felt equipped to delve deeper into understanding and living out their faith. This next journey promised to explore more intimate realms of spirituality, examining how personal experiences and deeper soul-searching could further enrich their understanding of faith.

Thus, the monks looked forward to continuing their spiritual education, anticipating how the new lessons would enhance their personal journeys and strengthen their community, inspired by the wisdom of Tobias and guided by the thoughtful teachings of Sophea.

Chapter 110

One crisp morning, as the monks embarked on their routine outing through the quiet streets of the village, Kesia felt a compelling urge for deeper understanding that couldn't wait. Veering slightly from the group, she slipped unnoticed into a small internet café. Her heart raced with a mix of excitement and guilt from sneaking away, but her quest for knowledge urged her forward. Sitting down at an outdated computer, Kesia opened a browser and quickly typed in her burning question about the nature of Wisdom.

After a few clicks, she found herself chatting with an advanced AI, ChatGPT4, asking pointedly, "Who is Wisdom? Is it God, the Holy Ghost, archangels, or something else?"

The response on the screen was enlightening: "In biblical texts, Wisdom, often personified as 'Sophia' in Greek, is portrayed as a unique manifestation of divine attributes and principles.

It is not straightforwardly identified as God, the Holy Spirit, or any archangel but rather occupies a special place in scriptural exegesis. Wisdom, or Sophia, spans several books and serves various theological and literary purposes, acting as a bridge between the divine and the human, guiding, teaching, and enriching those who seek her."

Armed with this newfound understanding, Kesia felt a rush of clarity and excitement. She thanked ChatGPT4 and hurried back to rejoin the monks, her mind buzzing with ideas and questions.

At their next gathering in the monastery's great hall, as Sophea prepared to lead another session, Kesia's newfound knowledge felt like a pressing weight in her chest. As the lesson concluded, she stood up, her voice slightly trembling with the gravity of her revelation.

"Holy Hannah! Sophea, you are Wisdom," Kesia exclaimed, her statement ringing out in the sudden silence of the hall.

The monks turned in surprise, while Sophea, maintaining her composure, smiled gently, recognizing the depth of Kesia's insight. "Kesia, tell us what you have learned," Sophea invited, her eyes twinkling with a mixture of curiosity and encouragement.

Kesia explained her excursion and the conversation with the AI, sharing the insights she had gained about Wisdom being a divine attribute that manifests to guide and teach. "It dawned on me," Kesia continued, her voice steadying with confidence, "That what you impart to us, Sophea, the guidance and the teachings, is the living embodiment of Wisdom. You help us bridge our understanding between the earthly and the divine, much like Sophia in the scriptures."

The room was filled with a profound silence as each monk pondered Kesia's words, feeling the weight and truth of her realization. Sophea nodded thoughtfully, acknowledging the compliment and the responsibility it entailed.

"Thank you, Kesia, for your brave and insightful words," Sophea responded warmly. "Wisdom is not a single entity or person—it flows through all of us when we open ourselves to divine guidance and seek to understand the deeper truths of our existence. In teaching you, I too learn, and we all grow together, woven into the very tapestry of Wisdom itself."

The session ended with a reflective mood as the monks dispersed, each contemplating the dynamic and omnipresent nature of Wisdom in their lives. Kesia felt a newfound respect for the teachings and for Sophea, realizing that her quest for knowledge had led her to appreciate more deeply the spiritual journey they were all on together.

Prayer to Archangel Uriel,

Archangel Uriel, divine angel of the light, please raise my frequency by surrounding me with your radiant love-light energy. Empowering my body, mind, spirit, and soul on every level with your sunbeam energy of enlightenment. Grant me inspiration to seek the truth and turn my knowledge into wisdom.
Amen.

Acknowledgments

First and foremost, I wish to express my deepest gratitude to the divine muse that whispers through the breeze and guides the pen with an unseen, but ever-felt presence. The journey of writing "Wisdom of the Soul" has been transformative, and it is with a humble heart that I offer thanks to those who have walked with me on this path.

To my family and friends—your unwavering support and endless encouragement have been the pillars upon which this project has rested. Your belief in my vision, even when the road was obscured by the fog of doubt, helped illuminate the way forward. I am eternally grateful for your love and patience.

I extend my sincere appreciation to my wonderful team at Maximilian Enterprises, especially my editor, whose keen insights and suggestions helped refine and sculpt this narrative into its final form. Your dedication to this story has been a beacon of professionalism and passion.

A special thank you goes to the cultural consultants and historians who provided invaluable expertise that enriched the authenticity and depth of the story's setting and characters. Your contributions have been integral to the soul of this book, ensuring accuracy in the midst of creative interpretation.

To the artist, Jennifer Louie who crafted the cover and the visual representations within these pages, your talent has given Wisdom of the Soul a face that mirrors its spirit—thank you for your remarkable artistry.

My gratitude extends to the academic and spiritual communities whose works on theology, philosophy, and spirituality have informed and inspired the conceptual foundations of this novel. Your research and writings were crucial in weaving the intricate tapestry of this story.

I must acknowledge the contributions of artificial intelligence in this creative process, specifically OpenAI's ChatGPT, which provided assistance with initial brainstorming, factual verification, and even some aspects of narrative structuring. This technology has opened up new avenues for creativity that were previously unimagined.

And finally, to you, the reader—thank you for embarking on this journey through the pages of Wisdom of the Soul. It is for you that these words have been woven into a story meant to entertain, enlighten, and inspire. May you find a reflection of your own journey within this narrative.

May we all continue to learn, to grow, and to understand the deeper narratives that guide our souls through the cosmos of collective experience.

With all my gratitude,
Dr. Constance Santego

Bibliography

The Bible (New International Version)
   The primary source for biblical quotations and
   references, particularly from the Books of
   Kings and Proverbs.
Aristotle. Nicomachean Ethics.
   Discusses virtues and ethical living, which
   parallels the discussions of virtues in the
   book.
Aquinas, Thomas. Summa Theologica.
   Offers insights into theological virtues,
   particularly faith, which is explored in depth
   in the later chapters.
Durant, Will. The Story of Philosophy.
   Provides an overview of philosophical
   thoughts that complement the discussion of
   wisdom and ethical considerations in spiritual
   contexts.
Eliade, Mircea. The Sacred and the Profane: The
Nature of Religion.
   Explores the concept of sacred space, relevant
   to the discussion of temples and spiritual
   sanctuaries in the book.
Heschel, Abraham Joshua. God in Search of
Man: A Philosophy of Judaism.

Discusses the relationship between God and humanity, offering a perspective on divine wisdom and human understanding.

James, William. The Varieties of Religious Experience.
Examines different aspects of religious life, including how faith and wisdom play out in personal experiences.

Jung, Carl G. Psychology and Religion: West and East.
Provides a psychological analysis of religious and spiritual experiences, touching on themes of personal growth through wisdom.

Lewis, C.S. Mere Christianity.
Offers a defense of Christian faith and morality that complements the discussions of spiritual virtues.

Smith, Huston. The World's Religions.
Discusses core teachings and philosophies of major world religions, providing a comparative backdrop to the virtues discussed in the book.

Tillich, Paul. The Dynamics of Faith.
Deeply explores the concept of faith as a central element in personal and communal religious life.

Underhill, Evelyn. Mysticism: A Study in the Nature and Development of Spiritual Consciousness.
Explores the nature of spiritual experiences and the development of spiritual

consciousness, relevant to discussions of inner peace and wisdom.

The Author

Dr. Constance Santego

Dr. Constance Santego is an esteemed author, educator, and holistic healer whose work spans across several disciplines including spiritual wellness, ancient mythologies, and personal development. With a doctoral degree in Natural Medicine, Constance has dedicated her life to exploring the intersections of spirituality, health, and human consciousness.

Born and raised in a small town steeped in folklore and surrounded by nature, Constance developed an early fascination with the stories and rituals that define different cultures. This curiosity blossomed into a lifelong pursuit of knowledge, leading her to travel extensively, in places as diverse as Greece, England, Mexico, and Spain.

Constance's academic journey is complemented by her practical experience in the healing arts. She is a certified Reiki Master, a practitioner of many modalities, and has conducted numerous workshops on meditation, energy healing, and mindfulness. Her holistic practice aims to integrate the body, mind, and spirit to foster well-being and spiritual growth.

Literary Contributions

Dr. Santego is the author of several books that explore spiritual themes through a blend of narrative fiction and insightful commentary. Her works often weave together elements of ancient myths with modern existential questions, creating a rich tapestry that resonates with readers seeking deeper understanding of themselves and the universe.

Wisdom of a Soul, her latest novel, continues this tradition by exploring the themes of balance, power, and transformation. It draws heavily from her scholarly research into mythological stories and her experiences in mystical practices. Through her narrative, she invites readers to contemplate the cosmic balance of light and darkness, and the individual's role within this eternal dance.

Future Projects

Dr. Santego is currently working on her next book, which promises to delve deeper into the spiritual journeys of historical figures across various cultures. She continues to contribute to academic nonfiction, sharing her insights on holistic health and spiritual wellbeing.

Constance lives in a serene lakeside town, where she enjoys her family time, herbal gardening, and writing. Her life's work reflects her passion for bringing light and healing into the world, guiding others through their spiritual journeys with compassion and wisdom.

Also Available

Play the game Ikona and test
your Virtues and Sins
For additional information on
Constance Santego's wide range of
Motivational Products, Coaching Sessions,
Spiritual Retreats,
Live Events and Educational Programs
Go to
www.ConstanceSantego.ca

Follow me on:
Instagram - Constance_Santego &
Facebook - constancesantegoo
YouTube Channel - Constance Santego
Subscribe and receive free information &
Meditations